GOOD LITTLE GIRLS

ALSO BY RITA HERRON

Romantic Suspense

The Keepers

Pretty Little Killers

Graveyard Falls

All the Beautiful Brides
All the Pretty Faces
All the Dead Girls

Slaughter Creek Series

Dying to Tell
Her Dying Breath
Worth Dying For
Dying for Love

Contemporary Romance

Going to the Chapel

GOOD LITTLE GIRLS

The Keepers, Book 2

RITA HERRON

Montlake
Romance

Published by Montlake Romance, Seattle

www.apub.com

Amazon, the Amazon logo, and Montlake Romance are trademarks of Amazon.com, Inc., or its affiliates.

ISBN-13: 9781503902152
ISBN-10: 1503902153

Cover design by Caroline T. Johnson

Printed in the United States of America

GOOD
LITTLE
GIRLS

CHAPTER ONE

Tinsley Jensen was tired of being a shut-in. Tired of living in fear.

Tired of *not* living.

How could she live when she was too frightened to go outside the beach cottage she'd rented and explore Seahawk Island? Set on the coast of Georgia, it was beautiful, peaceful, and relaxing, and it had been a favorite vacation spot of her family's when she was little.

Now she'd become so antisocial that her friends and fiancé had abandoned her. She traced her finger over the photograph that she kept on the table of her and her younger sister. She'd even cut off communication with Carrie Ann.

The wind whistled through the eaves, rattling windowpanes and sending a chill through her. Dusk settled over the sea, the twilight hour a reminder that soon night would envelop her, cocooning her in the endless loneliness.

Outside, a seagull swooped down onto the sand in search of food. A sailboat glided away into the distance. The last fisherman of the day packed up and left the dock, visible from her window.

A few feet away, volunteers from the sea turtle patrol, a local group who devoted their time to rescuing injured sea turtles, knelt to dig up a loggerhead nest. Onlookers gaped in awe as the babies burst through the shells. Families crowded around. Two little girls she'd seen playing on the beach all summer squealed with delight as the volunteers gently scooped the babies into their palms, then placed them in a large bucket.

Memories of the happy times from her childhood surfaced. She and Carrie Ann on the beach, chasing waves and riding bikes.

She wanted to talk to Carrie Ann so badly she ached. Her sister had been calling lately, but she hadn't answered. What could she say?

I'm still here, trapped. Frightened.

Stay away from me. He might be watching.

She had always been the strong sister, the one who took care of Carrie Ann. She couldn't see her until she could stand on her own two feet again. Or walk out the door . . .

Angry that she was missing out on life while her attacker was free, she inhaled a fortifying breath.

Those tiny baby turtles had broken out of their shells and were fighting to reach the sea.

She had to break out of her own. Stop allowing the Skull—the man who'd abducted and held her hostage—to dominate her thoughts and run her life.

It had been months since she'd escaped him. There had been no word since from the police that he'd taken another woman. Or that he was anywhere near Seahawk Island.

Maybe he'd moved on and forgotten about her . . .

All summer she'd watched people walking their dogs in the early morning. She'd seen families playing on the beach, chasing waves, building sandcastles. The mother with those two little girls, dancing and laughing, reminded her of her own family.

She couldn't remember the last time she'd laughed.

Then another memory came to her. The last time she'd volunteered with PAT, Pets as Therapy. She'd carried a Yorkie to visit an elderly patient in a nursing home, a woman who'd given up on life.

The moment she eased the dog into the woman's arms, though, life had sparked in her eyes.

If that frail ninety-year-old lady could fight to live, so could she.

Even Tinsley's parakeet, Mr. Jingles, perched in his cage by the window, was stunted by her withdrawal from the world. She'd opened the cage door, offering him freedom. But he hovered inside just as she did.

"We can do this," she whispered.

A shadow fell across the window. Night was coming.

The crowd outside parted, then formed two lines, leaving a path for the baby turtles to crawl to the ocean. She snatched her camera. She wanted to see them up close.

Determined, she took a step toward the door, but suddenly her lungs squeezed for air. Fear seized her, its invisible hands immobilizing her.

Cursing herself, she reached for the doorknob, then turned the lock. But she was shaking all over, and her knees buckled. The room spun. The doorframe blurred.

She staggered sideways and clawed her way toward the couch. Gasping for air, she fell onto it and dropped her head between her knees. Sweat beaded her face and neck. Her heart raced. A sob of frustration welled inside her, but her throat was so dry the sound died.

The medication for her panic attacks sat on the kitchen table a few feet away. It felt like a million.

Knowing she couldn't reach the medication, she grabbed the bottle of green tea she'd opened earlier. With trembling hands, she tipped it up and drank deeply.

Seconds passed. The room spun again. Perspiration trickled down the side of her face.

She focused on the door, willing herself to try again.

But the knob was turning.

Someone was outside, trying to break in.

Dammit, she needed the .22 she'd bought when she'd moved here. She had to protect herself.

Terrified, she jerked her head toward the window.

The Skull. He was there. His evil eyes were watching her through the eyeholes of his black mask.

A scream lodged in her throat. Her phone was on the end table. She needed help. She'd call Agent Wyatt Camden. He'd protected her a few months ago when a vigilante killer had struck on the island.

A rapping sounded on the window. Glass vibrating.

She blinked, certain she was seeing things.

But he was there.

The man who'd tortured her—his masked face pressed against the window.

Tears filled her eyes. Her body trembled. Dammit, she had to fight. *Call Wyatt.*

He was on speed dial. She managed to hit the number, but the window rattled again, and the Skull's eyes peered at her, mocking her.

His voice taunted her from the past: *Good girls don't cry . . .*

God . . . She'd cried, and he'd punished her for it.

Her phone slipped from her clammy hand and hit the floor. The room swam into a sea of grays. Shadows filled her vision.

The glass was breaking . . . He was coming inside . . . his dirty hands reaching for her . . .

She forced herself to stand. She needed that pistol. But his laughter echoed through the room, and she stumbled.

Then her legs gave way, and she tumbled into the darkness.

◆ ◆ ◆

Family meant everything to Wyatt Camden. Even more so since his father's death five years ago.

Yet he was proud of his old man. Twenty years on the Savannah police force, and he'd been one of the good ones. He was brave, strong, courageous. Everything Wyatt aspired to be.

Too bad he'd been killed in the line of duty.

His mother had fallen apart when the news came. The one bone of contention between her and his father had been the danger he faced daily.

Wyatt could be killed on the job, too. He'd almost died after being stabbed by that bastard, the Skull.

His father's words echoed in his head. *Show no weakness, son. Emotions are for wimps. Men must be strong.*

So he'd worked like hell in physical therapy and fought his way back to active duty.

That ordeal had made him question whether or not he'd ever marry. He sure as hell didn't want to put a woman through the pain his mother had suffered.

Except part of him wanted a family of his own.

It didn't matter now. He was married to the job.

He pushed away his dinner plate with a groan. "Mom, that was great, as usual."

She gave him that sweet, concerned look that made his stomach knot. "Don't you want some more, honey? You need your strength."

Wyatt gritted his teeth. He didn't want sympathy or to be babied.

Ever since he'd been injured, his mother had plied him with meals. She claimed it was the way of the South.

Recovery meant hearty food. Grieving meant casseroles. Family dinners meant gorging on pot roast, potatoes, and gravy. And peach cobbler. It was a wonder he didn't weigh three hundred pounds.

He started to carry his plate to the kitchen, but his mother motioned for him to stay seated. She insisted she liked waiting on her boys, that it gave her purpose, so they'd silently agreed to let her.

His brothers, Cody and Dominic, grinned as his mother cleared the table. Family dinner was a required weekly event in the Camden house, as it had been when his father was alive.

It was even more important to his mother now that he was gone.

Dammit, Wyatt missed him.

"How's Little League going?" Cody asked.

Wyatt couldn't help but smile. He loved those kids at the Boys' Club. They needed him. "Good. We could use another hand if you want to help."

Cody nodded. "Sign me up."

Dominic set his coffee cup on the table. "I would help, too, but I'm getting ready to leave for NCIS training at FLETSC."

Before his mother could return with the pie, Wyatt checked his phone for messages. She insisted no phones or work discussion during dinner, but he'd felt antsy the past few days, like something bad was about to happen.

The screen displayed a number he didn't recognize. But the name "Tinsley Jensen" appeared. *Damn.* Her disappearance had been the biggest case of his career. The investigation had dragged out for months as he and his partner, Hatcher, had chased one false lead after another. During that time, he'd learned everything there was to know about Tinsley. He liked what he'd discovered.

She rescued dogs for a living. He was a canine lover himself. Had always had a stray around growing up. He'd have one now, but he wasn't home long enough to take care of it.

He and the police had exhausted lead after lead until the case was about to go cold. Then Hatcher's first wife, Tinsley's friend, had been abducted and the stakes raised.

He and Hatcher had worked around the clock to find both women. They'd been too late for Hatcher's wife. Tinsley had been hanging on by a thread.

One look into her sad but determined eyes, and he'd fought like hell to free her.

Rescuing her had nearly cost him his leg. But hell, danger went with the job. He thrived on the adrenaline rush. The chase.

The reward of taking another predator off the streets.

Heart pounding, he pressed "Voice Mail." Instead of a message, a muffled sound echoed back. Then white noise, and the phone went silent.

Fear mushroomed in his chest. Tinsley hadn't called him in months. Not since that awkward night he'd guarded her when a vigilante killer had struck.

Although those murders hadn't been related to the Skull, the killer, who belonged to a group called the Keepers, had been drawn to Tinsley's website, *Heart & Soul*. A website where she expressed her feelings regarding her abduction. A place where other victims shared their experiences. Victims who bonded over the violence that had uprooted their lives.

A member of the Keepers had turned vigilante and had left a body on the dock by Tinsley's cottage as a sign that justice was being served.

His mother swept in with the pie, but he pushed away from the table.

"I'm sorry, Mom. I have to go."

He gave her a quick kiss on the cheek, said good night to his brothers, then hurried to the front door. Outside, he hit the sidewalk running.

CHAPTER TWO

They called him the Skull. He liked the name. It made him sound tough. Scary.

And important.

He'd evaded police for months. Had worn a disguise. Smart. His victims couldn't identify him.

Which gave him the advantage. He could walk up to them in the grocery store or at a coffee shop, and they had no idea who he was.

Only one had survived, though. He'd thought about her ever since.

He paddled the canoe away from the dock near Tinsley Jensen's cottage, his heart pounding.

She probably thought she was safe hiding out in the cove, thought he had no idea where she was.

He'd known all along. He'd done his homework. Tracked her from the minute she was released from that hospital.

And he'd been watching her ever since.

Something was wrong tonight. Someone else was there. When he saw the silhouette on the walkway to her cottage, he'd retreated into the shadows.

He hoped to hell whoever it was hadn't seen him. He'd been so careful these last few months. Meticulous in keeping a low profile.

Need clawed at him day and night, relentlessly feeding the darkness inside him. It had taken all his will to keep the rising hunger inside him at bay.

It was almost time to be with her again. The Day of the Dead would mark their anniversary.

The shadow on the dock turned and looked straight out toward the ocean. Toward him.

He cursed, ducked low, and paddled down toward the pier where he'd parked his car.

Fuck. He couldn't be with her tonight.

But he would be soon.

And nobody would stop him.

CHAPTER THREE

Wyatt's pulse raced as he drove across the causeway onto Seahawk Island. He called Tinsley back, praying she'd answer. But the phone rang several times and went to voice mail, raising his anxiety, and he sped around another vehicle.

Nightmares of her ordeal and rescue plagued him constantly. If he'd found Tinsley early in the investigation, she wouldn't have suffered the atrocities inflicted by her abductor.

She wouldn't be totally free until the Skull was caught and in prison—or dead.

He'd prefer the latter. Criminals escaped prison, were released on parole. He didn't want that fear hanging over Tinsley.

Anger nearly choked him as he remembered the bruises and scars on her body. The monster who'd tortured Tinsley didn't deserve to breathe the same air as a human.

Seagulls swooped low in the sky as he left the causeway and drove through the heart of the island, the Village, with its shops and restaurants. Dusk had come and gone, the last slivers of red and orange streaking the sky as night settled in. Spring and summer had brought tourists and vacationers to the coast, giving life to the stores, pier, park, and community swimming pool. Now that fall had arrived, the crowds had thinned. But with milder temperatures in the seventies, people still flocked to the island for rest and a reprieve from their busy lives.

He slowed to let a biker cross, then veered onto the side street leading to Sunset Cove.

Wyatt scanned the street as he approached. No cars in sight. The two other houses in the cove looked vacant. Lights off. Blinds and curtains drawn.

The breeze from the ocean picked up, making the palm trees sway. Waves crashed onto the shore and dock, the wind beating at the wooden railing and porch.

He parked, then pressed Tinsley's number again. The ringtone buzzed in his ears. Still no answer.

He climbed the steps and glanced at the side window. The shutters were closed.

Body tense, he scanned the porch, dock, and property. A lone figure in a dark jacket was jogging down the beach, nearly lost in the shadows.

A jogger or someone who'd possibly hurt Tinsley?

He rapped on the door, then peeked through the front window facing the ocean. It was dark inside, a single light burning from the back. Tinsley's bedroom.

Tinsley hated the dark. She'd slept with a light on since the attack.

He knocked again, then jiggled the doorknob. The door creaked as it opened.

Fear pulsed through him. Tinsley never left the door unlocked. *Never.*

He pulled his gun and held it at the ready as he inched inside.

Tinsley was lying on the floor near her desk, unconscious.

He raced to her and knelt, then felt for a pulse. Weak. But at least she was breathing.

Heart hammering, he reached for his phone to call an ambulance, but she moaned and her eyelids fluttered.

Gently, he rolled her to her side and tilted her face so he could examine her for injuries. "Tinsley, it's Wyatt."

Her eyelids flickered, eyes widening.

"You called me. I was worried and rushed over."

Her gaze darted from side to side, then settled on his face.

He gently grazed his knuckles along her cheek. "What happened?"

She whimpered and tried to sit up. He took her arm to help her, but she pulled away, her eyes wide with fear.

Dammit, he'd forgotten she didn't like to be touched.

She scrambled back against the couch and propped her back to it as she rubbed at her temple. "*He* . . . was here."

Wyatt tensed. She didn't have to tell him who *he* was.

"You saw the Skull?" he asked gruffly.

She nodded, her lower lip quivering. "At the window . . . looking in. Then he broke the glass . . ." Her voice cracked. "He was reaching for me . . ."

Wyatt jerked his head toward the front window, then the side windows. None of them were broken.

Tinsley's gaze followed his, shock flashing across her face when she saw that the windows hadn't been shattered.

"I'll check." He scanned the room, searching for footprints, sand, a dusty fingerprint—any sign that someone had been inside. But other than the door being unlocked, nothing was disturbed.

A bottle of prescription pills sat on the end table by the couch. He examined the label. A narcotic for anxiety.

Had Tinsley taken the meds and imagined she'd seen the Skull breaking in?

◆ ◆ ◆

Confusion clouded Tinsley's mind as she stared at the window overlooking the ocean.

It wasn't broken. No shattered glass. No one coming through . . .

But she'd seen the Skull.

Hadn't she?

"Are you certain you saw him?" Wyatt asked.

Anger hit her hard and fast. He didn't believe her.

She nodded. Although with the window still intact, how could she be sure?

She dug her fingers into the edge of the couch and pulled herself to her feet. Still dizzy, she had to take several deep breaths to steady herself.

Wyatt was watching her as if she was crazy.

She supposed locking herself inside this house made her appear unstable.

Maybe she *was* losing her mind . . .

Wyatt cleared his throat as he approached her. His big masculine body overpowered the room, filling her space with his woodsy scent.

Reminding her that she wasn't strong enough to fight him off.

Emotions flickered in his eyes as if he realized he frightened her.

Humiliation washed over her. But she refused to apologize. She'd been brutalized by one man. She didn't know whether she'd ever trust another.

He stepped back, giving her space, then claimed the club chair across from her. With one hand, he gestured toward her prescription bottle of Ativan.

"What were you doing before you saw him?" Wyatt said in a quiet voice.

"If you think I drugged myself into hallucinating, you're wrong." She squared her shoulders, struggling for calm. "I haven't taken one of those in months."

His gaze locked with hers. "Half of the bottle is missing."

Tinsley shook her head. "That can't be. I didn't like the way they made me feel and stopped taking them." Her hand shook as she reached for the medication. She removed the cap, her head throbbing as she looked inside.

He was right. Half the pills were missing.

"I don't understand," she murmured. "This bottle was full."

A tense silence stretched between them.

"Let's retrace the evening," Wyatt said. "Tell me what you were doing before you thought you saw him."

Tears of frustration clogged Tinsley's throat, but she swallowed them back.

That monster's voice taunted her—*Good girls don't cry. If they do, they die . . .*

"Tinsley?" Wyatt said in a low voice.

Mouth dry, she grabbed her bottle of tea and took a sip. "I was watching the sea turtle patrol. They were releasing baby hatchlings."

A small smile tilted Wyatt's mouth, and Tinsley's stomach fluttered. Wyatt Camden was a handsome man. Big. Strong. Tough. Once upon a time, she would have thought his smoldering eyes, shaggy hair, and muscles were sexy.

Sexy was the last thing she wanted now.

"My brothers and I used to watch the volunteers release the babies when we were little," Wyatt said. "My mom even donates to the Georgia Sea Turtle Center."

"It's a good cause." The conversation sounded so normal that she wanted to ask more about his family. After all, he knew everything about her.

But she couldn't make this personal. "A crowd had gathered to cheer the babies out to sea." She gestured toward her camera. "I . . . told myself if those babies could make it, I could leave the house."

His eyebrow shot up. "You were going outside?"

Emotions welled in her chest. "I wanted to," she whispered.

A tense heartbeat passed, sympathy flickering in his deep-brown eyes. "Go on," Wyatt said quietly.

She inhaled sharply. Talking about herself was always difficult. She'd learned to live alone. To be alone. Not to trust anyone or to share her vulnerability.

Her fiancé had run when she'd opened up to him. He'd wanted a whole, normal woman.

That ship had sailed the day the Skull abducted her. She wasn't whole or normal anymore. She never would be.

"Tinsley?"

"I reached for the doorknob. I wanted to go out and breathe the salty air, b-but I got dizzy." She rubbed at her temple, disgusted with herself. "The room started spinning, so I staggered to the couch. When I looked up, his face was pressed against the glass, watching. He was smiling, then he broke through the glass . . ."

Her chest ached again. The air was trapped inside. She couldn't breathe.

"It's okay," Wyatt said softly. "You're safe now, Tinsley. He's gone."

She hadn't realized he'd moved, that he was sitting beside her. His hand was on her back, rubbing circles.

For a moment, it was comforting.

Then the fear returned and she pushed him away, then looked at the window again.

Another strained moment. "I don't see signs that anyone broke in."

"You think I'm crazy, don't you?" Panic sharpened her tone. "That I made it up?"

Wyatt shook his head. "I don't know what happened. Maybe the wind rattled the glass so hard you thought it shattered."

He gestured toward the entry, concerned. "The door was unlocked when I arrived. Did you unlock it?"

Tinsley rubbed her forehead again, her mind a blur. She'd reached for the doorknob. Had she unlocked the door? Yes . . . "I did, but then I got dizzy . . ."

"You could have been dreaming? Sleepwalking, maybe?"

15

She prayed he was right. "Maybe."

He stood, jaw set, his dark eyes piercing her. "I'm glad you called. I want to help you." He moved toward the door. "I'll look around outside."

◆ ◆ ◆

Wyatt didn't know what to believe.

Tinsley had been hiding out for months, ever since she'd been rescued. She was afraid the Skull would return for her and suffered from nightmares and anxiety attacks.

The Keeper had frightened her even more by leaving a body on the dock in front of her place.

Those factors could possibly trigger delusions.

Wyatt stepped outside, pulled a small flashlight from inside his jacket, and shined it across the porch floor. His boot prints marred the wooden surface.

But no others.

Dammit. He didn't want it to be true that the Skull was back. He didn't want Tinsley to have a breakdown either.

Although if he was locked inside a house for months, he would go out of his mind.

He thrived on open spaces, on adventure activities like biking and hiking and whitewater rafting.

He aimed the flashlight along the door and searched for evidence someone had jimmied it, but he didn't see any dirt or prints on the doorframe or knob.

The Skull was smart, though. He hadn't escaped the law because he was careless. He would have worn gloves. Covered his tracks.

Still, Wyatt spent the next half hour searching, walking the steps and dock, looking for any hint that the bastard had been on the premises.

Just as he was about to return to Tinsley, his phone buzzed. His boss, Deputy Director Roman Bellows from the FBI's Savannah field office.

He quickly connected. "Yeah?"

"SPD phoned us. They've got a case they want our help with."

His instincts kicked in. If they wanted the Feds, it was serious. "What is it?"

"A crabber found some bones in the marsh."

"They were murders?"

"Don't know yet, but it gets more interesting." Bellows paused. "The heads of the skeletons had been removed."

"You mean they were separated from the rest of the body?"

"I mean they're missing."

A coldness swept through Wyatt. The Skull had kept Tinsley in a dark place, a room where three skulls had stared back at her from ropes strung from the ceiling.

Skulls that clacked together and tinkled like wind chimes made of bones.

CHAPTER FOUR

Carrie Ann Jensen hurried along Savannah's River Street, her pulse hammering. Why wouldn't her sister talk to her?

Sure, she'd let Tinsley down after the attack. She hadn't said or done the right things, but she hadn't known how to handle seeing her sister so traumatized. Still, she'd tried and tried to make amends, but Tinsley didn't want anything to do with her.

Desperation clawed at her just like it had those first few weeks her sister was missing. Then she hadn't known where Tinsley was or whether she'd ever come back.

She'd prayed and worried and bugged the police to keep looking for her until one of the damn cops had warned her not to call him again, had told her she was acting like a psycho.

She was *not* a psycho.

Granted, she had problems with anxiety and impulse control. Sometimes she was as down as a dog, and other times so jittery she thought she was coming out of her skin. Those days she went shopping. She'd become obsessed with buying things online and had ended up with boxes of unopened items that she had no idea why she'd ordered.

Her insomnia had gotten so bad that she went days without sleeping, and then she couldn't eat because her stomach was wrecked. She'd hit the bottle to help calm her down and knock her out. But then she'd have the hangover from hell, and when the alcohol mixed with her antidepressants, sometimes she blacked out.

Twice she'd woken up in a cheap hotel with some loser she didn't know and would never have slept with if she hadn't been blinded by alcohol.

That had scared the bejesus out of her. The last time, the fuckwad had gotten rough with her. She'd fought him off and ended up with a black eye and a busted rib, but the bastard hadn't gotten what he wanted.

For the first time, she'd really understood what it must have been like for Tinsley to have a man force himself on her.

That's when she'd decided to call Tinsley. She wanted to tell Tinsley she understood now. Besides, when she started coming unraveled, her sister always grounded her.

But how could she make amends when Tinsley wouldn't even speak to her?

She wrapped her arms around her middle and rocked herself back and forth, her breathing choppy. That damn rib still made it hurt to breathe.

Two teens sporting body jewelry and sleeves of tattoos pushed past her. A big wrestler type guy in a black jacket with a hoodie looked down at her as if she might be his dinner.

She shot him an icy look, then ducked into a shop, desperate to escape him.

Fall decorations hung throughout the store, Halloween costumes and orange and black lights and masks . . .

Vampires and zombies and superheroes and . . . a skull. Skull masks . . . all different kinds . . .

Panic charged through her. She shoved her way through the crowd, constantly checking to see whether the big brute in the hoodie was following her as she rushed out the side door. No hoodie guy, but the beady black eyes of the skulls were watching.

Laughter echoed behind her. They were laughing at her. They knew what she'd done. Just like in her nightmares.

Knew she was on the ledge.

Knew she'd been a bad sister.

That she was coming unglued . . .

Talking to Tinsley was the only way to put her back together again.

CHAPTER FIVE

Wyatt clenched his phone with clammy hands as he told Deputy Director Bellows about Tinsley's call. Finding skull-less skeletons the same night Tinsley thought she'd seen her abductor at her door made the hair on the back of his neck stand on end.

"You think the Skull was at her place?" Bellows asked.

Wyatt scanned the beach from the porch, still searching. The cottage looked quaint, homey, a nice place to retreat and relax.

Except Tinsley hadn't ventured outside to enjoy the scenery these last few months.

"I don't know," he said. "It's possible someone was out here, but there's no evidence of a break-in. I'll check on her again, then drive out to the marsh."

Wyatt hung up, then kicked sand from his boots and knocked on the door.

Under the circumstances, he was nervous about leaving her alone. Would she be safe tonight by herself?

The door slowly creaked open. Tinsley's violet-blue eyes looked up at him expectantly.

"I'm sorry, but I didn't find evidence he was here," Wyatt said.

Her face looked pale in the sliver of moonlight slanting across the porch. "Thank you for looking."

He shrugged. "Maybe someone was outside, but if it was the Skull, why didn't he come in? You were alone, vulnerable."

She winced, and he realized she must hate feeling that way.

"He wanted me to know that he's close by," she said. "You don't understand how sick and twisted he is. He taunts his victims, likes to watch them squirm. The fear gets him off almost as much as the pain he inflicts."

Wyatt's jaw hardened. He didn't doubt that for a moment. "I have to go to a crime scene. But I'll come back later and stand guard for the night."

Tinsley clamped her teeth over her lower lip, a nervous gesture he'd seen her do before.

"You don't have to come back," she said softly. "I . . . didn't mean to trouble you."

He swallowed hard. The guilt over not saving her sooner got to him. His mother said he thought he was responsible for the whole world. She was right.

All in all, not the worst flaw he could have. But emotions could hinder an investigation.

"You are not trouble," he said softly. "If I'd killed that bastard the first time, you wouldn't be living in fear now."

Her expression softened. "It's not your fault, Wyatt. You nearly died saving me."

It wasn't enough. He always closed his cases. Got the bad guys. "I am going to find him one day," he promised. "But I do have to go now." In fact, whoever took those skeletons might be connected to the Skull.

He couldn't discount any possibility. "I'll call the local police department on the island and have an officer drive by."

She cut her gaze back toward the window. For a moment, she looked so frail that he was tempted to pull her up against him and comfort her.

But he kept his hands by his sides. Touching her wouldn't give her comfort.

The last thing he wanted to do was to hurt Tinsley.

"Having someone drive by might help," she said.

She didn't sound convinced. Then again, Tinsley wasn't naive. She'd survived a monster.

A monster who wanted Tinsley. He'd told her she'd never escape him. That if she did, he'd come back for her.

Wyatt didn't doubt that he would either. The bastard might have lain low the last few months, but the anniversary of the night he'd kidnapped Tinsley was drawing near.

He'd taken her on the first day of the Day of the Dead celebration.

His MO suggested he followed the holiday religiously. He'd sent sugar skulls to the police to let them know he had a victim. Had created an altar of flowers and a paper-skull string and told Tinsley that she should honor the dead.

Wyatt wouldn't let Tinsley fall prey to him again.

Tinsley locked the door as Wyatt left, her body trembling.

She'd always been independent, had helped others. She'd been active and social and loved people and dogs.

Now, being in the same room with someone, especially a male, completely unraveled the calm she'd struggled so hard to regain.

She moved to the window to watch the late-night beachcombers. Sad that she lived vicariously through strangers. That those strangers had become like family.

Her sister's face taunted her, and she rubbed the sea turtle pendant she wore on a silver chain around her neck. One lazy Sunday evening, on a trip to Florida, she and Carrie Ann had found the sea glass with their father. They'd been so excited that their mother had crafted necklaces out of the glass.

Hers shimmered with the deep blue of the ocean and shades of turquoise, while Carrie Ann's was a pale green with gold streaks.

When she was held prisoner in that horrid room, she'd forced her mind to escape to better times. To when she was little and she and her sister had built sandcastles and chased seagulls and boogie-boarded on the waves. To the long lazy days they'd sailed with their father. He'd taught her and her sister how to tie sailing knots when they were little. She and Carrie Ann used to make a contest out of it, to see who could untie the knots the fastest. They'd even practiced in the dark.

Toward the end of her captivity, though, the good memories had faded. She'd fallen into despair. She'd thought she'd never see Carrie Ann again.

She'd wanted to die. She'd *prayed* to die.

Then Wyatt found her, and she'd been rushed to the hospital, and for a brief moment in time, she'd been happy to be free. But the physical injuries and emotional scars, the publicity and the police interrogations, took their toll.

Her fiancé walked away. He hadn't signed up for the emotional basket case she'd become.

She'd pushed Carrie Ann away, too.

Liz Roberts's business card mocked her from the side table. The counselor/victims' advocate had good intentions. But talking about what happened to her hadn't changed anything.

Her website was her only source of comfort—at least she'd found a sisterhood in her readers. People who didn't judge. Who didn't blame Tinsley for drawing a psycho to her as her fiancé had.

People who needed her because they were suffering, too.

She slipped into her desk chair and began another entry.

We all have little girls inside us. Innocent. Trusting. Loving. Eager to please.

Once, we had silly girlish dreams of our first kiss. Our first date. Of falling in love. Of a white wedding dress and a man who loved us with all his heart.

Then something happens—a defining moment. A person. An event. A tragedy. A violation.

It changes us, steals our love of life, our trust and hope, our future.

Then we become people we don't recognize anymore. People we don't like.

People we don't want to be.

But we're trapped inside the memories and pain. It weaves a web around us, one so tight and confining that there are times we can't breathe.

Times we don't want to breathe anymore.

The innocence is gone.

And in its place is distrust. Fear. Despair.

I grieve for the girl I once was. For the woman I wanted to be.

Only the shell of that person remains.

I hate him for doing this to me.

I hate myself for not being stronger.

But I can't erase his voice from my head.

"Be a good girl and don't cry."

He said that as he tied me spread-eagle on the floor. Then he took pictures of me and hung them on the wall as if I was his private porn show.

"Daddy said I could never get a good girl, that I'm a loser. But he's wrong. I have you." He shoved my legs apart and rammed inside me. "Even good girls have bad in them. Just like she did."

I tried to scream, but he clamped his hand over my mouth. "You like it, don't you? You like it when I fuck you hard."

No . . . I silently screamed.

His eyes turned feral, sinister, sick. "Say it. You like it, don't you?"

But I didn't say it. I refused.

And he punished me for not obeying.

Wyatt had learned early on to wear boots on the job. An agent never knew where he'd be on a crime scene or what he'd be stepping into when he arrived.

The marsh held its challenges anyway. The alligators, for one, prowling and hiding, waiting to strike. The muddy soil sucked at his feet like quicksand. The murky water was a breeding ground for mosquitos, gnats, and no-see-ums, the tiny, ravenous midges that plagued the island.

Still, cast in shadows with the weeds and sea oats swaying in the wind, it held a certain beauty.

Not tonight, though. The loamy scent hinted at death. Bones had been found. Bones that needed answering for.

Flashlight beams from the evidence response team skated over brittle marsh grass, adding a ghostly feel.

He didn't know why a graveyard had been built so close to this marshland, but this graveyard and church had been here long before the last hurricane, which had caused erosion and altered the landscape.

His leg throbbed and felt stiff as he trudged through the overgrown sea grass and weeds.

Biting back the pain, he headed toward a uniformed officer who stood in ankle-deep water with a grim expression on his face.

He flashed his credentials. "Special Agent Wyatt Camden. You called us."

"Sure did. Detective Ryker Brockett."

Wyatt recognized him. He'd worked the vigilante murders.

Brockett gestured toward a small wooden bridge over a deeper section of the water. A middle-aged man in jeans and a Braves hat stood looking out at the scene, his complexion ruddy.

"Crabber said he put his net in, and when he pulled it up, bones were caught in it."

An image formed in Wyatt's mind. "I guess that was a shock."

The detective nodded grimly. "He was shook up but curious, so he jumped onto the bridge, then heard bones cracking beneath his shoes."

"Ah, hell." He felt for the guy. Then again, the crabber could have been the one to dig up the bones, then staged the scene to make himself look innocent.

"These bones were in unmarked graves?"

Brockett nodded. "The other graves are old but intact with stone markers. There're no signs that these skeletons were in coffins, which raises more suspicions."

Damn right it did.

"If anyone else shows up, keep them away from our crime scene," Wyatt said. He half expected Marilyn Ellis, the news anchor who'd covered the vigilante murders, to barrel in with her cameraman.

"Will do. ME should be here soon. Said he'd call a forensic anthropologist to help excavate the bones and transport them back to the lab for analysis."

"Good. We'll need all the help we can get."

Wyatt shined his flashlight over the ground to make sure he didn't step on any of the bones as he strode to the bridge where the crabber stood. Some perpetrators enjoyed wreaking havoc, then watching the police scurry to dig up clues and track down the culprit. He'd wait till he talked to the guy to make that call.

From a distance, it was difficult to read the man's expression. Closer, with his flashlight illuminating the man's face, he noted sweat on the crabber's brow and forehead. His breathing was also raspy and choppy.

"Sir, I'm Special Agent Wyatt Camden." The wooden boards creaked as he moved closer. "I understand you found the bones."

The man slowly turned and extended his hand. But it wasn't excitement or awe in his expression. His eyes were glazed, cloudy. Vacant.

The truth dawned. This man wasn't looking at the crime scene in shock—he was blind. Instead, he'd been listening to the sounds of the workers.

"I'm afraid I did find them," the man said in a low voice.

"Tell me what happened," Wyatt said.

The man lifted one hand to shift his hat, and Wyatt spotted scars on his fingers. A long one ran across the palm of his hand as if it had been sliced wide open. It was fresh, too. The skin was still red and puckered.

"Friend of mine dropped me off so I could crab."

"Do you come to this spot a lot?"

The man shrugged. "I've got a couple of different places I go. Last week I had good luck here, so thought I'd try it again."

"Was anyone here when you arrived?"

"Don't think so," he mumbled. "Then again, I could have missed someone if they were hiding. But I didn't hear voices or a car."

"Then what happened?" Wyatt asked.

"I tied the chicken necks inside the net, then dropped the net in." He patted the pocket of his jeans and removed a pack of unfiltered Camels. "Had a smoke or two while I waited."

"What time did you get here?"

"Dusk."

"You said you didn't hear a car or boat. A canoe could get close to here."

"Sorry. Didn't hear anything but the wind and the birds. And some tree frogs."

"What happened next?"

"I pulled one of the nets up to check, but . . . there wasn't a crab inside. At first, thought I'd caught a stick, but . . . it didn't feel like a stick." He coughed, then lit up a cigarette. "I ran my fingers over it, then realized I had bones . . ."

"You touched them?"

"Yeah." Revulsion darkened his voice. "Just one of them. Freaked me out, and I dropped the net. I heard it splash, then figured I'd better retrieve it and call someone."

Wyatt spotted a net on the bridge, a chicken neck inside, one lone crab tangled in the weave. "Was this the net?"

"No, one of them other guys took it." He held up his hands. "They took my prints, too, and my shoes."

"They need to compare prints and forensics to eliminate you," Wyatt said.

The man lifted his chin and looked up at Wyatt, and for a moment, he felt as if the man could see him.

"Why you reckon someone would steal bones?"

Wyatt didn't like any of the answers that came to him.

CHAPTER SIX

The Keeper smiled as she drew a sketch of the Skull. A narrow head. Scrawny body.

Beady eyes. Eyes that belonged to a coward.

He didn't know it yet. But they were going to play a little game of cat and mouse.

Except this time, he would be the mouse.

Tonight, she had set her plan in motion. Thanks to television news coverage of the Skull, she knew details that would help.

The Day of the Dead was significant to him. A string of paper skulls, *papel picado*, adorned an altar. A shrine was made with marigolds and crimson flowers meant to honor those who'd passed. Sugar skulls were also used as decorations.

Unlike Halloween, the Day of the Dead was a time of reflection. Peace. Quiet.

Except the Skull had turned it into his time of kidnapping and torture.

She clicked onto Tinsley's *Heart & Soul* website. Tinsley had written a new post. Fear and pain echoed from her words.

I grieve for the girl I once was. For the woman I wanted to be.

Only the shell of that person remains.

And I hate him for doing this to me.

Tinsley had to face the demons. According to her blog, she thought hiding out in the sanctity of the cove with the ocean breeze, salty air, and kids' laughter would rejuvenate her soul.

Yet she lay trapped in the agony of her memories like a hermit crab trying to climb above the surface when the sand is mired down by a heavy boot, preventing its escape.

She would be unleashed from her misery soon.

Although she might have to suffer first to earn her freedom.

But it would all be worth it in the end.

After all, she wasn't the only one who'd suffered.

CHAPTER SEVEN

The last sliver of sunlight faded from the powder-blue sky, casting a blanket of gray across the waves as they crashed onto the shore.

Tinsley rubbed her arms to ward off the chill invading her.

The anniversary of her abduction was approaching.

Maybe that was the reason she'd thought she'd seen the Skull outside the window.

She searched the beach and dock for signs that he'd returned. He might not have been here tonight.

But he would come back for her. It was only a matter of time.

Where had he been during the winter months? And the long summer?

Lying low until the tourists left the island? Until it was nearly deserted?

That was already happening. She felt the changes in the cooler air seeping through the screens. Saw it in the ebb and flow of the tides.

Vacationers had returned to school and work. The days were starting to grow shorter as fall set in.

Self-disgust ate at her. Once upon a time she'd loved autumn with its vibrant shades of colors. Invigorated by the crisp cooler air, she'd enjoyed long walks with whatever rescue dog she'd housed at the time.

But *he* had ruined that for her.

Now she didn't want summer to end. The days had been long and hot but filled with happy families on the beach. Families that she could pretend to be part of. That made her feel less alone.

And there had been hours and hours of sunlight to keep the darkness at bay.

Those lazy days had brought a sense of peace and lulled Tinsley into thinking that she might one day heal. That maybe he'd forgotten about her.

Summer might be his time of rest, too.

Since her attack, she'd studied the pathology of serial killers. She pulled one of the research books she'd ordered online from her shelf and flipped through the pages, searching for the chapter about rituals. There was a method to the madness of a predator.

The changing of the seasons might be significant for the Skull. Had something traumatic happened to him in the fall? Maybe he'd lost someone . . . the people he chanted to during that damn celebration . . .

She shivered again. With the days growing shorter, night seemed to last forever.

She hated the darkness. The long hours of emptiness and uncertainty.

Those nights triggered memories of being held captive, of the dank interior of the room where he'd kept her.

Of the sound of his voice, hollow and flat, echoing from the doorway. Of the taunts and demented words he'd whispered in her ear as he'd forced himself on her.

Say you like it. Say you want me to fuck you.

She'd bitten her tongue until it bled to keep from giving in to him.

As soon as he'd spent himself, he'd crawl away and curl into a fetal position. While she'd lain there, limp and helpless, she'd seen horror and self-disgust in his eyes. He'd punished her.

But then he'd punished himself. Said he hated that he'd taken her.

That he couldn't stop himself.

It was her fault. She was temptation. A devil in disguise.

Trembling from the memories, she stripped her clothes and headed to the shower. She'd scrubbed herself a million times since she'd been free, but his scent and the feel of his hands and body lingered.

Just as the scars did.

She stared at herself in the mirror, hating the way she looked. Another victory for him.

He'd scarred her to keep her from tempting another man into sinning by wanting her.

♦ ♦ ♦

Wyatt rubbed his bleary eyes as the evidence response team searched the crime scene.

They had to set up lights, rope off the area, and photograph the grounds and gravesites without disturbing the graves any more than necessary.

Mistakes would be made, though. The first responding officer had probably trampled part of the scene already. So had the crabber who'd found the body. Elimination footprints had been taken.

Wyatt's partner, Hatcher McGee, met the medical examiner as he approached, and they walked toward Wyatt. Dr. Patton had worked the vigilante killings with Hatcher. The man was good but not an expert on bones.

"So far we think three skulls are missing," Wyatt said.

"According to the local lore surrounding Skull's Crossing, three were found years ago," Hatcher said.

"You think these are related?" Dr. Patton asked.

Wyatt shrugged. "That's possible, although this unsub didn't leave skulls. He stole them."

Hatcher scratched his head. "True."

Wyatt shifted. "The man who abducted Tinsley had three skulls hanging in the room where he held her."

Hatcher crossed his arms. "We assumed those belonged to his previous victims. Maybe he stole them from a graveyard, but there weren't reports of grave disturbances like this."

Thunder crackled, and lightning zigzagged across the inky sky, streaking the area and making it look ghostly. Wyatt tried to form a mental picture of someone digging up these skeletons, and a possible motive.

"It's almost Halloween," he said, throwing out the obvious and less sinister possibility. "Could be kids or teens wanting to prank someone."

Hatcher and Dr. Patton nodded agreement, although silence stretched as another clap of thunder rent the air, and Wyatt's mind dove to dark places.

"I'm going to check on that forensic anthropologist." Dr. Patton retrieved his phone from his pocket and stepped aside to make the call.

Wyatt heaved a wary breath.

"You have to be wondering the same thing I am," Hatcher said bluntly.

Wyatt nodded, the unease in his gut tightening. "Tinsley phoned me earlier. She thought she saw him outside the cottage."

Hatcher's sharp intake of breath punctuated the air. "Dammit. We knew he'd resurface sometime."

Wyatt studied the workers combing the marsh, his pulse hammering. "He could have taken these skulls as a statement to us that he's back."

Or perhaps he needed them to re-create the place where he held her.

Because he was setting up a new hellhole to take her to when he abducted her . . .

The date on the calendar mocked Tinsley as she wrestled for sleep. Last year at this time she'd been excited about the fund-raiser for the rescue shelter. All her planning had paid off, and the event had gone off without a hitch.

She'd been on top of the world as she'd walked to her car.

But then the Skull had abducted her, and she'd been introduced to a kind of violence she'd never imagined.

Finally, she threw the covers aside, slid from bed, and padded to the living room. The walls were closing in on her again. After being held in that confined space, she hated being locked in these three rooms.

But she didn't know how to break through the terror that paralyzed her. The panic attack she'd suffered earlier proved she wasn't ready.

Would she ever be?

Releasing a weary sigh, she peeked through the shutters onto the porch.

The wind rattled the glass panes, raindrops trickling down the window like a river of snakes. Thunder boomed, and another downpour rushed from the sky, beating the tin roof of the cottage like nails.

Something hit the porch floor, and she jumped. Heart racing, she leaned closer to the window and peered toward the steps. Another loud thump.

Branches from a tree had snapped off in the storm.

Too jumpy to go back to bed, she stepped into the kitchen and put on water for some hot tea. While it heated, she opened up her computer. Several responses to her website filled the screen.

The teakettle whistled, and she grabbed a tea bag from the canister on her counter, placed it in her favorite beach mug, then filled the cup with hot water. A headache pulsed at her temple, and she swallowed a painkiller, then sat down in front of her computer.

Emotions clogged her throat as she read the sympathy-filled comments. Ironic that here, locked in this space, she'd made dozens and dozens of friends. Granted, they were all faceless and anonymous, no one she would invite over for coffee or lunch, but having contact with these strangers gave her a safe haven for her feelings. Here, she didn't have to put on an act and pretend she was normal.

I hate the man who destroyed my life just as you do, Tinsley.

I was a victim of the River Street Rapist. When he left me in that alley, I wanted to curl up and die.

Then the paramedics found me and assured me I would be all right.

But I'm not all right. I don't think I ever will be.

He stole so much from me. My trust in men. My sense of safety. My life as I knew it.

Now every time I walk to my car or go for a run, I'm constantly alert, watching, waiting for an attack.

My boyfriend asked me what happened before the man raped me. If I'd flirted with him. Smiled at him on the street. If I was giving out vibes that I wanted to talk to him.

That hurt the most.

But I asked myself the same questions.

A hundred times, I retraced every second of the hours leading up to the moment he snatched me.

Had I seen him in the restaurant where I'd had dinner? Had I spoken to him at the bar when I ordered my drink?

Had I invited him to rape me?

No . . .

No woman invites a rapist to attack her. Rape isn't about sex, it's about violence. Power.

The woman was right. The counselor Tinsley had worked with had assured her of the same thing.

Another comment appeared, and she began to read.

The Day of the Dead will be here soon, Tinsley.

It is a time of reflection, a time to honor the loved ones we've lost.

A time to remember that death comes for all of us.

Will you visit your parents' graves and honor them this year?

She slammed her laptop closed. When the Skull had chanted and sung to the dead, he'd asked her whether she visited her parents' graves. Had he written that post?

CHAPTER EIGHT

The photos the Skull kept of Tinsley made his body hum with need. She had been a good girl. Kind, giving, delicate as a flower.

Just like Janine.

Grief robbed his breath. He'd known wanting Janine was wrong, but he'd wanted her anyway.

He thought Tinsley could replace her. Fill the void in his life. Make him happy.

But she'd refused to say she wanted him. That she liked his touch or having him inside her.

That had angered him the most.

He'd wanted her to love him. Wanted them to be a family.

Now she'd locked herself away in a cottage at Sunset Cove. As if a locked door could stop him from taking her if he wanted to.

And he definitely wanted to.

The dark urge was building in him again. The hunger to see her. Touch her. Take her.

Make her his.

He ran his fingers over the bones of the skulls, smiling as the sound of the girls' screams echoed in his head.

Those skulls had once held the brains of living beings. The mind was an intricate part of the body. The brain controlled everything, from motor skills to emotions to pain.

His was warped, they said.

They had punished him. And when that hadn't worked, they'd run tests. Tried to fix him.

Given him shock treatments to kill the devil inside him.

But he was what he was, and there was no changing that.

The Feds would call the skulls he kept his trophies.

They'd speculate that he'd been abused as a child. That he'd suffered some horrific traumatic experience. Maybe he'd been tortured or locked in a cage.

They were wrong.

He'd had a normal mama and daddy. He hadn't been beaten or burned or had his head smashed in when he was little. His mama loved him, had nursed him when he was a baby. She'd cleaned his cuts and driven him to band practice and taken him to Sunday school.

She'd been a do-gooder with a tender heart for animals. Maybe she'd loved them a little more than she had him.

That had been her flaw.

He didn't blame her, though. No, he loved her.

Early on, he'd known he was different. Sinister thoughts crept into his mind at odd times. Voices whispered inside his head, telling him to hurt others.

At first he'd run from the voices. Tried to ignore the urges. He'd fought the beast inside him. But his anger and rage had intensified daily.

Then one night his mother had insisted he take care of a sick stray she'd brought home. They already had six filthy animals in the house. Some of them cried and mewled like babies and kept him awake at night. He tried to cover his head with his pillow to drown them out. When that hadn't worked, he stuffed cotton balls in his ears.

Mama rocked and held those damn animals like babies.

The voices in his head screamed that it wasn't fair.

She'd promised to take him Christmas shopping the next day. She'd canceled a dozen times already. He'd wanted that video game system that all the boys were getting that year, but she'd said he couldn't have it. That they could use that money for the rescue center. She'd said he needed to learn a lesson about not being selfish.

Then she'd brought that mangy animal in and told him he'd have to stay up with it that night. She had to sleep because she had surgery the next day.

The damn scrawny cat had fleas and sores on its body. Knots and bugs inside its long, matted hair. And piercing green eyes that made him think it might be possessed by the devil.

Still, he'd wanted to please his mama. He'd brought the animal food and water and tried to brush out the tangles in its ratty hair.

But the damn thing had hissed at him, its devil eyes alight with evil. Then it had scratched the hell out of him, and he'd snapped.

Killing it had been merciful. The cat was no longer sick. It was resting.

He'd destroyed the devil living in it.

Once he gave in to the beast inside him, he felt a sense of peace. It took a strong person to do what he'd done.

He wasn't the monster they thought. He had eased the cat's suffering.

Just as he would soon ease Tinsley's.

Frustrated that he couldn't get close to her tonight, he left the island. Hunting there was too risky.

Savannah's nightlife was in full swing as he parked. Halloween decorations adorned the storefronts. Voodoo dolls, pirates, monsters, and ghosts . . .

The streets teemed with visitors and locals. Music blasted from the bars.

He had to be discreet. Avoid anyplace with cameras.

Satisfied with the alley behind a coffee shop, he dug his hands into his pockets, then slipped inside and ordered a coffee. He needed his head clear. Didn't want to smell like whiskey.

After all, he was looking for a good girl.

Not one of the whores slurping down cheap pink drinks with umbrellas from the pub or expensive martinis from the Olive Glass where the millennials gathered.

He settled outside at a corner table to watch. Agitation built as group after group of coeds walked past.

Short skirts rode up their butts. Breasts hung out of tight knit tops. They wobbled unsteadily on heels that no fool should ever try to walk in.

Obsessed with their cell phones and social media, they were oblivious to him or any other man.

Still, those tight nipples made his cock twitch and harden.

It was wrong to want them.

He shifted and dragged his gaze back to the outdoor seating. A petite girl in jeans and a T-shirt claimed a table near him. Her wavy brown hair and funky glasses made her look wholesome but sexy.

He studied her as she sipped a latte. She appeared to be alone.

He pasted on his most charming smile. Meeting girls had always been hard for him. All the small talk. Flirting. Games.

He didn't like games.

Just as he was working up the nerve to talk to her, a girl with short spiked hair, a cropped top, and boy jeans appeared and threw her arms around the petite girl. Then they fused mouths in a kiss.

He threw his cup in the trash and stalked back toward the parking lot.

He was wasting his time here.

She wouldn't have been right anyway. Not when he wanted Tinsley.

He climbed in his car, slammed the door, and sped toward Sunset Cove to see whether she was sleeping.

CHAPTER NINE

Wyatt shook rainwater from his hair, his uneasiness growing. He wanted answers. Wanted to know whether those skulls were connected to Tinsley's case.

His instincts screamed that they were and that Tinsley was in danger.

He jammed his hands into his jacket pockets, his gaze traveling across the marsh as he walked back to his SUV. Storm clouds had rolled in around midnight. The team had been forced to halt their search during the worst of the downpour but had resumed as soon as it eased. The rain and mud made forensics more difficult to retrieve and identify, but they'd done their best.

At least they'd confirmed that their initial count of three missing skulls was accurate.

Had the skulls belonged to murder victims? If so, had the killer returned to collect them?

Hopefully the forensic anthropologist and ME could make IDs, and they'd investigate from there.

A car engine sounded from the road. A white news van rolled up and parked, and then a woman and cameraman climbed out.

Marilyn Ellis, the investigative journalist who'd been a thorn in their side on other investigations.

She'd repeatedly pressured Tinsley for an interview, but Tinsley staunchly avoided the press.

Yet here Marilyn was, ready to pounce on the story about the missing skulls. How the hell did she even know about them? A police scanner?

Marilyn made a beeline for Hatcher. Big mistake. Hatcher detested her. His partner motioned to the uniformed officer to keep her away from him—and the crime scene.

Then Hatcher strode toward Wyatt. "I'm heading home. Korine isn't feeling well."

Hatcher was the toughest guy he knew, but he was a worrywart regarding his wife's pregnancy.

"Take care of her," Wyatt said, and meant it. "I'll go by Tinsley's and check on her when I leave here."

He just hoped Marilyn didn't put two and two together and assume these missing skulls were connected to Tinsley.

After her rescue, Tinsley had been so traumatized that her memories had been sporadic and fuzzy. The doctor had said she'd been drugged. She'd also repressed the details because of the trauma.

He'd advised them to give her time. That she would remember when she was ready.

But those details she kept locked away could be the key to finding the bastard who'd tormented her. He might have to push her to remember . . .

Marilyn headed toward Detective Brockett, and Wyatt jumped in his car. The detective could take care of her.

Raindrops pelted his windshield as he drove across the island to Sunset Cove. Early-morning joggers and walkers were already hitting the sidewalks and beach, oblivious to the fact that a serial predator might be hunting again.

He scanned the area as he neared the cove, then turned into the cul-de-sac and parked. For a minute, he simply sat and studied the cottage where Tinsley had imprisoned herself.

The past few months the Skull had lain dormant. No word from him. No sightings. No other victims.

Wyatt wondered whether the monster had left Georgia and gone to another location to hide—or to hunt.

Was he back now?

Wyatt got out of his vehicle and headed toward the cottage. They believed that the Day of the Dead was significant to him, but how? Did the celebration have a personal meaning, or had the Skull fixated on it because it had to do with death?

Wyatt climbed the steps to the porch, scanning the neighboring cottages, the dock, and the beach in case the Skull was watching.

The storm had tossed sand and debris onto the porch; rivulets of water streamed down the windowpanes.

The shutters were closed.

Was Tinsley awake? Had she slept at all last night?

He raised his hand to knock, then hesitated. Once he told her about the missing skulls, she'd wonder whether her abductor had taken them.

Could he rouse that fear in her again without verifying that the two were connected?

◆ ◆ ◆

Tinsley's heart hammered as she watched the early-morning news. Marilyn Ellis stood by a strip of marshland, the wind tousling her hair.

"We're here this morning at Seaside Cemetery, where dozens of bodies dating back to the Civil War were once buried. The last hurricane tore up the topography, rearranging sections of beach and adding to the erosion problem, and uprooting graves. Workers had just

46

restored the graves and smoothed ruffled feathers of family members whose loved ones had been defiled by nature. Unfortunately, last night the graveyard was disturbed again. Only this time it wasn't a force of nature that wreaked havoc but mankind." She paused while the camera panned across the marshland. Cast in early-morning shadows and gray skies, it looked downright eerie.

"Local police and the FBI have joined forces to search the area where three skulls were reported to have been taken, the heads severed from the skeletal remains."

The sound of footsteps on the porch startled Tinsley and dragged her attention from the news. Another sound, another footstep.

Someone was out there . . .

She wasn't expecting a delivery or a visitor, not this early in the morning.

Shoulders stiff with tension, she grabbed the fireplace poker and tiptoed to the door. A knock sounded just as she leaned closer. She jumped back, braced to fight if an intruder burst through.

Another knock.

Heart racing, she gripped the poker tighter and checked the peep-hole. Tall. Brown shaggy hair. A wide jaw.

A blue FBI jacket drenched in rainwater.

Relief surged through her. Wyatt.

She quickly reached for the doorknob. As soon as she saw his grim expression, she knew where he'd been.

"You were at that graveyard, weren't you?" she asked, emotions thick in her throat. "I . . . saw the news . . ."

His gaze shot to the television, and then he wiped his boots on the doormat and stepped inside. "That was the call I answered."

Fear crawled up her spine. Last night she'd thought she'd seen the Skull on her porch.

She'd worked so hard to forget him. To push the memories away. To regain her sanity.

Any sense of safety she'd started to regain vanished. The Skull was back. And he'd taken those skulls so she would know it.

◆ ◆ ◆

Wyatt made it a point to never let a case get personal. Never get involved with a witness or suspect. Emotions dulled the mind and interfered with focus.

But all those months he'd studied Tinsley, hoping to find a clue as to why she'd been chosen as a victim, had gotten to him.

He'd seen pictures of her receiving awards for her humanitarian efforts with rescue animals. Photograph after photograph of her working with PAT—several shots of her with veterans suffering from PTSD, a blind woman in need of a guide dog, an elderly woman with diabetes who needed a gentle reminder to check her blood sugar before it dropped to a dangerous level. Of Tinsley carrying therapy animals into the children's hospital.

God, those pictures of her at the hospital tugged at his heart. There was one with a little blonde-haired girl in a wheelchair, another with a toddler wearing leg braces, and then one with a cancer patient . . .

Tinsley Jensen was a damn saint.

He'd felt like he'd known her before he'd even met her. That had never happened to him before. Hell, he'd never even been tempted by a suspect or a victim or a witness.

But he liked Tinsley. She hadn't deserved to be in the hands of a depraved psycho.

Working day after day, chasing leads while she was missing, he'd collapsed into bed at night, haunted by images of what might be happening to her.

The fear on Tinsley's face now tugged at his heartstrings.

She closed the door, then walked to the breakfast bar. "Do you want coffee?"

"Coffee would be good. Black," he said, his mouth watering.

She removed a mug from the shelf above the coffee maker and poured it full.

Their fingers brushed as she handed it to him.

Awareness shot through him; alarm flashed in her eyes as if she'd felt it, too, and didn't like it.

Who could blame her after the way she'd suffered at that bastard's hands?

Needing to distract himself, he sipped his coffee while she filled a mug for herself. No sweetener or cream for her either.

Silence stretched, thick with fear and questions. She crossed the room, picked up the remote, and clicked "Off." When she turned to face him again, she traced a finger around the rim of her mug. "You think he took the skulls, don't you?"

"I don't know," he said. "It's possible."

"Don't lie to me," Tinsley said. "After what he put me through, I deserve to know if he's found me."

"The truth is that I really don't know. It's too suspicious not to take precautions. But it's also possible that vandals, maybe teens looking for a way to celebrate Halloween, had their own kind of fun in that graveyard."

Tinsley squeezed her eyes shut for a moment, her face strained as if she wanted to believe that theory but didn't quite buy it. He ached to comfort her, to assure her he'd never let that bastard touch her again.

But he couldn't do that, especially when he had no idea where the Skull was hiding. Without an ID or image of his face, the bastard could be right next door, and they wouldn't know it. Although they'd searched for months, all they really knew was that he was male, sadistic, and that he had a thing about skulls.

They believed he'd abducted three other girls before Tinsley. At least the police had received three sugar skulls. Tinsley had also described seeing three skulls hanging in the room where he'd kept her, suggesting he'd murdered them.

But the bodies of those girls had never been found.

She tucked a strand of hair behind her ear, her expression so pained it struck him that she'd been waiting ever since she'd escaped for the moment her kidnapper would come back for her.

That maybe she needed to finish this before she could truly move on.

"I wanted to forget him," she said in a low whisper. "But I can't." She walked over to the window and opened the shutters.

Outside the sky looked bleak. Gray. Filled with another storm on the horizon.

Wyatt cleared his throat. "I'm sorry, Tinsley. If I'd caught him that day—"

"You've already apologized," she interrupted, her voice cracking. "I owe you my life, Wyatt."

"You don't owe me anything," Wyatt said, a knot in his belly. "But I want to find this creep and stop him before he hurts you or anyone else again. I'd like to put a trace on your phone in case he contacts you. Is that all right?"

"Of course."

"Also, I need you to tell me everything you can remember about your captivity."

She shook her head in denial. "I can't go back there and relive it. I . . . just can't."

Wyatt slowly walked toward her. He wanted to hold her so badly his hands literally ached.

That would be a mistake, though. He never crossed the line on a case. And this one was too important for him to start now.

Besides, Tinsley wouldn't welcome his touch. In fact, he might make the situation worse if he touched her.

So he curled his fingers around the hot mug instead and forced his voice to remain soft. She needed a safe place to open up. No judgment.

"I understand your reluctance, and frankly, I don't want to hear the details. But anything you can share might enable us to find him."

Their gazes met and locked. Emotions flooded her face, then resignation.

"All right." She sank onto the couch.

He braced himself to remain detached as she began to talk.

CHAPTER TEN

Marilyn Ellis settled into the chair in the room at the psych hospital that had been prearranged for her interviews with Cat Landon, a.k.a. Belinda Winters. Her arrest for a series of vigilante killings had revealed that she belonged to a chat group called the Keepers who were incensed over what they deemed injustices of the law. Cat had left the justice symbol, a double *SS*, on the foreheads of the ones she'd punished as a sign that justice had been served.

Online, the Keepers supported exacting that justice themselves.

Although Cat had insisted she'd acted alone, the Feds still had doubts.

Marilyn had worked damn hard to earn time with Cat, just like she'd worked to climb her way to success at the news station. Except with Cat, she'd had to get permission from the Feds to talk to her.

They'd warned Marilyn that if she learned of other victims, or of other active Keepers planning more vigilante murders, she had to come forward or face prosecution.

She was no goddamn snitch, though.

Her boss at the local TV station in Savannah knew that. She had a reputation as a barracuda and as being the one woman on the team who'd sacrifice herself for a story.

All true. And the very characteristics that might earn her a lead anchor spot. Being part of a muckraking team had taught her a lot.

But she had a hard time being a team player.

Her boss, Edwin Polk, had laid out the terms for her just this morning. "If you want the lead spot instead of Denton, you have to bring me something big. A story that no one knows about."

She was working on it.

And she'd get it, no matter what she had to do. Some thought she had a God complex. Others said she was a thrill seeker.

A few simply called her a bitch.

She didn't deny any of those labels.

Still, no one knew the truth about Marilyn Ellis. And no one ever would.

Even Cat didn't realize the connection they had.

Marilyn might tell her one day. But for now it was her secret to keep.

She liked secrets.

She especially liked exposing the secrets of others.

The door opened, and a male nurse named Samson escorted Cat inside. Months ago, when Cat had first been arrested for the murders of a judge, a pedophile, and a driver's ed teacher who'd sexually harassed his students, a lawyer named Kendall James had jumped in to represent her. She'd used the fact that Cat had been molested as a child to garner a plea with the DA, so Cat was serving time in a psychiatric hospital instead of a maximum-security prison.

Cat spent her days with nutcases instead of violent offenders. A waste for a brilliant woman with a photographic memory.

Marilyn had done her part to paint a picture of Cat as a victim.

Besides, all those cocksuckers Cat had killed had deserved to die.

Marilyn greeted the young woman with a smile, waiting to see what kind of mood Cat was in today.

During their first interview, Cat had been defensive and combative. Later, when she realized that Marilyn was on her side, she'd relaxed.

Cat glanced warily at Samson as he remained in the doorway.

"I've got it from here," Marilyn said, dismissing him. "You can leave us alone."

From the beginning, Marilyn had insisted that she conduct her interviews in private. Although a staff member always watched through the glass partition in case the situation turned volatile.

Or in case Marilyn slipped Cat a weapon so she could escape.

But they couldn't hear what was said.

Cat ran a shaky hand through her tangled hair, and Marilyn noticed a fresh scar on her wrist. Other bruises marred her lower arm.

Had she been fighting? Or . . . had she tried to commit suicide?

The first two months, the hospital had kept her under a suicide watch, but the last time she'd seen Cat, she'd seemed to have moved past that stage.

"I thought we were finished," Cat murmured.

She was talking about the interviews. But Marilyn wasn't finished by a long shot.

She squeezed the woman's shaky hands. "We've only just begun."

In fact, the interviews had been a smokescreen to find out more about the Keepers.

Not for the police.

For herself.

CHAPTER ELEVEN

"I don't know where to start," Tinsley said. "We went through this a dozen times after I was rescued."

"Sometimes, with the passage of time, people recall different details, maybe something they didn't remember at first. Even the slightest thing can be important." Wyatt paused. "Start from the beginning. Do you think you'd met the man who abducted you before?"

Tinsley rubbed two fingers along her temple, struggling to recall that time. A time she'd prayed to forget. "I don't know," she said honestly. "Sometimes he made comments that suggested we had."

"Like that?"

"When he was mad, he said that I shouldn't have ignored him."

"Was there anything else?"

Memories nagged at her, escaping the locked box where she stored them for her own survival. "He said he liked it when I wore my hair in braids." She heaved a breath. "But I haven't worn my hair in braids since I was twelve."

An awkward silence followed.

"Was there something significant about that time?" Wyatt asked.

Her heart wrenched. "My parents died when I was twelve. A car accident. They were my whole world, and my sister's. One minute they were there; the next, gone." She hesitated and took a breath.

Images flashed behind her eyes. *The policeman at the door. Gram doubling over with a sob. Carrie Ann screaming . . . Nights and nights of her screaming.*

The funeral home with strangers patting her shoulder. Mama's and Daddy's hands . . . so cold. Stiff. Hard. Their lips that looked like plastic.

A white lacy blouse. Church clothes that didn't look like Mama. No sweet perfume on her neck. No prickly beard on Daddy.

Her birthday that year passed without celebration. Then Christmas. No live tree 'cause Daddy wasn't there to cut one. Carrie Ann growing hysterical that they couldn't find the ornaments they'd made the year before. Gram burning the cookies . . .

"I'm sorry about your parents," Wyatt said, dragging her back to the present.

She nodded, numb. "My grandmother moved in with us. It was a . . . difficult time."

"He could have met you when you were young. Or sometimes predators research their targets," Wyatt said quietly.

"You think we attended school together?"

"It's possible," Wyatt said. "Or he met you somewhere else, and once he fixated on you, he dug up whatever he could find on you. Maybe he found a picture of you wearing braids in a school yearbook."

"I suppose," she said with a small shrug.

Wyatt sighed. "Let's talk about the day he took you. Walk me through what you did."

Tinsley tensed. "Why? You think I did something that made him choose me?"

Wyatt set his coffee mug down, his gaze meeting hers. "Listen to me. This was not your fault. But the more we know about him and the reason he chose you, even if it was random, the more it will help us put together a profile. Little things that might not have seemed important at the time may be significant to his pathology."

Tinsley clung to Wyatt's words: *Not your fault, not your fault, not your fault* . . .

She closed her eyes, forcing herself back to that day. "It was a beautiful fall day," she said softly. "We were hosting an adoption event at the park. I remember the crisp, cool air, the leaves falling, the smell of hot chocolate at the stand near where PAT set up their booth."

"PAT?"

"Pets as Therapy," she replied. "Everyone who volunteers is dedicated to rescue animals. We train the animals, then take them to hospitals, nursing homes, children's centers, the VA hospital, and other places to help people with depression, mental illness, dementia, loneliness, and other issues. The rescue center PAWS hosted kids' games, a food truck, and an area where people could spend time with the animals available for adoption." A smile tugged at her mouth. "We even had a pet parade for adoptive parents to bring their animals dressed in costumes."

"What time was it?" Wyatt asked.

"It started at noon and went until six. Each month we host similar events in different locations to drive adoptions."

"Were there a lot of people attending?"

She nodded. "We had a huge turnout. By the end of the day, all the rescues were spoken for."

Wyatt made a low sound in his throat. "He could have been there at the park. Maybe he talked to you or was watching you during the event."

Tinsley's heart stuttered. She'd probably talked to a hundred different folks that day. She could easily have met him during the event and not remembered. Was that what he meant when he said she'd ignored him?

◆ ◆ ◆

Wyatt had read the police report taken at the hospital after Tinsley had been admitted. He'd wanted to interview her himself, but he'd been bleeding badly from where the Skull had stabbed him during Tinsley's rescue. Doctors had rushed him into surgery to save his life and his leg. When he'd come to, he'd been dosed with painkillers and moved to a rehab facility to start physical therapy.

Meanwhile, Hatcher had been so distraught over his wife's death that he'd been out of commission as well.

The day they finally found Tinsley still haunted Wyatt. The Skull's partner, whom they hadn't known about at the time, had abducted Hatcher's wife, Felicia. Wyatt and Hatcher had finally traced them to a location and stormed in. But Hatcher had been too late to save Felicia. She'd died at the hands of the Skull's partner, right in front of his eyes.

Hatcher, obsessed with getting justice—revenge—had tracked down the bastard and killed him.

With Wyatt and Hatcher out of the picture temporarily, a detective from the Savannah Police Department had met with Tinsley to question her. According to the report, Tinsley had been in shock and too traumatized to give them much.

Tinsley's fiancé, Jordan Radish, had rushed to the hospital and stayed with her around the clock the first two days. But he had a rock-solid alibi for the time of her abduction, and they'd cleared him immediately.

"There were hundreds of people in and out of the booths—kids and families, teenagers. That morning we sponsored a 5K run to raise money for PAWS. At least five hundred people signed up for it."

Wyatt raked a hand through his hair. "He could have been anywhere in that crowd."

"Maybe he tried to talk to me and I didn't have time," Tinsley said.

"That's possible, but again, it's not your fault. His brain is wired differently. Predators can misconstrue a smile, an action, a word. Virtually anything can set them off."

Tinsley nodded. "We keep a list of everyone who adopts a pet as well as applicants and people interested in volunteering," Tinsley said. "People who love rescue animals are usually kind and tenderhearted." She shivered. "He was none of those things."

No, he wasn't.

No matter how hard he tried, Wyatt couldn't erase the disturbing images of her battered body and bruised face from his mind.

"That list might help," he said. "Think back to that day again. Did anyone stand out? Someone who seemed antagonistic toward you or upset?"

Tinsley closed her eyes again, her face strained as the seconds passed. Wyatt waited, giving her time to sort through the past. "I don't recall anything significant."

"Do you run background checks on the applicants?"

Tinsley sipped her coffee. "Not really. Our goal is to find homes for them, not put people on the spot."

"I understand, but you must be careful about placement."

"That's true. Interested parties fill out a questionnaire, and we interview them. We get a good sense of what the people are like, what their home is like, and their plans to take care of the animal. We also request pictures of the home and yard. If the person has another pet, we suggest they bring the pet in for a meet and greet with the rescue they've chosen to see if they're compatible."

Wyatt considered that information. "Did you have to turn down any applicants that day?" That seemed like a stretch for a trigger, but who knew what made this guy tick?

Tinsley pursed her mouth in thought, walked to the coffeepot, and refilled their mugs. Then she claimed a seat again.

"Now that you mention it, there was a small incident. I didn't think anything about it at the time, but some guy reached out to pet a mixed-breed dog we had, and it snapped at him. It was strange because the dog, Hershey, was usually friendly and liked everyone."

Wyatt's instincts kicked in. Animals sometimes had a sixth sense about who they could trust.

"What happened then?"

"The guy got upset," Tinsley said. "I remember pulling Hershey back and soothing him. The man said we should put that one down, but I told him we didn't do that. Not unless the animal was extremely dangerous and was examined by a vet first."

"How did he take it?"

Tinsley shrugged. "He walked off in a huff."

It could be nothing. But if that guy had been pissed, he could have perceived the entire situation in a negative light.

Would that be enough to trigger him to kidnap and hurt Tinsley?

It seemed far-fetched, but if no other leads turned up, it was something to pursue.

◆ ◆ ◆

Tinsley shifted restlessly. Adoption days were positive, heartwarming, and wonderful, for both the owner and the rescue animal. It had been a wholesome family event.

To think that a predator had been there was unnerving.

According to her therapist and the police, though, predators were everywhere. Pedophiles lurked in the park, near children's playgrounds and schools. Sexual deviants found victims in alleys, on the street, in bars, or even on the job. No place was safe.

That was the reason she'd locked herself between these walls.

She'd tried so hard to understand the man who'd violated her. Had studied the damn books on her shelf, read about psychosis and ritualistic behavior.

But she might never understand, because as Wyatt said, the bastard was wired differently. He could have a mental imbalance, be bipolar or schizophrenic. Or a sociopath. Or any combination.

He'd been violent one moment, then illogical, scattered, and obsessive-compulsive the next.

The crying jags and angry rants after he raped her were especially disturbing. He'd apologized for hurting her, claimed he felt guilty about what he'd done.

Then he'd taken that guilt out on her . . .

She inhaled sharply. She had to get him out of her mind. He had controlled her then.

She refused to let him control her now.

He did, though. As long as she lived in fear, he still held her hostage, a prisoner to the pain.

"I'll need contact information for the PAWS group, and PAT, and copies of those lists," Wyatt said.

Tinsley snagged a business card from her desk and handed it to him. "Call Susan. I'll let her know you'll be in touch so she can pull together the lists."

He tapped the card between his fingers, as if he was stalling and wanted to ask her something else.

She summoned her courage. "What is it?"

His gaze slowly rose to hers, his expression troubled. "I need to know exactly what he said to you when he held you. He may have inadvertently given you a clue that you're not aware of."

A shudder coursed up her spine. The things he'd said were ugly. Demeaning. Could she share them with Wyatt?

She had to. Putting the Skull away was the only way to slay her demons.

CHAPTER TWELVE

Dark storm clouds shrouded the morning sunlight from the solarium window in the sanitarium, mirroring Cat's mood. Odd to have such a sunny, supposedly cheerful place in a nuthouse anyway.

Cat detested the sunshine and the staff's fake smiles and the lunatics here who looked at her like she was one of them.

Maybe she had one foot on the crazy train, but she hadn't completely climbed aboard.

She was just pissed off at life and her mother and the court system, and at the man who'd taken advantage of her as a child.

She'd hated for so long that she didn't know how to feel anything else.

Seth Samson, the psychiatric nurse who took care of her meds, smiled as he handed Cat her morning pill along with an envelope from her mother. "How are you doing today?"

How was she doing? Her hand shook where she held the letter, so she quickly jammed the envelope in her pocket. She was fucking sick of this place and the staff's condescending looks of pity and disgust. But admitting that would land her in restraints, and she could not bear that again.

So she zipped the foul language inside.

"I've been thinking about calling my mother and making amends." Making them believe that would earn her points.

"Good for you, Cat. That's progress. I'll let the counselor know." He slipped from the room to refill her water.

You do that, Seth. Tell them I'm getting all well now. That I'm not going to kill anyone else.

She could play the game.

Not that she had when she'd first come here. She'd been brutally honest and said whatever was on her mind. Told them all to go to hell.

The staff had been tough on her, kept her restrained, in solitary confinement. The patients had been afraid.

Their wide eyes and nervous glances dogged her wherever she went. Was she going to steal a plastic knife off a lunch tray and stab one of them in the jugular? Or maybe she'd strangle them with her bare hands . . .

Laughter bubbled inside her. She didn't kill good people. She'd tried to tell them that. But anyone who hurt or molested children or raped young girls was fair game.

That bitch Marilyn had encouraged her to behave so she could get out of this crazy ward one day. Why Marilyn cared she didn't know. Cat sensed the woman had her own agenda.

One day Cat would find out what it was. It was the only reason she'd agreed to talk to her. That, and well, hell, she was bored out of her mind.

The fuckers had cut her off from the world. No news. No communication.

A travesty for an Internet queen like her.

Marilyn told her what was going on. The reporter couldn't seem to help herself. She puked up gossip and news and crime stories as if her head would explode if she didn't pass on the gory details.

Cat started smiling and pretending she was taking her meds. She was cordial to the staff. Cooperated in therapy and fed the counselors exactly what they wanted to hear.

She lied like the big fat liar they wanted her to be.

Just like her mama, Esme, had lied all these years and pretended nothing had happened to Cat as a child, that the psychiatrist who was supposed to help her hadn't mauled her with his filthy upper-class hands. That Mrs. Davenport's money had been worth sacrificing her daughter's sanity.

Even the people like Seth and Marilyn who understood why she'd taken the lives of those horrific people—and they had been bad—wanted her to get well. Wanted her to show remorse. Forgive her mother. Promise she'd never be a bad girl again.

The only thing she regretted was getting caught.

There were others who needed to be taught a lesson, too. Thanks to her newfound friends, she wasn't as out of touch as the cops thought.

"You won't believe what's happening," Seth said in a low whisper as he hurried back into the room and refilled Cat's water cup.

"What?"

"Yesterday, the police found a graveyard where someone stole the skulls of three people buried in the marsh."

An image of Tinsley Jensen locked in that little cottage at Sunset Cove taunted her. When she'd read Tinsley's *Heart & Soul* website, she'd found a soul sister.

The Keepers had a list of those who'd gotten away with their crimes. Ones who needed to pay with their lives.

The man who'd abducted, raped, and tortured Tinsley was high on their list.

Rage at Marilyn clawed at her. Why hadn't Marilyn told her about the bones? "Do they have any idea who took them?" she asked.

The nurse leaned closer, his gray eyes darting around the solarium. No doubt he'd get in trouble for sharing the news story.

"Not yet," Seth said. "Didn't that man who abducted the Jensen woman hang his victims' skulls from the ceiling?"

Cat nodded. Although they hadn't recovered those skulls, because they'd never located the place where the bastard held Tinsley.

If the Skull was coming out of hiding, the Feds would jump on the case.

The Keepers had to find the bastard first.

CHAPTER THIRTEEN

Wyatt grimaced as he watched Tinsley. The painful memories were taking a toll. Maybe he'd made a mistake by pushing her.

But the only way to find the Skull was to learn everything about him. Understand what made him tick. Understand his victimology.

"Do you want to go on, or do you want me to leave?"

Tinsley swallowed hard, then folded her arms and went to look out the window. A distant look glazed her eyes as if she were miles away. The tide was in, waves crashing against the shore. A lone jogger in a gray hoodie paused with his dog, then threw a tennis ball, and the dog chased after it.

"He's out there somewhere," she said in a low voice. "He's free, while I've locked myself in here." When she pivoted to face him, determination darkened her eyes. "What do you want to know?"

"Everything," he said quietly.

Her face paled, and she rubbed her arms, drawing his gaze to the scars on her fingers and her wrists.

"All right."

As a cop, he had to ask tough questions. As a man who found her attractive and despised what the Skull had done to her, hearing the details would be difficult.

But he wanted to find this bastard and lock him up so he couldn't hurt her again.

"Tell me about that night after the rescue event."

She squared her shoulders. "After we finished with the applications and packed up, a couple of the volunteers had said they were going to the pub nearby for drinks. But I was exhausted and rushed to my car. I'd parked a block away in an alley behind an abandoned warehouse. I was putting a box in the trunk of my SUV when I heard footsteps behind me." She went still, her breath catching. "Before I could turn around, he grabbed me from behind. I tried to fight . . . but then I felt dizzy and . . . he must have injected me with some kind of drug, because I passed out."

Wyatt tensed. "They tested you for drugs when you were admitted to the hospital. I'll check and see what they found."

"He gave me injections at other times," she said with a shiver.

"Heroine? Meth?" Wyatt asked.

She shook her head. "I think it was pain medication," she murmured. "When he drugged me, he said, 'I can give you pain; I can take it away.'"

Interesting. Could mean that the unsub worked in the medical field where he had easy access to meds. An avenue to explore.

"Did he talk as if he was a doctor? Or a nurse, maybe?" Hell, he could be a first responder, PA, nurse assistant, even a medical student or pharmacist.

Tinsley rubbed her forehead. "Not that I recall. I do remember that he seemed ritualistic."

Wyatt raised a brow. "How so?"

"He talked about death, about reflecting on lost loved ones. He created a shrine with flowers and candles and those sugar skulls."

He'd read that in the file. "The Day of the Dead seemed significant to him. Did he explain why?"

Tinsley shrugged. "He talked about honoring our mothers and fathers when they passed. He also mentioned his *abuela*."

Wyatt tightened his fingers around his coffee mug. "He used the word *abuela*?"

Tinsley nodded. "Yes, when he told me about the Day of the Dead celebration. And I heard him tell the man who took Felicia that his *abuela* had taught him about the rituals."

Wyatt studied her. Norton had been there. "Did you see this man?"

She shook her head no. "They were talking outside the door where he held me." Her gaze met his. "That man took Felicia because of me."

"We don't know that," Wyatt said, hating the guilt in her voice. "He could have kidnapped her to get to Hatcher. Our names were in the news as the agents working the case. Norton and the Skull may have cooked up a plan to divert our attention."

"When he carried me to that old shanty in the swamp, I thought he was going to kill me. I wanted it to be over. But then I realized Felicia was there." Her voice cracked. "I didn't want her to die."

"I know that. So does Hatcher." The anguish in her voice nagged at Wyatt. He knelt in front of her and placed his hands over hers. "For what it's worth, I'm glad you survived."

He expected her to pull away from him, but she didn't. Instead, she gave a self-deprecating laugh. "But I didn't survive, did I?"

Wyatt cleared his throat. "Yes, you did. You're the strongest person I've ever met. And you're going to help me find that bastard and make him pay."

◆ ◆ ◆

Tinsley stiffened as she stared at Wyatt's hands on top of hers. Her breath quickened, and the familiar stirrings of panic tightened her chest.

She jerked her hands away and curled them in her lap.

"I'm sorry, I didn't mean to make you uncomfortable," Wyatt said gruffly.

The sincere regret on his face made her angry at the man who'd ruined her for another man's touch. And angry at herself for letting him. "I'm sorry I'm not normal," she said, anger sharpening her voice.

"You are normal," Wyatt said. "Any woman who suffered through what you did would feel the same way. I promise not to touch you again unless you ask."

She would never ask.

That realization made her even more furious.

"You did good today," Wyatt said. "You gave me two things to look into. He may have some kind of medical training or have grown up around someone who did. That's a broad field, but he could be a CNA or a nurse, a paramedic, an orderly, a med tech, or . . . even a doctor."

She had wondered that at the time. He'd seemed knowledgeable about treating her injuries when he'd lost his temper and beaten her. But how could a doctor or nurse or anyone in the medical field torture a woman?

"He also used the Spanish term for grandmother," Wyatt said. "That means he may have some Hispanic or Latin background." He paused. "Did he mention any other family? A sibling maybe? His mother or father?"

Tinsley bit down on her bottom lip as a memory teased her mind.

She'd passed out on the floor, still disoriented from the night before. The day before, he'd dragged her from the metal cage that had become her home.

He tied a rope around her neck like a leash, then attached it to the cement wall, leaving a short length for her to move around. If she tried to get too far away, the rope would tighten and choke her.

Footsteps pounded from another room. He was coming closer. Coming back for more.

Tears clogged her throat, and she fought a scream. No use, though. No one would hear her.

The door to the room squeaked open, and a sliver of light snaked into the darkness. The mask he wore was in place. He shuffled toward her, tossing the whip in his gloved hands.

She knew what was coming. She bit her lip to keep from crying out.

He wanted her to beg. She refused to do it.

He yanked her head back, then forced her onto all fours. She waited for the sound of his zipper, but this time she didn't hear it. Instead, something large and long slapped her rear, and he shoved her thighs apart.

A second later he shoved it inside her. She choked on a sob as he used it like his cock, ramming it inside her and out again.

Then his zipper, and she felt him against her legs.

She clawed at the floor, praying it would be over soon. But it seemed to go on for hours. When he finally finished, he tossed the object in the corner. Blood trickled down her thighs and splattered the floor.

Then he started to cry.

"I'm sorry, Mama," he choked out. "But she makes me do it."

He shoved her away. She collapsed on the floor, aching and throbbing.

He raged on and on for what seemed like forever. She lay limp, praying he'd leave her alone.

But he crawled toward her and stroked her hair. "I'm sorry, I know it's wrong." His sobs intensified, and he pressed his body against her back, curling up behind her and clinging to her as if she should console him.

"Tinsley, it's all right. I'm here."

Tinsley startled, jerking back to the present.

"He kept me in a cage like an animal." Humiliation heated her face. "Sometimes he dragged me out and tied me to the wall. Once he was done . . . he cried like a baby."

"He cried?" Wyatt asked.

She nodded. "He sobbed and kept saying he was sorry to his mama. He said he knew it was wrong, but I made him do it."

Wyatt's deep breath punctuated the air. "You did not make him do anything. He's a sick man."

"He was so angry with me afterward," she said, the memories flooding her. "As if he knew he'd done wrong but couldn't help himself."

"Abusers often do that," Wyatt said in a deep voice. "They beat their child or spouse or girlfriend, then apologize and sometimes shower them with gifts later. Most victims say they did something wrong, something that antagonized their abuser."

"That's exactly what he did," she whispered.

"The fact that he apologized to his mother means she may be the source of his rage," Wyatt said. "Unfortunately, his victims, and you, may have reminded him of her. That's the reason he chose you."

Tinsley twisted her hands together. "That makes sense."

"The timing of your abduction and his first kills are important. Since his fixation seemed to be on his mother, it's possible he'd just lost her before he began abducting and killing."

A pained silence stretched between them for a minute. Tinsley looked down at the scars on her hands as another memory tickled her consciousness. The skulls . . .

"He didn't talk about the skulls," she said. "But he did talk *to* them."

Wyatt arched a brow. "What did he say?"

She released a shaky breath. "He said, 'Watch me. See what you make me do.'"

CHAPTER FOURTEEN

Wyatt balled his hands into fists. Listening to Tinsley talk about the brutal way she'd been treated made him want to pound the monster's head in.

"Will you tell me the truth if I ask you something?" Tinsley said.

He slowly breathed in. As much as he tried to hide his disgust at the Skull, he was afraid Tinsley might misread his reaction as disgust for her.

And disgust was *not* how he felt about her.

"I promise that I'll always tell you the truth." He owed her that much.

"You believe Norton Smith, the man who killed Felicia, was connected to the Skull?"

"We think so."

His gut twisted as he gazed into her eyes. Beautiful, heartsick, lonely, pained eyes.

Eyes that made him want to slay dragons and whisk her off to a fantasy world where men didn't hurt women.

Fuck. He was breaking his own rules by caring about her. *Not good.*

"Have you found their connection?"

"Not yet."

"What *do* you know about Smith?"

Wyatt cleared his throat. "His nickname was Nortie. He grew up in an orphanage in the North Georgia mountains. His parents died in a car crash when Smith was four. Smith was in the car when it happened. He suffered a head injury and was trapped in the car with his dead parents for hours until he was rescued."

"That would have been rough for a kid."

Wyatt made a noncommittal sound. "The social worker who handled Smith's case thought he had brain damage. She suspected he was bipolar, that he might have had a psychotic break. But she hadn't seen him in years. As soon as he aged out of the system, he hit the streets. She had no idea where he'd been living or what he'd been doing since."

Tinsley massaged her temple as if thinking. "I should have asked *him* about his family. And other things. Then I might be able to help now."

Wyatt gentled his tone. "You did what you had to do to survive. Probing him about his family, or lack of, could have triggered more violence.

"Besides, there's also the possibility that the hype about your abduction triggered Smith's need for attention. He wanted the spotlight, to be famous like the Skull, so he discovered that Felicia was your friend and kidnapped her."

"You mean a copycat?" Tinsley asked.

Wyatt nodded. "Smith made a call to Hatcher," he said. "That deviated from the Skull's MO. He never phoned. He just sent a sugar skull to the police to let them know he had another victim."

Tinsley shuddered, and Wyatt wished he hadn't revealed that last part. But he'd promised her the truth, and keeping silent would only hinder the investigation.

His phone buzzed. He checked the number. The ME. "Excuse me. I need to take this."

Tinsley snagged an afghan from the couch and wrapped it around her as if she was cold. He pressed "Connect" as he stepped outside onto the porch and answered.

Dr. Patton said, "Stop by the morgue. The forensic anthropologist is here. She has information about those bones at Seaside Cemetery."

"I'll be there in a few." He hung up, then went to tell Tinsley.

◆ ◆ ◆

Tinsley felt shaky and uneasy as Wyatt left. Needing someone to talk to, she called Liz Roberts and asked her to stop by.

Wyatt hadn't confirmed that the skulls taken from the graves were connected to the man who'd abducted her, but her abductor had talked to the skulls in the room where he'd kept her as if he'd known them. As if they belonged to women he'd once held hostage.

Not as if he'd dug them up somewhere.

Determined to pull herself together, she looked at the beach outside. A gray mist covered the puffy white clouds and crystal-blue sky.

A long-legged brunette in jogging shorts and a T-shirt ran along the shore, headed toward the Village, a beautiful golden retriever running in sync with her.

Envy stirred inside Tinsley.

She missed working with animals. Having a dog here would keep her company. Maybe someday when this was over . . .

Remembering the upcoming adoption day planned at the park, she curled up on the window seat with her laptop, then accessed the rescue center's website. Three months ago, she'd started working with PAWS again. She'd had to, or she would have lost her mind.

The ad for the upcoming event glowed on the screen. The date was approaching. A year to the day from the last one.

Another 5K run, a bouncy house and games for kids, food trucks, a dog show and demonstration with a trainer, a vet table with Dr. Joyce Ferris. That woman had been a godsend. She donated her time and expertise to PAWS and PAT, giving the animals free shots, exams, spays, and neutering.

Tension eased from her shoulders as she spotted pictures of the pet parade from the year before. The event had been fun for families and the participants, who'd formed playgroups for their dogs among themselves. Not only had lifelong companionships been forged between owners and their pets, but also adoptive parents had made friends.

This year she'd suggested they bring in patients from a nursing home to play with some of the animals to demonstrate the importance of PAT.

She wanted to be there, petting the dogs, greeting people, and helping them find the perfect companion.

A knock sounded at the door, and she startled.

Don't panic. It's probably Liz.

She stood, her gaze catching another jogger on the beach. This one was a man in a dark hoodie. A chill chased through her. She'd seen him almost every day lately. He always slowed slightly as he passed, but he never got close enough for her to see his face.

The knock came again, and she rushed to the door and checked the peephole. Relief surged through her. Liz.

She let the vivacious blonde in with a tentative smile.

Just as she had before, Liz came bearing lattes and pastries. Tinsley pulled out a chocolate croissant and took a bite. Heaven.

She thanked Liz, and they settled on the couch and loveseat in front of the window. "I'm glad you called," Liz said. "I was planning to come by one day this week anyway."

"Did you see the news story about that cemetery being disturbed?"

Liz nodded, her expression turning to concern. "They haven't identified the bones yet or who dug them up, have they?"

"Not yet." Tinsley shifted restlessly.

Liz let the silence continue for a moment, the counselor's way of giving Tinsley time to sort through her thoughts.

"I thought I saw *him* outside the window last night," Tinsley said. "I . . . thought he was breaking in."

Liz arched a brow. "Was he here?"

"I don't know," Tinsley said. "The sea turtle patrol volunteers were releasing the babies, and I wanted to go outside so badly I could almost taste the salty air. Then I tried to open the door and walk out, but . . . suddenly I couldn't breathe. I felt dizzy, and . . . then I heard the window breaking and saw him coming in. I called Wyatt, then passed out."

"Oh, sweetie, I'm proud of you for taking a step today. It just sounds like you had a panic attack."

Tinsley bit her lip. "Maybe. When I regained consciousness, Wyatt was here. He thought I'd taken too much antianxiety medication, but I hadn't taken any."

Silence, thick with tension, stretched for a heartbeat. Finally, Liz broke it. "Did Wyatt find proof the Skull was here?"

"No." Tinsley dropped her head into her hands with a groan of frustration. "Maybe I'm going crazy."

"You're not going crazy," Liz said. "Although given the stress of being confined, along with the anniversary of your abduction approaching, it's natural that you're thinking of him, maybe even having nightmares. Your subconscious has protected you by repressing your memories, but they can return anytime."

Tinsley sipped her coffee, then set the cup on the end table. "I did remember a few things tonight and told Wyatt about them."

Liz's sigh punctuated the air. "That must have been difficult."

"It was." She raised her chin, struggling for courage. "But if it'll help find that monster, it's worth it. I'm ready to take my life back."

"I'm glad to hear that," Liz said. "You're making progress."

Tinsley hesitated, then decided she had to tell someone the rest. The words he'd spoken to her that had shamed her to the core. "When he raped me, he told those damn skulls to watch, to see what they made him do."

Liz blinked but didn't react. "God, Tinsley."

Tinsley fisted her hands in her lap. "And when he finished, he said I'd asked for it just like they did."

CHAPTER FIFTEEN

She'd asked for it.

Liz fought rage as she joined her best friends at the Beachside Bistro & Bar on the island. Most of the evening crowd seemed happy, playful.

But the mood at the table where her friends congregated was somber.

She couldn't get that conversation with Tinsley out of her head. Almost every single victim she'd worked with had been told the same thing by their abuser—that they'd asked for it.

"We heard about those skulls being stolen from the cemetery," Laura Austin, guardian ad litem, said.

Beverly Grant, a court reporter with the state court in Savannah, ordered a round of lemon drops and spinach dip for the table. "Tinsley must be freaking out."

"I can't believe the police never caught that bastard." Rachel Willis, parole officer, had an edge to her voice. "I wish I knew where he was."

So did she. Tinsley had suffered way too much to live the rest of her life in fear. Granted, she'd survived physically, but her mental state was still fragile.

Technically, Liz wasn't supposed to discuss a patient's private thoughts with anyone, including the police. Except Tinsley had posted her feelings on her website. The emotional posts had attracted numerous followers and drawn Liz and her friends closer together.

It had also put them in the limelight as persons of interest during the vigilante killings.

"Someone should do something," Rachel said.

Kendall James, a lawyer who'd managed to keep the four of them from prosecution a few months ago, shot a stern look around the table. She'd also represented Cat Landon. "Listen, girls, let the police handle this."

An awkward silence followed. Rachel's wary gaze skated around the bar as if searching for a predator. Maybe the Skull . . . or the River Street Rapist.

Both still needed to be dealt with.

Laura snapped a chip in half and dug it into the dip. Bev licked sugar from the rim of her martini glass, then sipped the lemon drop.

They were all avoiding eye contact with Kendall. All thinking the same thing.

That Cat would do something if she could.

Liz couldn't tell them that she'd been seeing Cat at the psychiatric hospital. That she understood Cat's side of the story. That even though she worked for the court system, it didn't make her immune to its faults.

That sometimes she wanted to take justice into her own hands.

That Cat had secrets. Secrets Liz was sworn not to tell.

CHAPTER SIXTEEN

Dr. Patton introduced Wyatt to the forensic anthropologist, Eve Lofton.

She gestured to the tables where they'd spread out the three sets of bones. "I've examined all three skeletons and found commonalities."

Wyatt folded his arms. "And?"

"All the bodies are female. I'd guess their ages as late teens."

Wyatt frowned. If the Skull had first abducted teens, why take Tinsley? She was in her late twenties.

"It's hard to say how long the bones have been there," Dr. Lofton continued. "There are a lot of mitigating factors to take into account."

Wyatt's mind raced with the implications. "Is it possible these remains belong to the three young women we suspect the Skull killed?"

"I can't give you a definitive answer to that question right now, but I think the bodies were in the ground for a few years."

They didn't think the Skull had been operating that long but couldn't be certain.

"How about cause of death?"

"Not yet. But there's one more thing."

"What?"

"The bones of two of the bodies belong to sisters."

Wyatt considered that information. "Okay. I'll have our analyst search for reports of missing sisters. If we get IDs, it might lead to the girls' killer."

◆ ◆ ◆

Too agitated to sleep, Tinsley settled in front of her laptop and posted to her website.

> He hung the paper skull decorations around the room, then knelt in the corner to sing to the dead. The scent of marigolds and those crimson flowers filled the room, suffocating me.
>
> I lay perfectly still in the corner, praying he'd leave me alone tonight. My body was bruised and sore, my will to live waning.
>
> The three skulls dangling in the dim light looked like shadowy ghosts staring at me with their vacant eyes.
>
> They had been here, too. Before he took their lives.
>
> They probably screamed and cried and begged him to let them go. But in the end, he'd murdered them.
>
> When was he going to kill me?
>
> I hoped it would be soon. Fast and painless.

I didn't think I could bear another day of his filthy hands on me. Of him grunting as he rammed inside me like an animal.

Of his demented chants and apologies afterward.

They were meaningless anyway. Because he would do it again.

I was so cold that I shifted, desperate to get warm. But that movement brought his crazed gaze back to me.

"The Day of the Dead is a time of reflection, to honor our loved ones." Anger darkened his eyes, but his face was hidden by that damn mask.

If I get the chance, I'll fight him, tear it off. I want to see the face of the monster beneath.

"You have no respect for the dead, or you would be quiet."

Fear clawed at me as he dragged me by the hair over to the flowers and shoved my face into the pungent mass. The odor made my stomach cramp. Or maybe it was that I hadn't eaten in days.

Sometimes he drugged my food, so I tried to go without. Maybe I'd starve to death. At least then the pain would be over.

Although he must have caught on to my plan. Last night he'd shoved some bread down my throat. I gagged and spit it out, and then he shook me hard and slapped me.

I was so weak that I collapsed against the floor. That angered him more. He stomped over to the skulls and started screaming.

"Stop laughing at me. It's your fault that she's here. Your fault that you're dead!"

He rubbed his hand over the mask, then stormed back to me. His rough hand jerked my head up. "You are the one, Tinsley. You're different than them. You can save me."

What was he talking about? I could save him from what?

Tinsley started to close the laptop, but a response to her post appeared.

I'm sorry for your suffering. I'm glad you survived, though. You are an inspiration to others.

Have faith. The tides are changing.

Soon justice will be served, and you'll be free.

"Can you tell me anything else about the bones?" Wyatt asked the forensic anthropologist.

Dr. Lofton gestured toward a femur, then a tibia. "All the girls suffered from multiple bone fractures."

"They were abused before they died," Wyatt said.

She nodded. "Could have been by the killer or by someone else. A family member."

"I'll have our analyst add that to the criteria in our search."

"I'll send DNA samples to the lab along with digital prints of the bones." She shoved her hands into the pockets of her lab coat. "I've also called a forensic artist who works with facial reconstruction. I can't promise anything, but if we can get a general idea of the girls' ages and sizes, we might be able to create sketches of each girl to plug into the system as well."

"Identifying the victims is a priority," Wyatt agreed. Once they did that, they could track down family and friends of the deceased and start questioning them.

Fatigue pulled at his muscles. "Keep me posted."

His phone buzzed as he left the morgue. Hatcher.

He answered and quickly filled him in.

"Korine and I were talking," Hatcher said. "You know she's been studying behavioral analysis the last few months. She suggested we compile a profile of the Skull and send it to all law enforcement agencies and to the media."

"Sounds good. Tonight?"

"Afraid not. She's been having a few contractions, so the doctor wants her to take it easy."

"I can't imagine Korine taking it easy." She was just as driven as they were. She'd probably be working up until she delivered if the doctor let her.

Envy stirred inside Wyatt. He was happy for his friend and his new wife. But the thought of the two of them having a baby made him itch to have a wife and family of his own.

Something he'd sworn not to do, not after the way his mother had suffered when his father was killed on the job.

His father had been right—emotions got in the way. And right now, he had to focus.

♦ ♦ ♦

Tinsley's phone buzzed. She didn't get many calls, so she checked the number.

Her sister again.

She pressed her fingers to her lips, reining in her emotions. She missed Carrie Ann like crazy.

But the distance between them was too far to breach now. Carrie Ann was better off without her in her life.

The phone trilled four times, then rolled over to voice mail.

Her throat felt dry, so she grabbed a bottle of green tea, poured it over ice, and took a long sip as she connected to voice mail.

"Hey, sis, it's me. I want to come to the island to see you." Carrie Ann's voice sounded muffled, as if she was outside and it was lost in the wind. "Please call me."

Tears burned the back of Tinsley's throat. Was she imagining it, or was there a note of desperation in her sister's voice?

She wanted to see Carrie Ann. Wanted to be close to her again.

But *she* was different now. He had changed her. Destroyed her sense of safety and confidence. Stolen her soul.

Carrie Ann didn't want to hear about the abduction and the weeks she'd spent in the hands of the Skull. And Tinsley didn't want to tell her about it. The shame and humiliation were too painful.

Besides, her sister might not be able to handle it. She'd been so fragile after their parents died. Teenage hormones had kicked in on top of her grief, and Carrie Ann had become irrational and erratic. More than once, she'd been sent home from school for fighting.

One day she was raging with anger, the next day sobbing, the next day withdrawn. Her mood changes kept the pendulum swinging at an unpredictable rate.

Tinsley had been her rock.

She wasn't a rock anymore. She was as brittle as the shells battered by the hurricane.

She would call Carrie Ann—when she was strong again and could be the big sister Carrie Ann needed. And when the Skull was no longer a threat.

She sent her a text.

Not a good time. Call you later.

The wind picked up outside, hurling debris across the porch. She kept her outdoor lights off in deference to the turtles. Bright lights from houses or other buildings could discourage mothers from nesting. Hatchlings were drawn to moonlight, but artificial light could confuse them and draw them toward land, where they could be eaten or run over.

The beam of a flashlight made her stiffen. A lone figure in a hoodie was shining it on the sand as he walked. The same man she'd seen before?

Nerves on edge, she clutched her tea and drank it while she watched. It was a man. Tall. Lean. Black sweatshirt. Jeans. His shoulders were hunched in the wind.

But she couldn't see his face.

She snagged her binoculars and peered through the lenses for a closer look. His features were hidden by the hood.

Then he paused and turned to look up at her cottage as if he sensed she was watching him.

Her heart jumped.

He wore a mask. Totally black, it covered his face except for white circles outlining his eyes. Just like the one the Skull wore.

Oh God . . . it's him . . .

The room began to spin in a dizzying blur. She staggered sideways. Grabbed the wall to hold herself up. He started walking toward her.

She reached for her phone but knocked it off the coffee table onto the floor.

A cry of frustration caught in her throat.

She glanced back at the beach. He was moving toward her. She had to hurry.

Trembling with fear, she stooped to retrieve her phone. But her foot bumped it, and it slid beneath the table. She cursed and ran to the box above the refrigerator where she kept her .22.

Her breath panted out, the world blurring again. She snatched the pistol, then staggered back toward the window.

He was gone.

Either gone or on the steps of her porch where she couldn't see him. Footsteps sounded outside.

Panic seized her. Her vision went foggy. The world swayed. Her legs suddenly gave away. The darkness clawed at her like quicksand.

A tapping on the window broke through the fog. His beady eyes pierced her through the holes in the mask. The windowpane rattled.

The paper skulls danced in the wind . . . Then the three human skulls, just like before . . . their vacant eyes staring back at her.

CHAPTER SEVENTEEN

The Keeper had set the plan in motion. The cat-and-mouse game had begun.

Nerves made her jumpy, but there was no turning back now. Something had to be done.

According to the details of Tinsley's abduction, the Skull built a shrine with flowers and sugar skulls and sang and praised the dead.

The Day of the Dead would soon be here. If he suffered from OCD as she suspected, he was thinking of Tinsley and wanting to reconnect with her.

Sacrifices had to be made to reel him in. One day Tinsley would understand and be grateful.

But another name topped the list of men needing justice.

Milt Milburn, the River Street Rapist. The bastard had raped several women, choosing his victims along the river walk in Savannah. Rumors had surfaced that his rich daddy had paid off the judge, and Milburn had been released on a technicality. Milburn and son had both been cocky enough to smile at the camera in victory.

But those rape victims had been traumatized, their lives changed forever.

Thankfully Cat, one of the Keeper's hands, had exacted justice on the judge who'd released Milburn. But Milt Milburn still walked free.

Like the Skull, Milburn had been quiet for months. The police knew where he was. But Milburn's father had threatened a lawsuit for harassment if they followed his son. So the police couldn't do a damn thing until he attacked another victim.

That meant another woman would suffer.

Maybe the fucking cops could live with that, but she couldn't.

A creep like him couldn't stay dormant for long. The need for violence was in his blood.

Predators might tell themselves they could stop. But most of them were too weak. They gave in to the dark urges. Couldn't resist the lure of the hunt.

She was counting on that.

She'd been watching him for weeks. Knew the bars he frequented. His cocky smile. His type of woman.

Meek. Trusting. Easy on the eyes.

She was not that type. Not anymore.

But hey, she could play the part.

She checked her wig in the mirror and carefully applied Kiss Me Pink lipstick before she climbed from the car. A breeze stirred the air, bringing the scent of the marsh and cigarette smoke from the bar.

She tugged her little black skirt over her hips, her chin lifted as if feigning disinterest as she strode inside. Men liked aloof women. Gave them a challenge.

Jazz music pulsed in the background, a sensual tune that sparked erotic movements on the dance floor.

He was here. Milt Milburn. The slime.

She'd spotted his little red sports car convertible in the parking lot. His dick was probably little, too. He tried to make up for it and prove his masculinity by using force.

His reign of terror would end tonight.

She spotted his smug face as soon as she scanned the patrons. He sat perched on the barstool at the end, his body angled so he could watch the door. Assessing the fresh prey as they entered.

The asswipe thought he was sophisticated in his *GQ* slacks and button-down shirt. A sterling-silver ring bearing the emblem for some snooty college he'd attended glittered in the dim lightning.

His eyes burned a hole in her as she sauntered to the bar, slipped onto a stool, and gave a shy smile to the bartender.

She'd much prefer bourbon, but white wine fit the profile of his victims, so she ordered a pinot grigio. Milburn was from an upper-class family. He was educated.

She thanked the bartender, paid for her drink, and then carried it to a table in the corner where it was dark. Better not to draw attention to herself.

Just as she'd hoped, he took the bait.

"Hey, gorgeous," he said as he slid into the chair beside her.

She blinked nonchalantly, not surprised he didn't ask. His victims said he was charming. That they'd liked him at first.

Until he morphed into an animal and took them against their will.

She sipped her wine, carefully keeping it out of his reach. She was in charge tonight.

He wasn't going to win.

"Where are you from?" he asked as he swirled his whiskey in his glass.

"Charleston," she said. Let him think she was a blue blood.

She feigned interest as he bragged about his competitive sailing adventures, then dropped in tidbits about his investment business.

All bullshit. He'd invested in being his father's son and living off his inheritance. Another rich brat who thought he could get away with anything because he had money.

So far it had worked for him.

But all good things came to an end.

By the third drink, she leaned on her hand, doting on him, acting as if she were tipsy. Little did he know that she could drink him under the table.

The seduction started with small strokes of his hand across hers. He scooted his chair closer, shoulders brushing. His lips caressed her hair.

She wanted to gag but forced a smile instead.

On the dance floor, couples gyrated to the seductive tune pulsing through the speakers. He swept her out to join them and pulled her close. His chest rose and fell with each breath, his excitement clearly building.

Two dances later, he led her toward the back door. "I need some air," he whispered into her ear.

She let him guide her through the crowded throng. Booze and the lure of the music lulled the patrons into a trancelike state where they were oblivious to what might be happening around them.

His hand grew tighter on her arm as he steered her into the alley. It was pitch-dark—no lights, no cameras. No one around. Far enough away from the parking lot and smokers' area so no one would see. Or hear.

He probably planned to rape her here and leave her by the dumpster. That was his MO.

He leaned in for a kiss, and her adrenaline spiked. She gently pushed away.

"A little soon for that," she said softly. "Let's go back inside and dance some more."

"I'm done with dancing, baby." The flirtatious gleam in his eyes turned to determination as he yanked her closer and slid his hands over her ass. He reached beneath her skirt, his filthy hands cold and mauling.

She shoved him harder this time.

Then he snapped. Gone was the slick, sophisticated charmer.

The River Street Rapist emerged. He yanked her purse from her and threw it to the ground, then hauled her against him.

His hands grew rough, punishing. He jerked her arms up above her head and pressed her into the cold brick of the building wall. Then he bit her neck.

Rage shot through her, and she kneed him in the balls. He bellowed in pain, then slapped her and called her a bitch.

He had no idea.

He lunged for her again, and she grabbed the knife she'd tucked inside her skirt and thrust it upward, straight into his belly. He grunted and cursed in shock and pain.

Eyes bright with rage, he dove toward her, his hands reaching for her throat.

She knocked him backward with a fist to his wound, then raised the knife and stabbed him again. This time in the heart, or where his heart should have been.

He grunted, blood spurting as he clawed for the wall.

She stabbed him again and again, smiling at the fear on his face when he realized he was going to die.

CHAPTER EIGHTEEN

Sunlight streaked the pine floor and lit the room, jarring Tinsley awake.

She blinked, but her vision was blurred, her head throbbing.

Confused, she peered around and realized she was on the floor near the door. The image of the Skull on the beach walking toward her house jolted her upright. She swayed, blinking the room into focus and massaging her temple.

Fear nearly immobilized her. She'd seen him outside the window again, had been going for her gun. Had he been inside her house?

If so, and she had passed out, why had he left? If it was him, he would have taken her . . . or raped her right here.

But if it wasn't him, who had she seen?

Pulse pounding, she looked around again, but nothing seemed out of place. The door was closed, the lock in place. Her laptop sat on her desk.

But her glass of tea was on the floor, the liquid spilled out.

Slowly, she dragged herself to her feet. The room swayed just like it had the time she'd called Wyatt.

He thought she'd taken her antianxiety medication.

She hurried toward the kitchen counter and checked her medication. With trembling hands, she unscrewed the cap and looked inside.

The prescription bottle was still half-full.

A shadow moved across the window.

She bolted toward it. Was he out there?

The porch was empty. But paper skulls dangled from her awning. And . . . skulls. Three of them were perched on the ledge by the window.

A scream lodged in her throat.

The chirp of her computer suddenly sounded in the quiet. Nerves rattled, she clutched at the sofa for support as she made her way to her desk.

A message—The women of Savannah are finally safe. The River Street Rapist is dead.

God . . . a photograph, too.

She stared in shock, emotions welling in her chest.

It was a picture of a man lying in a pool of blood. So much blood that it looked like a river of red.

◆ ◆ ◆

A shrill ringing jolted Wyatt from a deep sleep. He groaned and reached toward the nightstand by his bed, raking his hand for his phone. He knocked it to the floor, then scrubbed his hand over his eyes, leaned over, and retrieved it.

Tinsley.

Instantly alert, he quickly connected. "Wyatt."

"He . . . was here," Tinsley cried. "This time he left something."

Wyatt snatched his jeans from the floor and yanked them on. "Are you okay?"

"He left three skulls on the porch."

Wyatt cursed. "I'll be right there."

"There's more," Tinsley said, her voice edged with panic.

His phone was beeping with another call. Hatcher.

That couldn't be good.

He'd call him back after he hung up with Tinsley. "What is it?"

"Someone sent me a picture," Tinsley said. "It's . . . a dead man. I think it's the River Street Rapist."

Wyatt hit the floor running. "Keep the door locked. I'm on my way." He grabbed a clean shirt and dragged it on. Socks and boots next, then he strapped on his weapon and grabbed his jacket.

On the way out the door, he snatched his keys and hurried to his SUV. As soon as he peeled out of his driveway, he phoned Hatcher.

"Director Bellows just called," Hatcher said. "The River—"

"Street Rapist is dead," Wyatt finished.

"How the hell did you know?"

"Tinsley just called. Someone sent her a picture."

"Bellows said the killer sent photographs to Milburn's rape victims, too."

Wyatt turned onto the causeway.

"I don't like this," Hatcher said. "The killer left the justice symbol on his forehead just like Cat did before."

A coldness washed over Wyatt. "Another vigilante?"

"Could be the killer wants us to think that."

"Maybe." They had wondered whether Cat had acted alone.

"I'm headed to the SPD headquarters," Hatcher said.

"I'm on my way to Tinsley's," Wyatt said. "Someone left skulls on her porch last night. It could be the ones missing from those graves."

"Fuck," Hatcher said. "Another Keeper and the Skull on the same night?"

He didn't like it either.

They agreed to keep each other posted. Wyatt's pulse hammered as he drove past the Village. A few joggers and walkers were out; Morning Brew, the local coffee shop, was packed. Fishermen were scattered across the pier with their rods and reels, nets, and bait buckets.

A ship's horn sounded from a barge leaving Brunswick and heading into international waters.

He veered onto the side street leading to the cove, his gaze scanning in all directions, in search of a car or the Skull.

The sadistic man would enjoy watching Tinsley squirm. He hadn't attacked her yet, but he might be toying with her. Torturing her.

Waiting for the anniversary of when he'd first taken her to make his move.

◆ ◆ ◆

Tinsley brewed a pot of coffee while she waited on Wyatt.

Then she washed her face, brushed her hair, and changed into clean jeans and a pale-pink T-shirt. Despair nearly overwhelmed her as she stared at herself in the mirror. Her eyes looked sunken, her skin pale, the lack of sleep and sun taking its toll.

She hadn't noticed the way she looked in a long time. She needed a hair trim and a manicure and . . . maybe she could order some of that tinted moisturizer to give her skin some color.

Why?

It wasn't like she had company or needed to impress someone . . .

She hurried back to the kitchen. Those creepy paper skulls fluttered in the breeze, but the human skulls were even more sinister.

Did they belong to the women he'd killed before her?

The FBI and police speculated that he might have moved to another city or state this past year. He could have killed others and gone unnoticed. And these skulls might belong to those victims.

Either way, he was back. And he wanted her to know it.

A gust of wind tossed something onto the dock, and her stomach clenched. She stepped closer to the window to check it out. Relief spilled through her. It was just a branch that had broken off the tree in the yard.

A quick glance at the picture of that dead man on her computer screen made her panic return. Was there another Keeper?

Cat was in a psychiatric hospital. She couldn't have killed the River Street Rapist. So who had?

A knock sounded, and she startled.

"It's me, Wyatt."

She rushed to let him in. His big frame filled the doorway, the scent of his masculine aftershave wafting around her.

Her stomach fluttered. He smelled . . . nice. The kind of sultry, manly smell that once upon a time would have aroused her.

His dark-brown eyes skated over her in concern. "Are you okay?"

She nodded, although she wasn't okay, and they both knew it. "Those skulls . . . do you think they're more women he killed?"

A muscle ticked in Wyatt's jaw. "Forensics should be able to give us some answers."

"I don't understand," Tinsley whispered. "Is it him? Did he take them to taunt me?"

"I don't know yet, but we'll get to the bottom of it." His gaze shot to her computer. "That picture, when did it come in?"

"It came by instant messenger this morning."

Wyatt crossed to her computer to examine it. "It's him, all right. Milt Milburn." He hesitated. "The killer painted the justice symbol on his forehead, just like the Keeper painted on her victims." He turned to her, his jaw tight. "Whoever sent this also sent it to Milburn's victims."

Tinsley pressed her hand over her mouth to stifle a gasp. "It can't be Cat. Not unless she's orchestrating things from the mental hospital."

"I'll look into that angle," Wyatt said. "It's also possible that another vigilante replaced her. Hopefully our analyst can narrow down where Milburn's body was left so we can investigate."

Wyatt noticed the towel on the floor where she'd dried her spilled tea. He angled his head toward her. "Tell me what happened last night."

She bit down on her lower lip, then quickly swept up the towel and tossed it into the washer in the laundry room adjacent to the kitchen.

He poured them both coffee and handed her a mug. The gesture seemed . . . intimate.

Their fingers touched, a tingle rippling through her. Her chest clenched.

She would never be intimate with a man again.

"Tinsley?"

"I saw a man in a hoodie walking on the beach," she said, well aware her voice was strained.

Wyatt didn't speak. He simply sipped his coffee as if giving her time to gather her thoughts.

"I had worked on my website earlier and was having some tea. Then he turned toward my window . . . that's when I saw the mask."

Wyatt made a low sound in his throat. "A skull mask?"

She nodded, battling to control the fear. "I thought I was seeing things, so I kept watching him. Then he came closer, and I saw him smile and . . . I knew it was him."

"You saw him smile, with the mask on?"

"I know that sounds crazy, but it happened when he held me hostage. His black eyes lit up, and he . . . moved his mouth. He was laughing at me."

A tense silence fell in the room. "Go on."

"Then I got dizzy. I tried to reach the .22 I keep in the kitchen, but . . . I passed out."

Wyatt went still. "Where's the pistol?"

She quickly crossed to the refrigerator and pulled down the box where she kept it. But the gun was gone.

◆ ◆ ◆

Wyatt scrutinized the scene in Tinsley's house with a critical eye. Spilled tea, a masked man at the window, a missing gun.

He might think she'd imagined it, except this time the skulls were real. So someone had been there.

And whoever it was had been in her house.

"Did you take the gun out?" he asked.

Tinsley averted her gaze. "No. I passed out before I could reach it."

He let a heartbeat pass, hoping she'd say more.

"And before you ask, I didn't take any medication."

A case of the bottled tea sat on the floor near the door. "Did you have that same tea the other night when you lost consciousness?"

She cleared her throat. "Yes."

He examined the box. "Does a friend shop for you, or do you have groceries delivered?"

"I don't have friends here," Tinsley said, a defensive note to her voice. "The only people who've been in here are you and the counselor I'm working with."

Liz was one of the four women they'd questioned in the vigilante killings.

"Has she been here recently?"

Tinsley frowned as if she suspected where his line of questioning was headed and didn't like it. "She came by yesterday. But she didn't bring the tea. She brought coffee and pastries like usual. And she certainly didn't steal my gun."

He sensed she liked Liz and was getting close to the young woman. Tinsley could use a friend.

But at this point, Wyatt didn't trust anyone. Cat had been the lead FBI analyst during the vigilante killings and had intentionally manipulated the investigation.

Disturbing posts on Tinsley's website and in the private chat room where the Keepers met online contradicted Cat's insistence that she'd acted alone.

With the similarity of MO in Milburn's murder, they had to consider the possibility of an accomplice or that another Keeper had emerged to replace Cat.

"Who delivers the tea?"

"A local grocery on the island. I have a standing order each week."

"Do you sign for it?"

She nodded. "Usually. But come to think of it, I didn't hear the delivery guy knock this time. I just found the box on the doorstep."

"Don't drink any more of it until I have it tested."

Tinsley's eyes widened. "You think someone drugged my tea?"

Wyatt shrugged. "It would explain your dizzy spells." Although dizziness was associated with panic attacks. But with everything else happening, he couldn't discount the theory that she'd been drugged. Or that the Skull had found a way inside her cottage to taunt her.

He pulled his phone from his belt. "I'm going to call a tech to process your house. Maybe we'll get lucky and find some prints."

"If he was here," Tinsley said, "he didn't leave prints. He was obsessive about wearing gloves."

The certainty in her tone ate at him because she painted a picture of a cold-blooded sociopath who planned his crimes down to every detail. He didn't want to get caught.

But he'd taken a risk by coming to her house.

That could mean he was losing his edge. That his obsession with Tinsley would cause him to make mistakes.

Mistakes could be the key to catching him.

CHAPTER NINETEEN

Carrie Ann Jensen sipped her Moscow mule from the patio of the Pirate's Lair, a café built from an old pirate ship that drew tourists and locals in Savannah for its uniqueness and the ghost stories about the pirates from days gone by.

Two hoity-toity, blue-blooded socialites, who looked as out of place in the dockside café as she did in an antique China shop, gave her a disapproving look as if to say she shouldn't be drinking so early in the day. Diamonds and precious gems glittered from their hands and arms, while designer clothes showcased that they came from money. They sipped coffee and ate pastries and turned their noses up at everyone who was imbibing.

She didn't give a rat's ass what they thought. She was tired of being a good girl. Good girls got pushed aside. Stepped on. Bullied. Treated like shit.

They didn't just finish last; sometimes they didn't finish at all.

Just look where being good had gotten her sister.

She checked her phone, hoping Tinsley would return her call, but nothing so far. Not that she expected her to respond.

Tinsley had shut her out of her life as soon as she'd left the hospital.

It was her own damn fault, though. Carrie Ann hadn't handled seeing her sister broken and beaten very well. She'd cried and been too emotional, had said all the wrong things, asked stupid questions. Had run from the room, blubbering like a baby.

She couldn't bear to see her sister in agony. Couldn't look at the bruises on her body or the scars on her hands or the vacant, dead look in her eyes.

The nurses, doctors, and police had insisted Tinsley give them details that were so gory and private and painful that Carrie Ann had had to leave the room.

Naively, she'd wanted Tinsley to snap out of the shock and be her old self as if nothing had happened.

But it *had* happened.

Tinsley was traumatized. She'd needed Carrie Ann to be strong, to hold her hand while she cried, to listen when she talked.

But she'd failed.

After all Tinsley had done for her, she'd let her down. She hated herself for it.

When they were young, they'd been two peas in a pod. Gone everywhere together. Shared a room. Toys. Secrets.

She'd idolized Tinsley. Had tried to braid her hair like Tinsley's. Sometimes she'd snuck into Tinsley's closet and dressed in her clothes. She'd worn her headbands and bracelets and had even practiced walking like her big sister.

Then their parents had died in that stupid car accident, and her world had shattered. Carrie Ann had heard Gram talking about how bad it had been. How her mama's chest had been crushed and her daddy's arms and legs broken. How it had taken the mortician hours and hours and lots of heavy makeup and glue to make them presentable to the family. How the drunk driver who'd hit them had escaped without a scratch and fled from the police. Cocksucker had left the country the next day to avoid jail.

She'd wanted to hunt him down and kill him herself.

But Gram had sent her to counseling. Made her talk about her feelings.

Talking about her damn feelings hadn't brought her parents back.

Tinsley had always been the strong one. At night when she cried, she'd crawled into bed with Tinsley. Tinsley had soothed her and promised her that she'd never leave her.

Then she was kidnapped.

Selfish of Carrie Ann to fall apart afterward. She knew it was. But Tinsley was her anchor, and when her anchor was gone, she'd drowned.

She'd fallen apart at college. Had dropped out. Had started smoking weed to soothe her nerves. Until she'd been caught and threatened with jail time.

So back to counseling she'd gone. Another shrink. This one had been understanding at first, assured her that her feelings were valid, that violence against a family member had far-reaching tentacles. More months of counseling, and she'd realized that it was time for her to be the strong one. That Tinsley deserved an anchor of her own.

But all the backpedaling in the world hadn't earned Tinsley's forgiveness.

Why should Tinsley forgive her?

It was Carrie Ann's fault that her sister had been abducted.

She was supposed to help with the pet rescue event at the park that day. She should have been with Tinsley when she walked to her car.

But she'd had other plans. She'd ditched her sister with no excuse except she'd had better things to do.

Better than keeping Tinsley safe. If Tinsley hadn't been alone, that monster wouldn't have gotten his filthy hands on her.

She picked up her drink and chugged half of it, guilt gnawing at her.

Tinsley had no idea how close Carrie Ann was.

She would know, though. Soon. When the time was right.

Carrie Ann would make everything good again.

She had to.

It was the only way to free her sister.

CHAPTER TWENTY

Outside Tinsley's cottage, storm clouds moved in, stealing the blessed sunlight she craved. The Skull was gone now.

But Wyatt was still here. He'd come the moment she called.

She wrapped her arms around her waist in an effort to hold herself together. She had seen him earlier, hadn't she? Or was she hallucinating?

No, this time he'd left something on her porch.

Odd, too, that he'd been here and she'd received a picture of Milburn.

What was going on? Had another Keeper surfaced?

"Do you think that dead man's body is outside like the judge's was?"

Wyatt shrugged. "From that photo, it looks like he's in an alley." He gestured toward the dock. "But I'll have the team search your property as well as the surrounding area. They need to look for forensics on the person who left the skulls anyway."

"You don't think *he* did it?"

"I don't know," Wyatt said. "None of this makes sense. It's hard for me to believe he was actually in your house and didn't try to take you."

She shivered.

Wyatt cleared his throat. "It'll be all right. I won't let him hurt you."

Admiration for Wyatt blossomed inside her. He was honorable and brave and would sacrifice his life to save hers. Not that she was special. He was simply doing his job like he'd do for anyone else.

Tinsley offered him a smile of gratitude. "I just want it to finally be over."

If that meant facing the Skull and her worst fears, she'd do it. She had to fight back, or she'd never leave this house.

♦ ♦ ♦

Wyatt met the evidence tech and explained that they needed to search within a two-mile radius of Tinsley's, then process the exterior of the house, specifically the doorframe, windows, and doorknob.

Tammy Drummond, one of the crime scene investigators, frowned at the skulls. "Damn, that's creepy."

He nodded. "I want Lofton to examine them. If they match the bones we recovered from that graveyard, maybe we can identify them." And then investigate those three murders.

Inside, he wanted them to focus on the door again, then the kitchen, Tinsley's desk, the bottles of green tea.

"We need samples of the tea analyzed," he said. "I think someone drugged Tinsley." He pointed to the paper skulls, then the human ones in disgust. "Take these to the lab. Look for prints, and let's see if we can find where the paper ones were bought."

Special Supervisory Agent Roger Cummings, head of the ERT, nodded. "We're on it."

Wyatt explained about the photograph of the River Street Rapist sent to Tinsley and the rape victims and the justice symbol on Milburn's forehead.

Cummings made a sound of disgust. "Shit, that crazy Cat lady may have connections on the outside."

Wyatt stiffened. He didn't approve of the way Cat had handled things, but she'd had her reasons. She was FIH, his term for "fucked in the head," but she had suffered as a child. Her own sexual abuse drove her to seek justice for others.

His phone buzzed. Hatcher.

He quickly connected. "Yeah?"

"Bernie thinks Milburn's body may be somewhere on River Street, behind a bar or in an alley." Bernie was the analyst who had replaced Cat.

"Makes sense."

"I'm texting you an address," Hatcher said. "Meet me there. Korine is going to question the rape victims so we can clear them and their families."

"I'll get an officer to guard Tinsley's, then I'm on my way."

◆ ◆ ◆

Tinsley hated the sight of crime scene workers crawling all over her property and inside her house.

Would she ever be rid of them?

Not as long as *he* was alive and hunting . . .

Wyatt approached her with a grim expression. "Other than your gun, is anything missing?"

She shook her head, surprised the Skull hadn't been in her bedroom. He'd cursed her slinky underwear, told her she was dressing like a whore to entice him. He'd ripped it off and left her naked while he shamed her.

Another inconsistency in his behavior.

One moment he acted as if he wanted a good, wholesome girl, and then the next he was angry that she hadn't told him that she liked it when he fucked her.

"If you think of something else or discover anything he touched or took, let the ERT know." He jangled his keys in his left hand.

"Are you leaving?"

"Our analyst has a general location for us to search for Milburn's body." He lifted a hand to touch her arm, then seemed to think better of it and dropped it to his side. "I'll be back. But meanwhile, I'm posting an officer outside."

Tinsley nodded. She should be glad for the protection.

But the men outside were strangers.

She only felt safe with Wyatt.

But she bit her tongue to keep from telling him that. This wasn't personal to him, just a case. The Skull was the one who'd gotten away. The one who had nearly killed Wyatt.

He stepped to the door, then paused. "Call me if you need me."

She did need him. But she couldn't afford to admit that.

So she nodded, nerves bunching in her stomach as he left.

When had she started viewing Wyatt as her safety net? As her place of comfort?

As much as she fought it, she knew the answer. The night he'd stayed on her porch to guard her during the investigation into the vigilante killings.

He hadn't pushed her. Hadn't insisted on coming in. Hadn't asked questions or tried to touch her or encroach on her personal space in any way.

He'd simply been there. Strong. Silent. Steady. Understanding. Nonjudgmental.

Her stomach fluttered, an awareness of him as a man seeping through her. She wanted him to touch her. Hold her.

Wanted to be a normal woman again, not broken like the seashells on the shore ravaged by the storms.

◆ ◆ ◆

Wyatt met Hatcher on River Street.

Hatcher removed a copy of Milburn's death photo and flattened it on top of the low brick wall bordering the riverfront. "Bernie studied the shadows and lighting, then the surrounding buildings." Hatcher pointed to the map. "She thinks we'll find him somewhere along here. Maybe in back of one of the bars."

"Makes sense. He was probably out hunting."

"Except this time he became the hunted," Hatcher said with a sideways grin.

Both of them had been sick when Judge Wadsworth released the rapist on a technicality. The victims had been devastated and terrified he'd come back for them to get revenge.

"The Savannah PD did a preliminary search along the river, and they've checked the docks."

"Killer could have dumped him in the river after he or she took the picture and sent it. Without the body, it's harder to find evidence."

"And go to trial," Wyatt added. "Defense attorney could argue that the picture was staged."

"It's him and he's dead," Hatcher said matter-of-factly. "I have a feeling about this."

"Cat?"

"Possibly. She's smart and cunning," Hatcher said. "I spoke with the director of the hospital, and she said that Cat receives fan mail all the time."

Cat had followers. Supporters. Not a surprise.

Notorious criminals had always drawn admirers, copycats, women who wanted to marry them. Women who did marry them.

Cray-cray in his book.

They decided to divide up to search. Hatcher went left, and Wyatt went the opposite direction to comb the alleys behind the restaurants and bars.

For the next half hour, he scanned his flashlight into every crevice and corner along the river walk, into alleys, behind doors and trash cans.

The stale scent of booze, urine, and puke permeated the air, stifling, and a reminder of the nightlife in Savannah.

Nightlife the River Street Rapist had thrived on.

Poetic justice that it got him killed. A piece of fabric poked from beneath a bunch of boxes labeled with the name of a liquor distributor.

Wyatt pulled on latex gloves, then knelt and shined his light on it. In the picture, Milburn's clothes were so drenched in blood he hadn't noticed the color.

He eased aside the edge of the box. A cockroach raced out, the fabric a ratty bandana that was mired in dirt and mud.

A bandana wasn't Milburn's style. Italian loafers, polo shirts, and a Rolex watch fit the rich bastard.

He moved on to the next alley and found a homeless man snoring so loudly that his cardboard home shook.

Judging from the empty tequila bottle he clutched like a blanket, the old man would have been too drunk to remember anything, even if he'd witnessed a crime.

A strong stench wafted toward him as he passed another alley, the odor of vomit nearly overpowering.

He shined his light along the back wall. More boxes and garbage bags were jammed next to an overflowing dumpster.

Coughing at the stench, he tied a handkerchief around his nose and mouth, then shoved the garbage bags away and lifted the box edge.

Another bag—rotting food, drink containers, and disposable food cartons spilled out, flies and gnats buzzing.

A body was lying in the sludge. Garbage had spilled onto him, obscuring part of his face, and one of his hands was buried in something that looked like black beans and salsa. A rat was nibbling at his bloody chest.

CHAPTER
TWENTY-ONE

Wyatt and Hatcher snapped pictures of Milburn's body and of the surrounding ground and alley and wall beside the dumpster.

Then they gladly turned the processing over to the ERT. Detective Brockett from the Savannah PD, who'd been leading his officers in the search of the dock and river walk, ordered his men to canvass the neighboring bars and restaurants for witnesses.

An officer roped off the crime scene, then stood guard to keep curious onlookers out of the area. Another officer roused the homeless man and asked him whether he'd seen anything.

The old man looked glassy-eyed and shook his head wildly. He grabbed his bundle of belongings and staggered away as soon as the officer allowed.

Dr. Patton arrived just as the team pulled Milburn's body from the trash. Covered in discarded food and sludge, it was difficult to make out exactly what had happened. They photographed the body again, then the ME raked debris from the man's face and chest in order to examine him.

"From the picture the unsub sent, he appears to have been stabbed," Wyatt said.

Patton nodded, shining a light on the man's chest.

Wyatt counted seven stab wounds. "Reads like a crime of passion, someone with a lot of rage toward the man."

"Could be someone wronged by the bastard. But the double *SS* indicating the justice symbol on his forehead also suggests another vigilante," Hatcher said.

"How about a family member or boyfriend? Even a sister or friend of a victim might want retribution." Wyatt eyed the man's size. "Killer must be strong to have subdued him."

"Which could mean we're dealing with a male unsub."

"Or the killer drugged him," Wyatt said. Fitting, since Milburn had slipped a roofie into his victim's drink the first time.

"Cat may have found a way to communicate from the psych hospital."

A real possibility. Cat was a genius. She was also manipulative and cunning. "We'll pursue that angle, too."

"Over here, guys. I think I found the kill site." Tammy Drummond waved them over to the corner against the brick wall of the bar. "Look at the spatter." She pointed at the various spots, then at a larger pool on the ground. "Looks like he was stabbed here. Blood sprayed his clothes and the wall. Then he collapsed facedown. Blood pooled beneath him."

Wyatt scratched his head. "So his body was moved after the unsub photographed him. She—or he—wanted to keep Milburn hidden for a while, to allow the killer time to escape and to get rid of the murder weapon."

Wyatt noticed a spot of blood to the right, near the back of the dumpster. "Our unsub may have stepped in the blood. Let's see if we can get a good shoe print. Maybe we can match it to our killer."

"Copy that," Drummond said.

Footsteps echoed on the brick pavers, then voices. Wyatt pivoted, hands balling into fists as Marilyn Ellis tried to push her way past the crime scene tape. Her cameraman rushed up on her heels, camera aimed at them.

"Keep her back!" Hatcher shouted.

His partner detested Ellis.

Wyatt didn't trust her either.

◆ ◆ ◆

Tinsley's phone jangled just as the crime scene workers left with their photographs, the skulls, and her case of green tea.

What would she do if she couldn't rely on the delivery service for her groceries and other items she needed?

The phone rang again. She checked the number, expecting Wyatt. But it was Liz.

Anxious to talk to the counselor, she answered.

"I saw the news about the River Street Rapist on social media," Liz said. "Someone posted that he sent pictures to the rape victims. I called each of them to see if they wanted to talk about it, and I'm on my way for a group session. I just wondered if you'd heard and if you're okay."

"I'm all right. I received the picture, too," Tinsley said. "The FBI has already been here."

"I'm sorry," Liz said. "Do you want me to come over?"

Did she? Yes. But Milburn's rape victims needed Liz more than she did now. "No, you need to be with those women. I'm sure they're relieved he's dead, but the police may treat them like suspects."

"You're right," Liz said. "But I'm here for you, too, Tinsley."

Tinsley's chest filled with emotions. The counselor was the most heartfelt person she'd ever known. "I appreciate that. But Agent Camden was here. And the crime scene workers are outside now."

"Crime scene workers?"

Tinsley clamped her teeth over her lower lip, then explained about the skulls, her missing gun, and Wyatt's suspicions about her tea having been drugged.

A tense second passed. "Oh my God, Tinsley. Are you sure you don't need me now?"

"No, go ahead to the group session."

She hung up, then settled in front of her computer to update her website. Suddenly a flurry of posts came through.

> Tonight I'll sleep well for the first time in two years. I know it's wrong to wish a human dead, but Milt Milburn was no human.

> The cops should have kept him locked up. But they didn't. So someone had to do their job. Someone had to stop him before he hurt another woman.

> What do you think, Tinsley? He got what was coming, didn't he? Isn't the sight of his blood a beautiful thing?

Tinsley shivered and started to close her laptop. She couldn't blame these women for their anger and outrage.

Dark thoughts had obsessed her for months. Thoughts of what she'd like to do to the man who'd tortured her and ruined her life.

Those dark thoughts threatened to choke the soul out of her.

Another post flashed on the screen, and her lungs squeezed for air as she read it.

> I think about you every day, Tinsley. I remember how soft your skin was. The subtle feminine scent of your body.

The texture of your cunt milking my cock.

The taste of your salty tears as you fought me.

You wanted to be a good girl, didn't you? But you failed. And you had to be punished.

But that is in the past. We can start over again. It's almost time for us to be reunited.

Do you dream of me at night when your head hits the pillow?

I dream of you. And I look forward to when we are together . . .

◆ ◆ ◆

"Special Agent Camden!" Marilyn Ellis waved her hand toward Wyatt, pushing the limits of the crime scene tape as she leaned closer for a better view of what they were doing.

"Get her out of here!" Wyatt growled at the officer in charge of securing the scene.

"You can't make me leave," Marilyn yelled. "The public has a right to know that Milt Milburn is dead."

Wyatt and Hatcher traded frustrated looks. "You'd better handle her," Hatcher said in a low voice. "I've never hit a woman, but she might just drive me to it."

Wyatt didn't like the pushy newscaster either, but they couldn't avoid the media completely. He'd just have to figure out a way to use her—or control what she aired.

A small crowd had gathered behind her, another officer working to clear the area and prevent the onlookers from snapping pictures with their cell phones. Three uniforms from the Savannah PD formed a wall with their bodies to shield the body from the cameras.

Wyatt strode over to Marilyn, angling himself between her and the dead man. "You can't air anything about this scene until we identify the deceased and notify the family."

Marilyn lifted her chin haughtily, a smirk on her face. "Good try, but we both know who died here."

Wyatt frowned. Had she talked to the rape victims? He doubted it. After Milburn was released and the judge who let him go was murdered, the victims had retreated from the public eye.

"I don't know how or where you got your information—"

"Please," Marilyn said with a huff. "This murder is all over social media. Did you really think you could keep the death of an alleged rapist quiet?"

Wyatt cursed.

She shoved her mike toward him. "Whoever killed Milt Milburn sent a picture of him to the River Street Rapist's victims. Is it true that the killer painted the same justice symbol on Milburn's forehead that the Keeper did on her victims? Is there another vigilante killer on the loose?"

He gave her a go-to-hell look. "At this time, the police and FBI have no comment. Now please stay back so we can investigate."

His cell phone was ringing as he walked away. He checked the caller ID. Director Bellows.

"What the fuck is going on?" Bellows shouted. "Harold Milburn just stormed into my office and said social media is blowing up with pictures of his son's dead body. There's speculation about another vigilante killer, and people on Twitter are crucifying the police and FBI, saying they don't want us to spend taxpayer dollars to find a rapist's killer."

Dammit, just because Milburn had been a senator, he thought he could get away with anything or go anywhere.

"I don't know how word spread," Wyatt said. "Tinsley wouldn't leak the picture. Could have been one of the victims."

"Milburn's father has already hired a lawyer and is suing the Savannah Police Department as well as us for this clusterfuck."

"Milburn's father is a rich asshole who used his money to bail his son out time and time again. He created a monster."

"I agree, but he just lost his child, and he won't be appeased until he has someone's head on a platter." Bellows wheezed a breath. "That'll probably be mine."

"We can't control what people do these days, not when everyone has a camera and can capture what happens as it's happening."

"I know, it's a losing battle," Bellows said. "All the more reason we wrap this case up quickly. But I'm warning you, Camden. You'd better play it by the book. No illegal searches, so get your warrants in hand. Like it or not, we have to find Milburn's killer."

CHAPTER TWENTY-TWO

The Skull watched Joyce Ferris leave the rescue shelter where Tinsley had worked, her do-gooder smile on her face. Like Tinsley, she devoted her spare time to helping abused and homeless animals. The good doctor had received an award for her humane efforts just as Tinsley had.

The city loved Tinsley. The animal rights activists loved her. The freaking world loved her.

So did he.

But she'd barely noticed him.

Until he'd made her take notice.

Only Dr. Ferris wasn't Tinsley.

Her hair was a darker blonde. Her skin not quite as porcelain. She twisted it up in a knot on her head as if she didn't have time to fool with her looks.

Her lab coat had once been white but bore dark-red and yellow stains. She probably smelled like wet dog, feline piss, and crap.

She was the closest thing he could get to the one he wanted.

She'd have to do.

He cranked his engine and drove slowly, careful to stay two car lengths behind her so he didn't spook her.

She maneuvered through the city, then onto a side road that led toward the marsh. He knew where she lived. In a little bungalow off the beaten path with a yard for the rescues she took home.

Last count, she had five—three dogs, two cats.

A smile curved his mouth as she veered onto the mile-long drive to her cabin. Lucky for him that she liked to be isolated.

No one to see him. No one to interfere. He just had to wait until it was dark. Or come back later . . .

He parked alongside the narrow road, beneath an overhang of live oaks, and settled in to watch through his binoculars. So predictable. She greeted the dogs first.

Let them crawl all over her and lick her. Then playtime. She tossed an old tennis ball and laughed as they gave chase.

After she'd run around the yard with them for half an hour, she finally went inside. Lights flickered on in the hall.

She left the sheers open. Thought she was alone, that no one could see her.

He grinned again, anticipation building.

First he'd let her shower. Get clean for him. Spray herself with that body spray she liked so much. Lavender.

Nice, although he preferred rosewood. Reminded him of Tinsley.

He knew everything about Ferris. This wasn't his first rodeo. He'd been inside her house many times. She liked Greek yogurt, blueberries, and pinot grigio. She grew her own herbs. She liked books about real-life adventures, mountain climbing, and survival fitness. She preferred country rock music, although she had a collection of Beatles albums. Her clothes hung neatly in the closet. Boring jeans, sweaters, and shirts. Nothing frilly. Plain, sensible underwear. Although he had found two pairs of lacy black thongs buried beneath the cotton undies.

No husband or lover or boyfriend. She kept a vibrator in her bed-side table.

Dirty girl. She wouldn't need that once she got to know him.

The rumble of an engine echoed from an oncoming car.

What the hell was it doing out here?

He tugged his hat over his head and ducked lower in his seat as it passed. *Dammit.*

He didn't want to be seen. Too risky.

He started the engine, pulled onto the street, and headed toward the highway.

"You got lucky, Doc." A smile twitched onto his mouth. "But I'll be back. I promise."

He always kept his promises.

CHAPTER TWENTY-THREE

Wyatt stepped aside to phone the director of the psychiatric ward where Cat was confined, a man named Lamar Heard.

"I don't understand how I can help," Heard said.

"This scene reads like the Keeper murders that Cat Landon took responsibility for. We suspected at the time that there was a list of other targets. The justice symbol on this victim, and the fact that this case was related to Judge Wadsworth's murder, suggests we were correct."

"I can assure you that Ms. Landon is still here. She's being monitored daily."

"Has she had any visitors?"

A second passed. Heard cleared his throat. "You know I can't divulge patient information without a warrant."

Wyatt sucked in a breath.

"Does Landon have access to a computer or a smartphone?"

"As I just said, I can't divulge private information on a patient. But our policy is that patients earn computer privileges through good behavior and with a medical clearance from the doctor. Even when they are allowed to use the Internet or phone, they're monitored. We keep careful tabs on any Internet activity or communication with the outside world."

"What about staff? Is there anyone who's become close to her? Someone who defended her actions?"

"Not that I can think of, but I'll look into it."

"How about her therapist?"

"Agent Camden, she can't discuss anything shared with her in confidence."

Frustration gnawed at Wyatt. "I know that. But talk to her. If Cat is orchestrating more murders, we need to know. Lives may be in danger."

A long sigh. "I'll do that."

He glanced up and saw Marilyn Ellis and her cameraman hovering at the edge of the scene. She wouldn't give up. "I know that Marilyn Ellis has interviewed Cat. When was she last there?"

"We've been through this," Heard said tersely. "Call me back when you have a warrant."

The phone went dead.

The hair on the back of Wyatt's neck prickled as he looked up and watched the reporter. Marilyn could have visited Cat, discussed Milburn, then killed him. Once Wyatt got the time of death, he'd see whether she had an alibi.

He headed toward the woman, his mind racing. Sometimes criminals insinuated themselves into an investigation. And Marilyn had her ass all up in their business.

She perked up as he approached, obviously thinking he had information to share. Tucking her hair behind one ear, she pushed the mike toward him. "Special Agent Camden, what can you tell us about this murder?"

He gave her a cold look. "As I stated before, I can't discuss the investigation at this time. But I have some questions for you, Miss Ellis."

Her eager smile faded slightly. "Excuse me?"

"You've been interviewing Cat Landon."

She waved the cameraman away. "I have been covering her story."

"Is that all you're doing?" Wyatt asked.

She narrowed her eyes. "I don't understand what you're getting at."

"You've painted Ms. Landon as a victim and a heroine."

Marilyn lifted her chin. "She rid the world of dangerous men when the court system and police failed."

"She also tried to kill Agent Davenport and one of our crime scene investigators to cover her tracks. They were not dangerous."

Her silence reeked of barely suppressed anger. He'd hit a sore spot. But she recovered quickly and gestured toward the scene behind him. "The River Street Rapist was certainly dangerous."

"So you believe that Ms. Landon is responsible for this man's murder?"

"That's not what I said."

"You've made no bones about admiring Ms. Landon's work," he continued. "Perhaps you decided to continue where she left off."

The realization that he considered her a person of interest flashed across her face. "What are you accusing me of, Agent Camden?"

Wyatt gave her a pointed look. "Your quick appearance at this crime scene is interesting."

Her lips pressed into a thin line. "If you're fishing for information about my conversation with Ms. Landon, you're wasting your time. I don't reveal sources or information revealed to me in confidence." She plastered on her TV smile. "Although we could trade information if you'd like to get a drink and talk."

Wyatt forced himself not to react. If Marilyn Ellis thought she could play him, she was wrong.

Climbing in bed with her figuratively or literally would be dancing with the devil.

◆ ◆ ◆

Tinsley's fingers trembled as she typed:

I see his face everywhere I turn. Outside my window. On the beach.

In my bedroom at night when I should be sleeping.

Sleep isn't restful, though. It's a series of nightmares bound together by the memories of what he did to me.

I'm back there again. I claw a mark on the wall beside the others. I started it the day he locked me in the cage.

There are other markings. Three sets. The days his other victims were here before they died.

The first girl—sixty-three days. The second one—only fourteen. The third—ninety.

It's day thirty-nine for me. I'm not going to make it to ninety.

He's worn me down. I no longer cry when he touches me. No longer scream when he forces me onto all fours.

In my mind, I disappear into a world where pain doesn't exist, and he's touching someone else, not me.

My detachment incenses him even more.

At first when I was trapped, I fought him. I tried to rip off that mask. I wanted to see the monster beneath. Be able to describe him when I finally escaped.

I imagined sitting on the witness stand and staring him down. Smiling as the guards dragged him away in shackles and chains.

And walking free as he was sentenced to life in prison. Or death for those other women he murdered.

But today that fight is gone.

After he raped me again, he left me free of the chain. He knows I'm weak. Too weak to run.

I let him think that.

But I crawl to the window. Grime and fog coat the glass. Thick trees stand, jutted together like a wall. A sliver of light snakes through an opening between the weeds.

There . . . an opening. That's the way out. If I can just make it to the light . . .

I roll my hand into a fist and punch the window. Glass shatters. I hit it again and again. Slivers of glass fly everywhere.

Then the glass is gone. But there are bars . . . *No* . . .

I grip them with my hands and try to bend them, move them apart. Frustration builds inside me. But they won't budge.

Sweat beads on my skin. My hands are clammy, blood soaked. It's so hot I can barely breathe, yet I'm shivering.

The door screeches open.

I yank at the bars again. I have to get out!

But a cold wave of air rushes into the room. He's coming toward me.

He'll punish me for this.

Panic and despair make me heavy.

I'm done.

The broken shards of glass glitter in the darkness.

"Ah, Tinsley, dear, you can't leave me . . ."

But I'm going to. One way or another.

I grab a chunk of glass and slice my wrist.

His bellow bounces off the walls as he runs toward me. I switch hands and slice the other wrist.

Blood spurts. The room tilts. Blurs.

I'm falling . . . spinning and falling. Relief is so close by, I can touch it . . . The dark swallows me. But then the light will come, and I'll find peace.

He catches me. I gasp for air, but I'm too weak to fight.

Finally the dark sweeps me under. I beg for it to take me. No more pain. No more sorrow.

No more . . . him.

Colors dance behind my eyes. Flowers and puffy white clouds and warm bright sunshine. Then my parents. Holding out their hands, waiting for me in the light.

I reach for them. Our fingers touch. Soon Mama will wrap her arms around me, and everything will be all right.

But . . . something yanks me back. Pain knifes through me. I blink. Pray for the light again.

But it's not Mama's voice calling my name . . . It's his.

And the ugly darkness is back.

"You can't leave me, Tinsley."

Yes, I can. I have to.

But . . . his hands are on me. He's wrapping my arms in bandages. A sharp sting in my arm. Drugs again.

The pain will fade. He promises that.

But he'll bring it again. He always does.

Hatcher crossed the alley, his phone in his hand. "I just talked to Korine. She cleared the three rape victims who testified against Milburn."

Relieved, Wyatt gave a nod. "How about family members?"

"She's working on that and will keep us posted. So far, though, no leads."

Numerous people, both family and nonfamily members, had been irate over Milburn's release.

"I don't know if this murder is connected to the Skull," Wyatt said, "but I talked to Tinsley, and it started me thinking."

"She heard from him?" Hatcher asked.

Wyatt relayed what had happened with the skulls and his suspicions regarding the green tea. "I understand this is difficult for you, Hatcher, but we have to take a deeper look at Norton Smith."

Hatcher rubbed the wedding ring on his third finger. He and his first wife had been on the verge of divorce before her abduction. Hatcher had struggled with guilt over her death.

"I reviewed what we know about Smith," Wyatt said. "The logical place to start would be—"

"The orphanage where Smith grew up." Hatcher shifted. "I'll look at the murder book on Felicia and ask Bernie to pull everything she can find on that orphanage. The Skull may have met Smith there."

"I know that won't be easy, man. If you want someone else to handle it—"

"No," Hatcher said bluntly. "You and I started this case. We'll finish it."

◆ ◆ ◆

As night fell, Tinsley was so anxious that she plugged in a Zumba video and worked through the routine. She used to enjoy running, but running in place only reminded her that she was trapped inside. The music video pumped up her energy and helped keep her muscles toned. She followed it with a tape on self-defense moves that she'd been doing daily.

She had to stay in shape—be prepared and ready to fight. She'd die before she let that monster take her again.

When she finished practicing the moves, she spread out her yoga mat and stretched.

As kids, she and Carrie Ann had danced and put on skits for their mother and father after dinner. Carrie Ann had loved being the star of the show. She'd flipped and flopped and twirled in her tutu and kept them all entertained. She had always been the happy, outgoing child.

Until their parents died.

Tinsley rubbed her finger over the sea glass turtle around her neck, longing for those innocent childhood days.

A wave of sadness and anger engulfed her. She would never be innocent again, or dance around the room like that child.

Or dream of wearing a white dress and having a family of her own.

Those dreams had died during the weeks of her captivity.

Her phone beeped again. A text. Carrie Ann.

News story about you and the Skull. Why didn't you tell me he's back?

Tinsley's heart stuttered. What news story?

She grabbed the remote and clicked on the TV, surfing the channels until she found Marilyn Ellis with a late-breaking story. It looked like she was in Savannah somewhere, maybe an alley, not the TV station.

"Tonight police and the FBI found Milt Milburn, the alleged River Street Rapist, stabbed to death. His body was left in an alley on River Street. Although federal agents and police refused to comment, sources indicate that the victims who testified against Milburn received photographs of the dead man. Tinsley Jensen, the only surviving victim of the infamous Skull, also received the same photograph."

Tinsley gasped as a picture of her appeared on screen.

"A few months ago, police connected the deaths perpetrated by a woman they called the Keeper to Tinsley Jensen's website, *Heart & Soul*, and arrested one of their own, FBI analyst Cat Landon. Has another vigilante killer surfaced to pick up where Cat Landon left off?"

Guilt over Cat Landon's actions still plagued Tinsley. *Was* there another vigilante?

Marilyn Ellis continued: "Just this morning, the FBI responded to Ms. Jensen's house and found three skulls left on her porch. In earlier interviews with the police, Ms. Jensen stated that her abductor created a shrine of paper skulls, flowers, and candles in celebration of the Day of the Dead. With the Day of the Dead approaching, this raises the question—has the Skull returned for Miss Jensen?"

CHAPTER TWENTY-FOUR

The Skull ran his hand over his bald head as he paced in front of the TV.

God . . . he was so wired. He'd been eager for the good doctor tonight. So desperate to feed the raging animal inside him. To satisfy his hunger until he could have Tinsley again.

That fucking news anchor Marilyn Ellis bolted into his thoughts. What was she saying? Something about him leaving skulls on Tinsley's porch?

Bitch. She painted him as a monster. But he wasn't. He was a good man. He cared about people. He listened to their problems and sympathized when they told him how and where they hurt.

Then he did everything he could to make them feel better.

And now what was she saying? That he was back?

Sure, he'd been watching Tinsley. But he had not left anything on her doorstep. He wasn't that stupid.

So what the hell was going on?

He went to his trophy wall and soaked up the sight of the photographs he'd kept.

First Linnea—she'd looked the most like his mother, Janine, with her light-blonde hair and green eyes . . . and that killer smile . . . He'd taken her on impulse. A big mistake. She hadn't been sweet or loving or any of the things a good girl was supposed to be.

She'd had to die.

Then Sonya. She'd worked at a nursing home. Had been sympathetic to the elderly patients, a friend to the ones suffering from dementia. But her patience had stopped there. She cussed like a sailor. She hadn't liked animals. Or men.

Then Gail. Sweet and soft-spoken. A Sunday school teacher. A truly good girl.

Too good. She thought sex was dirty.

But that was wrong. Even good girls liked sex. His mother had, and she'd been a good girl.

Like Tinsley. She had been the best. The *one*.

He'd wanted her to be the last.

She would be.

But that Ellis bitch said he'd been to Tinsley's.

Either she and Tinsley had lied.

Or . . . someone was pretending to be him. An impostor.

He balled his hands into fists. He would not have that! No one could imitate him. No one.

Because no one knew what made him tick. Why he took the girls. What he wanted from them.

Norton Smith had tried to copy him, too. He'd made a mistake befriending that weirdo, but at the time he'd wanted to connect with someone who shared his dark needs. Smith had wanted to be like him. Except Smith was obsessed with being noticed. He'd wanted to be famous.

But Smith had it all wrong. Thought it was about hurting the women.

It had been about showing them that he was good enough for them. That he would always take care of them, especially when they were hurting.

Smith hadn't even been original enough to create his own MO.

If someone else had put skulls on Tinsley's porch, it was another impostor.

He plunged his fist into the wall.

No one would have Tinsley but him. They were meant to be together. He'd known it the first time he'd met her.

But there was no way he could go to Tinsley's tonight, not when the place was probably crawling with cops.

Furious, he snatched his keys and stormed out the door. He would go back to Dr. Ferris's house.

She wasn't Tinsley, but she could satisfy his dark hunger tonight and tomorrow and however long it took until he could have his true love.

CHAPTER
TWENTY-FIVE

Wyatt and Hatcher were finishing talking to the police officers who'd canvassed the bars and restaurants when a man in a suit and tie pushed past the police barrier.

Milt Milburn's father.

Instead of cornering Wyatt or Hatcher, though, he headed straight to Marilyn Ellis.

Wyatt watched her face light up with excitement at the idea of interviewing Milburn. Then Milburn tore into her about the way she'd described his son, and her expression turned to discomfort.

Still, she was a pro. Even if Milburn attacked her verbally or physically today, Marilyn would put up with it. Drama made good TV.

Detective Brockett stepped up to Wyatt and Hatcher. "The officers haven't found any leads with the canvass," he told them. "A couple of waiters and a bartender noticed Milburn having a drink but didn't remember anyone specific being with him. The place was packed. Two women Milburn approached recognized him and immediately told him off. Then Milburn disappeared into a dark corner, and the bartender lost track of him."

Ellis's voice cut into the conversation, and they fell silent to listen to the interview. "We're here live at the scene of what we believe to be a homicide investigation." Ellis angled the microphone toward Milburn's father. "This is Mr. Harold Milburn, the father of Milt Milburn, the young man found dead here tonight."

Milburn snatched the microphone from her. "I want this town to know what an abominable job the Savannah Police Department and the FBI are doing. Instead of calling me or having the decency to inform me in person, I learned from social media that my son was murdered." He gestured toward Marilyn as if she were a piranha. "Not only did law enforcement and the press malign my son's good name and character with false allegations that destroyed his career, but now they've shown no respect for my family by allowing the press to be present during such a painful time."

Ellis simply let him vent, well aware that his reaction would hype ratings. Wyatt shifted. She basked in the limelight, even if the truth got skewed.

Wyatt and Hatcher followed alongside the transport team to shield Milburn's body from the camera as they loaded him into the hearse.

Milburn's father spied them and shot past Ellis. Marilyn and the cameraman trailed him like hound dogs following the scent of blood.

"Get started on the warrants for Milburn's phone and computer," Wyatt told Hatcher. "Bernie can help us search them and Milburn's contacts in case the unsub made contact online or via phone or text."

"Copy that."

Hatcher positioned himself by the body to keep Milburn at bay as the angry man approached.

"I want to see my son," Harold Milburn demanded.

Wyatt swallowed hard. As much as he detested Milt Milburn, no father should see his child in this condition. "I'm sorry, Mr. Milburn, but I don't think that's a good idea. When we get him to the morgue and clean him up, then you'll be allowed to have some time with him."

"How dare you try to keep me from my child," Milburn shouted.

Wyatt shot Ellis a warning look, hoping she'd turn off the camera, but no such luck. "I understand you're upset, Mr. Milburn, and I apologize for the way you learned about your son. We will do everything possible to find out what happened to him and see that justice is served."

"Like you cared about justice when those tramps maligned my son's character." He grabbed the mike from Ellis again. "Mark my words. You and the police will be held accountable for crucifying my boy. Milt did not rape anyone. The judge released him because those girls lied. They dress like whores and flirt and rub all over men, then cry rape when it's over. They got exactly what they deserved."

Wyatt saw red.

Now he understood why Milt Milburn had the attitude he did. *Like father, like son.*

He rolled his hands into fists to keep from slugging the man and reminded himself that Harold Milburn was in shock and grieving.

They'd investigate Milburn's murder because it was their job to do so.

But another case took priority: finding the Skull.

♦ ♦ ♦

Tinsley punched the TV off. She didn't want to hear another word from that pushy Marilyn Ellis. She'd staunchly refused to grant the woman an interview, but the stubborn reporter continued to hound her.

How had she known about the skulls left on her porch?

Wyatt . . . no. He wouldn't have told her anything. He was too professional. And . . . protective.

Her phone buzzed again. Carrie Ann once more.

Call me, sis. I'm worried about you.

Tinsley frowned. Her sister had certainly been persistent lately.

But Carrie Ann needed the old, reliable, strong Tinsley. And that woman was dead.

After that news story, Tinsley at least owed her sister a text. She stood and stretched, then paced to the picture window overlooking the ocean. The wind was howling, palm trees swaying, the sky dark and ominous.

She studied the beach, scrutinizing every inch for the Skull, but it was late and the beach appeared empty.

An officer had been left to guard the house. She was safe.

So why did she feel so on edge?

Hands trembling, she slumped down onto the window seat and typed a text to her sister.

Not sure where that reporter got her information, but unclear if the Skull has reappeared. FBI has been to the house and have posted a guard outside.

Don't worry. Stay safe yourself.

No need to tell Carrie Ann about Wyatt's suspicions regarding her tea being drugged. Not until she knew for certain what was going on.

Wyatt and Hatcher had warrants within the hour and headed straight to Milt Milburn's condo. They needed to execute the search before Milburn's father had time to erase incriminating evidence.

The ERT impounded Milburn's Ferrari and was processing it. Not that they thought the unsub had been in it, but it was possible. They had to explore every angle.

He and Hatcher flashed credentials at the security guard at the gate to the building. When they explained the reason for their inquiries, another guard escorted them to Milburn's and let them in.

The exclusive complex was pricey with ultracontemporary million-dollar condos, at odds with the rich history of the city. Milburn's unit faced the Savannah river walk.

Disgust tasted bitter in Wyatt's mouth. No doubt the bastard sat on his private patio, his libido raging as he hunted for prey.

"We can take it from here," Hatcher told the guard as he lingered at the door.

"You want me to help, I can," the guard offered.

Hatcher shook his head. "It's an official investigation. We have to go by the book. Already Milburn's father is planning to sue us and the SPD."

"Sounds like him," the man said in a derisive tone.

"You know the Milburns?"

"Just in passing. They didn't hang with the staff or anyone without money."

"Did the police talk to you about the rapes when the son was charged?"

The man nodded. "Yeah, but I never saw him bring women back here. I guess he preferred hotels or . . . whatever."

Dark alleys, Wyatt finished silently.

The man stepped back outside, and Wyatt and Hatcher entered the foyer, a two-story grand entrance with a chandelier that resembled dripping diamonds. Expensive paintings, Oriental vases and rugs, and white couches that looked as if they'd never been used filled the space. The entire décor was white. In fact, it looked downright sterile.

Interesting.

"I'll check the kitchen and den," Hatcher said. "Looks like his home office is over there."

Wyatt nodded and veered toward it as they both started their search.

He checked the desk first and found basic office supplies. A cherrywood filing cabinet held financials on several companies, a testament to Milburn's role as an entrepreneur and investor. On the off chance his murder wasn't related to the Keeper or the rape accusations against him, Bernie would check financials. If Milburn had cheated or swindled clients, one of them could have killed him and used the justice symbol to throw off the police.

Wyatt couldn't assume anything at this point.

He gave a perfunctory glance at each file, then decided he'd have the ERT carry them to the lab.

He slid into the man's leather desk chair and opened his laptop. The prosecutor had secured warrants for his computer and other electronic devices when Milburn was first arrested but hadn't found anything at the time. He'd suspected Milburn had wiped them clean.

Milburn had obviously purchased a new computer since.

As Wyatt expected, it was password-protected. *Dammit.*

He searched drawers, then beneath the desk, and found a file taped to the underside.

No password had been written down, although he did find a list of numbers and dates, so he tried a combination of several of them. Finally, he got in. He checked the man's browser history. Several financial sites, startup companies, research projects.

Nothing incriminating.

Frustrated, he searched the desk drawer, then walked over to the bookcase. Milburn had a collection of first editions. All the books on the shelf were meticulously lined up except for one, which was off-kilter.

He reached for it and pulled it out, then spied a box behind it. Curious. He pulled the box out and opened it.

CDs.

His heart pounded, and he carried them back to the computer. Seconds later, he inserted the first one.

His stomach churned at the images that appeared. Photos of young women strolling the river walk. There were candid shots of the ladies with friends, drinking, laughing. Having fun.

Had he been stalking them? Looking for his next victim?

Wyatt removed that CD and slipped in another. More photos . . . this time random women in sexual poses engaged in S&M.

A third CD, and he hit pay dirt. Pictures of the three women Milt Milburn had been accused of raping. Candid shots of them at their homes, in their houses, in their bathrooms when they thought they were alone.

He'd stalked them before he'd raped them.

The next set made his stomach turn. Pictures of the women, drugged and lying in erotic poses where he'd placed them for the camera.

Poses—evidence—that no one had known about at the trial.

Pictures that would have cemented the case against Milburn and sent him to jail. But the DA had obviously never found them.

He grimaced. Instead, Milburn had walked free. And he'd probably intended to rape again—most likely the woman he'd met in the bar hours before his death.

Instead of in jail, though, he was dead. And he definitely would be burning in hell.

Exactly where he belonged.

♦ ♦ ♦

Tinsley's computer dinged, signaling that she had a message.

She hurried from the bathroom to look at it, and her pulse pounded at the sight on the screen.

A picture of a woman tied up in a dark room inside a cage.

Fear shot through her, then horror. *Oh God* . . . it was Dr. Ferris.

See what you forced me to do, Tinsley. Since I can't have you, I'll have to make do with your friend.

A scream lodged in Tinsley's throat. He had taken Felicia from her. She couldn't lose another friend to him . . .

CHAPTER TWENTY-SIX

He took his time. The important thing was that Tinsley knew he hadn't forgotten the weeks they'd spent together.

That he really wanted *her*.

But for now, her friend would do. She fit what he was looking for. She was a good girl. She devoted her life to rescue animals.

How could he not admire her for that?

That was like Janine, too. So giving. So loving. So eager to help others.

The familiar twinge of desire stirred inside him. It was wrong, the way he felt about his mother. Sons were supposed to look up to their mamas, admire them, obey them.

But he'd lusted after his. Had wanted to replace his daddy in her bed.

It all started when his daddy let him watch one night. He'd seen his big daddy, naked, his thick cock ramming inside her, and he'd gotten so hard he'd come.

He couldn't help himself after that. He'd fantasized about doing the same thing to his mama that his daddy had done.

It was the beast.

Daddy said watching was okay, but not touching.

Sometimes when his daddy worked late, he'd sneak into the bedroom and watch his mama undress in the bathroom. When she'd dropped her clothes to the floor and stood there naked, he'd wanted to rake his hands over her big breasts. To touch her smooth skin and suck on her nipples.

He'd wanted to kiss her down there where his father said only he could lick her.

He'd dreamed about sticking his tongue in her after that.

The next time his daddy had worked late, he'd slipped into her bed when she was asleep. She'd woken up just as his tongue plunged into her pussy and he tasted her wetness.

She'd screamed and thrown him out of bed so hard his head hit the corner of the dresser.

His father had walked in and called him a pervert. Then he'd dragged him outside to the dog run and told him if he wanted to lick something, to lick the dog.

Anger shot through him at the memory. He'd hated his daddy after that.

And he'd wanted his mama even more. One taste of her, and he'd never forgotten . . .

But she never looked at him the same way after that. Had locked the door to the bathroom and bedroom when she undressed.

But he hadn't been able to control his urges. He'd tried to sneak into her bed again.

The next day, they'd punished him and sent him away.

His pulse hammered at the thought.

The beast screamed at him again. He hadn't deserved to be sent away. To be denied. To be shamed. Not after what he'd seen his daddy doing in bed with her.

He peeked in on Dr. Ferris to make sure she was secure. Yes, she was all tied up. Just waiting for him.

The anticipation must be killing her.

Laughter bubbled in his throat at the thought.

Adrenaline fueling his excitement, he stepped into the bathroom. Time for his cleansing ritual.

He hated the dirty, smelly, sweaty hair on the animals. Cat and dog hair clung to every piece of furniture in the house. And to him.

He'd become obsessed with shaving when he was a teenager, when Daddy had pushed him out into the dog run and made him stay there all night.

The next morning when his daddy let him inside, he'd showered and scrubbed himself raw. He wanted all the dirty, sweaty hair off his body.

Infatuated with the process, he'd researched customs of other cultures, a topic that had intrigued him from the moment he'd read about the Day of the Dead celebration. He'd been fascinated by the ritualistic shaving practices of ancient Rome and Greece.

Hair, especially beards, was a symbol of status.

In some countries and religions, shaving represented a passage into manhood.

So his own rituals had been born. He imagined himself as some stately Roman patriarch in a ceremony where his minions watched and revered him as his maids shaved his body clean.

He stripped naked, then faced himself in the mirror, examining his head and face and neck. He must be clean all over. Washed and groomed, his skin freshly showered and free of stubble.

Not wanting to cut himself, he used his electric razor on his head. The buzzing sound aroused him, brought images of him naked and bald as a baby.

Next he squirted a handful of shaving cream into one hand, then lifted his hand and inhaled the minty scent. *Heaven.*

Carefully, he lathered his face and neck until his eyes were the only visible part of his face. Everything had to be shaved except his eyebrows. He'd shaved those at first, but it drew too much attention. People thought he was a cancer patient and asked too many questions.

It bothered him to look at them, but it was a small price to pay for his freedom.

Slowly and meticulously, he raked the razor across his skin, removing the fine layer of beard stubble that grazed his jaw and neck.

When his face was completely smooth, he stepped into the shower. A fresh can of shaving cream sat in the soap dish along with a new razor.

He covered his chest first, then his arms and legs. Finally, his ass and pubic hair.

The water swirled with the discarded hair and shaving cream, disappearing down the drain, sucking away the dirt, sweat, and dead skin.

Satisfied, he dried off, then stepped to his dressing area and unlocked the cabinet that held his masks. The one he'd worn for Tinsley had been all black with white-rimmed eyes.

Another was black with white teeth painted on the mouth. Another had crossbones on the cheek. Streaks of red that looked like blood dripped from the mouth of another.

Three were missing. The three that belonged to the women he'd had to say goodbye to.

He traced his finger over the one he'd worn with Tinsley, then lifted it and pressed it to his cheek. Tinsley's scent.

His cock swelled. Twitched. Ached for her.

"Soon we'll be together again," he murmured. "Very soon."

He carefully placed the mask back onto the skeletal bust and chose another.

Next he pulled on his black bodysuit, removed a hypodermic from his supply, then headed toward the good doctor.

Once he sedated her, he could cleanse her as he'd done himself.

But he would make sure she was awake when he joined with her.

After all, he wasn't a pervert as that fucking reporter suggested. He wasn't into necrophilia.

He wanted her to be alive and awake so she would know exactly what was happening.

CHAPTER TWENTY-SEVEN

Tinsley clutched her chest and struggled for a breath. No . . . this couldn't be happening.

He couldn't have kidnapped Joyce. That woman was a godsend to the shelter. She loved people and animals and life itself.

Praying she was mistaken, she called Joyce. Joyce's phone rang and rang, but no one answered.

Her stomach tightened with fear as she looked at the picture on the computer again. Another message came through. A link to a live video stream.

She clicked on the link, tears blurring her eyes.

The woman was tied in the cage again. Tinsley couldn't see her face clearly. But she had medium-length hair, wavy, sandy-blonde . . .

Then slowly she lifted her head and looked up. Her eyes were wild with fear, a scream dying in the gag stuffed in her mouth.

Tinsley choked on a sob. It was Joyce.

A faint stream of light filtered through the room as the door opened, just enough for her to recognize him.

He was wearing the black bodysuit. A mask, this one with wide white teeth. And he was holding a hypodermic.

She knew what was going to happen. First he'd drug her, then bathe her and shave her body . . .

All except for the hair on her head. He kept that. He liked running his fingers through it. Had said that the only place hair belonged on a woman was her head.

Nausea shot to her throat. She couldn't believe it was happening. "Why are you doing this?" she cried. "Why? Joyce never hurt you!"

Rage and helplessness nearly immobilized her. But she fought the terror. She hadn't been able to save herself or Felicia. Maybe she could save Joyce.

Hands shaking, she clawed for her phone. But it slipped from her fingers and slid beneath the chair. Frantic, she dropped to the rug to retrieve it.

She snagged it, accessed her contacts, and called Wyatt. The phone rang three times, and then she heard his voice.

"Tinsley?"

"He has the vet who volunteers at the rescue center," she cried. "Wyatt, you have to save her."

◆ ◆ ◆

Déjà vu struck Wyatt. Just a few months ago, the Keeper had used a live video stream to reveal a man she held hostage.

They'd managed to save him in time, but could they do it now?

They had no clue who the Skull was, where he worked or lived, or where he'd held Tinsley.

"Wyatt, did you hear me?"

Tinsley's panicked voice jerked him back to the phone conversation. "I heard. I'll contact our analyst and see if we can trace where the post is coming from."

"He also sent me a photo of the doctor tied up," Tinsley said. "I'm going to forward it to you now along with the video link."

He swallowed hard at the image that appeared. "I'll get this to the lab along with that link." Although tracing these posts was damn near impossible. Bernie had been working on trying to trace a *Heart & Soul* post that had sounded as if it had come from the Skull, but so far she hadn't had any luck.

"Please hurry," Tinsley whispered. "He's going to rape her and torture her, and he wants me to know it. To see it and know he's doing it because of me."

Sick fuck. "Listen to me, Tinsley. This is not your fault. We will find him." And hopefully the woman before he killed her.

Although judging from what he knew of Tinsley's ordeal, the woman would suffer first.

"Tell me everything you can about her."

"Her name is Dr. Joyce Ferris. She runs the Best Friend's Animal Clinic and volunteers with PAT."

"Is she married? Involved with anyone?"

"No husband or family. She lives alone."

He glanced at Milburn's desk. Hunting for this asshole's killer was wasting time. He didn't give a damn what the jerk's father said.

He cleared his throat. "You're okay with us tapping your phone?"

A tense second. "Do whatever you need to do to find this bastard."

"Is the officer still outside?"

The sound of her breathing rattled over the line. Then her voice. "His car is in the cul-de-sac."

Hell, that was too far away. What if the Skull came in on boat?

"I'm going to have him check the property and beach."

"You think he was here already?"

"I don't know, but I don't want to take any chances. Hatcher and I are at Milburn's condo, searching it. I'll get in touch with Bernie and have police check Dr. Ferris's home, office, and phone. Maybe he contacted her, and we'll get a lead." He'd need warrants, too. Had to do this by the book as Bellows had warned him about with Milburn.

"I hope so," Tinsley said, her voice cracking.

"Hang in there. I'll be there ASAP."

A sniffle. "Please find her," Tinsley said, her voice low. Pained. "She doesn't deserve this."

Emotions welled in Wyatt's throat. "Neither do you." He wanted to say more, to do more. To be with her and comfort her.

But the best way to comfort her was to find the man responsible for tormenting her.

So he hung up and called the analyst. Hatcher stepped into the office as he was hanging up, and Wyatt filled him in.

Concern darkened his partner's eyes. "Go to Tinsley; I'll finish here."

Wyatt nodded. He couldn't concentrate here anyway. He showed Hatcher the porn photos he'd found, along with Milburn's private collection of his victims.

"The asshole got what was coming to him."

Wyatt agreed. But the law demanded they arrest Milburn's killer.

Tinsley's life, and Dr. Ferris's, were more important than tracking down someone who'd killed a serial rapist.

Tinsley tightened the belt of her bathrobe. The thick terry cloth warmed her, made her feel more secure.

Probably because she'd been cold and naked all those months in that cage.

Memories of his hands on her assaulted her. Him forcing her onto all fours, prying her legs apart, rubbing his disgusting self against her. Then inside her . . .

Nausea rolled through her. Poor Joyce . . . What was he doing to her now?

Joyce didn't have children or a husband, but she had wanted those things.

Tinsley covered her abdomen with her hand. Just as she had a year ago . . . before he'd ruined her for a man. And robbed her of the ability to have a family.

Rage seethed through her. He had stolen a year of her life. And her future.

She couldn't let him take that from Joyce. But what could she do to stop him?

Maybe if she sent him a note, he'd leave Joyce and come after her. Then Wyatt could catch him.

She lifted her fingers above the keyboard, her breath erratic as emotions pummeled her. But the video post had disappeared.

And she had no idea how to contact him.

◆ ◆ ◆

Wyatt called Detective Ryker Brockett and asked him to check the Best Friend's Animal Clinic for Dr. Ferris. "If you see anything that looks suspicious or indicates she was abducted from the clinic, call in the ERT. We need to find Dr. Ferris fast."

"Copy that."

"I'll go to her house and do the same," Wyatt said.

He phoned the local officer stationed at Tinsley's and asked him to check the beach and cove, then texted Bernie to get started on the warrants and to ask for help questioning Dr. Ferris's friends, volunteers at PAT and PAWS, coworkers, and clients.

Then he headed to her house. Leaving Savannah, he drove a couple of miles until he reached a stretch of deserted road that led toward more marshland.

The night seemed especially dark, the streetlights few and far between.

The doctor's house was a wood-framed bungalow that looked as if it had seen better days. A fenced yard housed several doghouses and kennel runs.

A German shepherd barked from one corner, and Wyatt parked and walked over, anger coiling inside him at the blood on its mouth.

Shit. He imagined what had happened. The dog had tried to protect the doctor. The Skull probably hit him to make him back off.

The dog whimpered and trotted toward the opposite corner, and Wyatt saw two other dogs lying on their sides in the yard.

Fuck. They'd better not be dead.

He shined his flashlight around the property, senses alert in case the man had stuck around. But he hadn't escaped the law because he was stupid.

This man was a planner. And he was patient. Otherwise they would have heard from him in the last few months.

He quickly checked the front door. Locked. As a formality, he rang the doorbell but wasn't surprised by the lack of response.

Concern for the dogs drove him back to the fence. The German shepherd remained at the edge, as if standing guard. Wyatt spoke in a low, soothing tone for a moment, assuring the animal he was a friend, then let himself inside the fence. Once inside, he stopped and let the dog sniff him as he spoke in a calm voice. "Shh, buddy, it's okay. I'm here to help."

The dog warmed up to him, and he petted him for a minute. "I know you're worried about the doc," Wyatt said. "I'll do everything I can to find her and bring her back."

He rubbed his head, then slowly walked over to where the other two dogs lay. A brown mutt and a mixed beagle. Both on their sides. He checked the brown dog for a pulse, relieved when he found one, then checked the beagle mix. He was breathing as well.

Still concerned, he called Bernie and asked her to send a vet to the house to take care of the animals.

Then he headed to the back door. He pulled on gloves, then shined the flashlight along the door and windows, peeking inside the exposed glass. Sheers hung open. She'd probably thought she was alone out here, that she had plenty of privacy.

That had worked against her when the Skull made his move.

He jiggled the door. Unlocked. Most likely, the Skull had taken her out through here.

He raked the flashlight over the sidewalk. No footprints or drag marks.

He eased the door open and peered inside, scanning the kitchen. The cabinets and floors were outdated, indicating the doctor hadn't cared about furnishings. She probably put the animals first.

No wonder she and Tinsley were friends.

Admiration for the vet stirred, strengthening his resolve to find her. The world needed people like her.

He shined the light along the counters and floor, searching for signs of an intruder, then eased through the hallway to the living area. A lamp overturned. Magazines strewn. A shattered coffee mug.

He could almost feel the struggle, hear Joyce Ferris screaming for help.

Pulse pounding as he imagined her fear, he inched down the hall to the bedroom. The bed was still made, although the small chair in the corner had been knocked on its side.

He peeked inside the bathroom and cursed. This was where she'd been taken. The toiletries on the vanity were overturned, a bottle of lotion on the floor as if she'd tried to grab whatever she could find to defend herself.

The shower curtain had been ripped from the rod, a towel saturated with water in the tub. Blood stained the corner of the sink where the woman must have been injured as he dragged her from the bathroom.

What disturbed him even more was the black outline on the mirror. An outline of a skull.

Beneath it, he'd written Tinsley's name in blood.

CHAPTER TWENTY-EIGHT

Something about the bloody message seemed off to Wyatt. The Skull had sent sugar skulls to the police to announce when he'd taken victims before. But he hadn't written in blood on the mirror or left a message.

This message read as if he was angry.

Was he evolving, or was he about to spiral out of control?

Hadn't he enjoyed the attention Marilyn Ellis had given him? Or was he angry that they were guarding Tinsley and he couldn't get to her?

Wyatt met the ERT at the front door, along with the vet and his assistant from the emergency service. Wyatt had also discovered two cats prowling around outside, but they seemed fine, just agitated.

Wyatt asked the vet to see whether he could pull DNA from the German shepherd for tests. The vet's assistant hurried to the mutt and the beagle mix. He listened to each dog's heart and palpated them for injuries.

"I think they've just been drugged," the assistant said. "It should wear off. But I'll transport them to the emergency clinic for tests and observation."

"We'll need a copy of any labs you run, especially the tox screen," Wyatt said. "This man has drugged his victims before to subdue them. Finding out how he gained access to the meds he uses could lead us back to him."

"Understood."

Wyatt watched as the doctor and assistant carried the animals to the back of the emergency vehicle.

"What do you know about Joyce?" Dr. Brudwig asked.

Wyatt scraped a hand over his jaw. "We have reason to believe that she was abducted by the man known as the Skull."

"Good God, poor Joyce."

Wyatt nodded grimly. "Time is of the essence. How well do you know Dr. Ferris?"

"Not that well," Dr. Brudwig said. "Just in a business capacity. But she was one of the kindest, most giving veterinarians I've ever met."

"Did she mention anyone following her or bothering her?"

Dr. Brudwig shook his head. "Not to me."

"When was the last time you saw her?"

"A couple of weeks ago at a staff meeting. She seemed fine and was excited about the upcoming event for PAWS." The man's eyes flickered with worry. "Please find her."

"We'll do everything possible. We're looking at her personal phone and computer as well as her work ones."

"You think she knew him?"

"It's possible. He could have met her at the clinic or rescue center. If she didn't perceive him as a threat, she might have let him into her house. That could have given him the advantage."

The doctor looked grim. "Do you want to question our male clients?"

Wyatt nodded. "That would help. I'll have warrants soon."

The doctor handed him a business card. "Tell your people to contact my receptionist. I'll see that she gives you whatever you need."

Wyatt thanked him, then texted Bernie with instructions for obtaining the files from the clinic and rescue shelter.

"Get warrants for the doctor's files so we can run background checks on each of the patients/pet owners who used the services of the

Best Friend's Animal Clinic. Also look at the volunteers and workers at the rescue shelter and anyone associated with the upcoming adoption event." A thought hit him. "Let's cross-check with anyone who attended or helped out at the event last year."

If a name popped on both lists, they might finally get a lead.

♦　♦　♦

No news from Wyatt. Every second that ticked by meant another second that Joyce was in that monster's hands. That he could be hurting her.

Frantic with worry, Tinsley turned to her website. If he was reading it and had contacted her earlier, maybe the FBI could trace his location.

A flurry of posts expressed relief that the River Street Rapist was dead.

> A shout-out to whoever ended that man's reign of terror.

> Finally, we can walk on the river walk and feel somewhat safe again.

> Don't forget that there are always other predators out there.

She skimmed more comments but was drawn to a different one.

> Every night when I go to bed, I see his face in my mind. He has never touched me, but he hurt my sister. I feel her pain as if he did those horrible things to me.

> I want to kill him with my bare hands. Some nights I do kill him in my dreams.

All the days she was missing, I searched the streets
for her face, praying she'd come back alive.

But when she did, she wasn't the same.

The sister I knew and loved was dead.

He will be dead soon, too.

A shudder rippled through Tinsley.

That post could have been about her and Carrie Ann. She had been lost when she'd returned from hell.

So lost she hadn't considered how much her sister had suffered when she was missing. How horrible the days had been when she'd waited for word on whether or not Tinsley was alive.

If the roles had been reversed, she would have been out of her mind with terror for Carrie Ann.

Just as she was for Joyce now.

A soft knock startled Tinsley. Then the doorbell.

She jumped, hesitating before she went to the door. The officer was supposed to be outside.

But what if . . . what if the Skull had gotten to the officer? He could have subdued him, then come to the door in disguise.

The low knock again.

She checked the peephole and nearly cried out in relief when she saw Wyatt on the other side.

She hurriedly twisted the lock and opened the door. Without thinking, she fell against him, her body trembling as he wrapped his arms around her and stepped inside.

Wyatt inhaled Tinsley's sweet scent, silently thanking the powers that be that she was safe.

He intended to keep her that way.

But her body trembled against his, a reminder that she was terrified and that she had reason to be.

He stroked her back, rubbing slow circles, amazed and grateful that she'd allowed him to hold her. But as that realization sank in, it must have also seeped into her consciousness.

She pulled away, a dazed look on her face. "I . . . I'm sorry."

He reached for her again, but she threw up her hands in a warning.

"You don't have anything to be sorry about."

She took a step backward, putting more distance between them, then lifted her hand to her cheek and rubbed it.

"Any news?" she asked in a pained whisper.

He wanted to tell her yes, but he refused to lie to her.

"We're getting warrants for her work and home computer and phone. Our analyst is going to compare her patient and volunteer list to the one from last year's fund-raiser, to see if anyone appeared on both."

"You think that's where he met me? And now that Joyce has taken over, he's fixated on her?"

"It's possible." He hesitated. "Think about it. Did the Skull make any references to the fund-raiser? Did his voice sound familiar?"

Tinsley twisted her mouth to the side. "I don't think so," she said. "Although there were hundreds of people at the fund-raiser that day. He could have been in the crowd or even spoken to me and I forgot." She gave him a beseeching look. "Were your people able to trace the video post he sent?"

"They're working on it." He ran his hands through his hair. "Was there anything you saw in the picture that might help us figure out where he's holding her?"

She shook her head no. "It was dark, just like it was when he held me. Do you think he has her at the same place?"

Wyatt shrugged. "If it's isolated, yes. Maybe there were sounds outside where you were? Birds? A train? Airplane?"

She dropped her head into her hands and rubbed her eyes. Silence stretched thick between them, fraught with emotions and fear.

"I think I heard a boat."

His pulse jumped. She hadn't mentioned that detail before. "What kind of boat? A motorboat. A barge? Cruise ship?"

"A small one. Like something you'd use in the swamp or an inlet."

There were a lot of houses near the river, a creek, inlets on the island and the outskirts of Savannah with water access.

An odd look crossed her face, and he cleared his throat. "Did you remember something else?"

She pressed her hand to her cheek again, her eyes haunted. "He has rituals."

Wyatt's stomach clenched into a hard knot. He didn't want to hear about them.

But he had to.

"Tell me about it," he said quietly.

She wrapped her arms around her waist and went to look out the window again. She'd closed the shutters, but she opened them and stared out into the dark night. Moonlight glittered off the palm trees, the wind gusts making them sway.

"He decorates for the Day of the Dead, builds the shrine with the paper skulls and flowers."

They'd talked about this before. "What other rituals?"

"He's obsessive about cleanliness," she said in a low voice. "He bathes his victims before he rapes them."

She sounded as if she were far away, describing something that had happened to a stranger. A coping mechanism.

"He scrubs his victims clean, even uses alcohol as if disinfecting the skin."

Maybe he was a germophobe?

"He also shaves himself and his victims."

Wyatt swallowed at the images she painted in his mind.

"He shaves himself?"

She nodded. "Meticulously. He said hair has no place on the body. Except for a woman's head." She shivered and touched her hair, fiddling with the strands. "He was bald but didn't cut my hair. He liked to run his fingers through it."

Wyatt stood ramrod stiff. He couldn't react, or Tinsley might stop confiding in him.

"The first time, he injected me with some drug that knocked me out while he performed his ritual."

"The first time?"

She nodded, her lower lip quivering. "After that, he made me stay awake. He wanted me to know everything he was doing."

Sadistic monster.

He inched toward her. The pain in her eyes nearly brought him to his knees.

Unable to help himself, he brushed his knuckles against her cheek. For a brief second, she closed her eyes and leaned into his hand.

Her soft breath punctuated the air. His stalled in his chest.

The fact that she'd allowed him to hold her when he'd first arrived, and now let him touch her, humbled him.

"It's over, Tinsley," he murmured. "You're safe."

His words broke the spell. She opened her eyes and stepped back again. "No, it's not. Poor Joyce. He's doing those things to her right now."

CHAPTER
TWENTY-NINE

Shadows darkened the patio of Sandlover's Cove, a local pub on Seahawk Island, as Carrie Ann parked. The bar overlooked the marsh and catered to locals who liked beer and seafood and enjoyed the late-night pub scene.

It was also off the beaten path and provided an easy place for Carrie Ann to hide. She'd had to get out of that hotel in Savannah. She'd been going out of her ever-loving mind. It had been too damn far from her sister.

Tinsley had refused to talk to her. Again.

Loneliness engulfed her, and she climbed out and crossed the gravel parking lot to the entrance of the pub. Paranoid that a predator might be watching, she scanned the surrounding area, then quickly ducked inside.

She tugged her pink cap over her head to hide her ugly hair loss. She couldn't help herself; when she was nervous or upset, she pulled it out without even thinking. Now she had bald patches that made her look like a freak.

The last shrink had tried to help her with it. Had given her medication. Antidepressants. Something to help her sleep.

But sleep was her enemy. When she slept, she had nightmares, vivid images of the things that monster had done to her sister. Images she couldn't get out of her head.

Once she connected to Tinsley's website, she'd started reading Tinsley's posts along with the others, and she hadn't been able to stop. She'd almost become obsessed with the dark thoughts.

Because they were so similar to her own.

If Tinsley knew what she'd been thinking the last few months, her sister would probably lock her in a loony bin.

But the best therapy for both of them was to rid the world of the Skull.

She slipped into a booth in the back, ordered a scotch, then booted up her computer. Seconds later, she found the chat room where the Keepers met.

Carrie Ann followed Marilyn Ellis's every broadcast. Marilyn not only asked tough questions but also, without even realizing it, kept her informed about Tinsley.

A few months ago, after not hearing from Tinsley, Carrie Ann had wondered whether Tinsley was still alive. Then Marilyn had aired that story about the vigilante killings and mentioned that one of the victims had been left in front of Tinsley's cottage.

Carrie Ann had been grateful to know where her sister was. And she'd been intrigued by the Keepers.

Cat Landon was her hero. Instead of tolerating the fact that bad men went free, she'd made sure they were punished. That took guts.

She wanted to be like Cat. Be a hero for her sister.

The waitress brought her drink, and Carrie Ann took a sip, then entered the chat room, her nerves pinging. Tonight's agenda: everyone was supposed to bring a list of problems that needed to be erased.

Taking action instead of sitting around and accepting the injustices felt liberating. Cathartic.

Voices and laughter from the pub blended with the sound of the ocean in the background. Two inebriated girls belted out a song, drawing laughter and clapping from their fellow coeds.

A dark-haired guy with a beard gave her a once-over. But when he saw her hat, he made a face and turned his attention toward a busty blonde on his left.

Bastard. Most men just cared about looks. They didn't stand beside you when you needed them most.

Tinsley's fiancé was the perfect example.

Not that Carrie Ann cared about this asshole in a bar. After what had happened to Tinsley, she was so not interested in a one-night stand. More than one of those had turned nasty for her.

She turned back to the chat room and the Keepers.

Maybe she'd add a couple of those bastards' names to the list.

CHAPTER THIRTY

The sound of rain drizzling added to the chill inside Tinsley. She couldn't shake the nauseating images of what the Skull was doing to her friend.

She pressed the palm of her hand to her eyes and struggled to remember more details about the place where he'd held her. But she'd been in the dark so long that she hadn't seen anything.

"Korine has been studying behavioral analysis the past few months," Wyatt said. "I want her to come by and talk to you and work up a profile."

She nodded. "If you think it'll help."

"It might. The profile is given out to law enforcement and the media," he said.

Joyce needed her to be strong now. "Tell her to stop by anytime."

Wyatt's phone buzzed. "I have to get this."

He stepped onto the porch, and she glanced through the window to watch him. The dark clouds shrouded the moonlight, an ominous feeling permeating the air as if a storm was on its way.

Wyatt came back in. His face looked grim.

God . . . not Joyce . . . He hadn't killed her already, had he?

"That was the lab," Wyatt said. "They have the results from your tea."

She took a breath. "And?"

"It was drugged."

Tinsley took a minute to absorb that fact. "So he was here," Tinsley said. "He wanted to subdue me. Why didn't he take me then?"

Wyatt's brows furrowed. "I don't know. Maybe he knew we were watching you, so he thought he'd scare you enough that you'd leave. Then he could make his move."

But she couldn't leave. She'd tried that already.

Wyatt moved up beside her. His gaze fell to where she rubbed the puckered, jagged lines on her wrists.

A tense second passed. He knew what had happened. "When?" he asked. "After you were found?"

No use denying it. He'd seen her file. She shook her head. "Day number thirty-nine." She swallowed, determined not to fall apart. It had happened. She was wounded. Scarred.

He knew that, too. He'd seen the horrid pictures, read the medical reports, her statement.

"I fought him at first, but finally I broke. I gave up. I . . . wanted it to end." Anger railed inside her. "But he wouldn't let me die. He saved me and doctored my arms and cried over me."

"Jesus." He lifted her hands one by one. Then he pressed a gentle kiss to each wrist, lingering as he gently ran his finger over the red, puckered flesh.

His touch and kiss were so sweet and tender that she couldn't move. Couldn't breathe.

Her gaze met his. She expected pity. Disgust. Revulsion.

Instead, there was understanding.

"If he gets me again, I'll kill myself before I let him touch me like he did before."

◆ ◆ ◆

Wyatt silently cursed. Part of him understood what Tinsley was saying. Another part of him wanted her to fight like hell to survive, no matter what.

"I'm not going to let him hurt you." Wyatt swallowed against the thickness in his throat. "I promise you that, Tinsley."

A sad look passed through her eyes. "I know you mean that, Wyatt. You're a good man. But you can't be with me every minute of every day."

He wanted to pull her against him again, to wrap his arms around her and never let her go. But he had to respect the distance she needed.

"If I can't, someone else can," Wyatt said.

"Don't you see?" Tinsley said in a pained whisper. "Being locked in here, having guards all the time, I'm still a hostage. He's still controlling my life."

He gritted his teeth. "It won't be forever," he said. "We'll find him and lock him up." But would they do it before he killed Dr. Ferris?

He stroked her arm. "Why don't you try to get some rest."

Anguish darkened her eyes as she looked up at him. "How can I sleep, knowing what she's going through?"

He didn't know how to answer that. Except to be honest.

"Staying up all night won't help her. If—no, *when*—we find her, she'll need you. I'll sack out on your porch and stand guard."

She ran her fingers through her hair, tousling the ends. "It's raining. You can't sleep out there."

He doubted he would sleep anyway. "I'm not leaving you alone." Of course, he could call for another local officer. But . . . he wanted to be here, dammit.

A wariness settled in her eyes, and then she gestured to the sofa. "You can stay on the couch."

His gaze met hers. "Are you sure? I don't want to make you uncomfortable."

Emotions flickered in her eyes. Then a fleeting second of awareness that made his body harden.

But he had to focus. Earning Tinsley's trust was more important than his own desires.

◆ ◆ ◆

Tinsley leaned against the door, her body trembling. Fear for her friend made it difficult to breathe.

But something else was happening. Something between her and Wyatt.

She released a pent-up breath. She'd been so distraught over Joyce's abduction that she'd turned to him for comfort. He'd touched her, and she hadn't balked or felt . . . ill.

And when he'd kissed the scars on her wrists, she'd felt tenderness in him that she'd never expected from any man.

Especially for her.

No one will ever have you but me.

The man in the Skull mask had told her that so many times that she believed him. She thought she'd die at his hands. Or that no other man would want her after seeing what the Skull had done to her.

Outside, the rain intensified, pattering against the roof. For a brief time when Wyatt held her, she'd felt safe. And she'd warmed to him, had felt an awakening in her body, as if she'd been asleep for a long time.

But he was only doing his job.

She removed her robe and reached for a nightgown. The image that stared back at her in the mirror looked different than it had before. The scars had faded slightly but remained. Her skin was pale from lack of sunlight. Puckered flesh and jagged lines crisscrossed her belly.

But her eyes flickered with something like . . . hope. Awareness. With the possibility that maybe she wasn't as dead on the inside as she'd believed.

Guilt quickly squashed that hope, and she dragged on her nightgown, crawled into bed, and pulled up the covers. Normally she left her door open so she could hear any noise from the front of the house.

It seemed odd tonight that she'd closed it, and that the man who'd stayed to protect her was on the other side.

Wyatt had nearly died saving her once. If she couldn't trust him, who could she trust?

She inhaled a deep breath, slid from bed, and unlocked the door. She eased it open just a fraction, then tiptoed back to her bed. But as she curled beneath the covers, images of what the Skull was doing to Joyce flashed behind her eyes, and tears blurred her vision.

She rolled to the other side, pressed her hand to her mouth, and released a silent scream, forcing herself to lie perfectly still the way she'd done when she'd known the Skull was watching.

◆ ◆ ◆

Wyatt tensed at the sound of the door opening.

He held his breath, expecting her to come into the kitchen. Maybe she wanted water or to check her computer again.

Or she might want to talk.

He waited, then heard the bed creak as she returned to it.

He breathed out, grateful she hadn't come back into the room. He wanted her to sleep. To rest.

He needed the distance from her.

Maybe the unlocked door was another step in winning her trust.

Or hell, maybe she was claustrophobic and needed the open door to breathe.

You're overthinking it, man. Focus on the case.

Needing air, he stepped onto the porch, senses honed for detecting trouble. Raindrops splattered the sand, the tides pummeling the beach and washing driftwood and shells onto the shore.

His mind turned to those skulls that had been left on Tinsley's porch and to the bones in the cemetery. If those girls had been murdered, another killer had gotten away. How had the Skull known they were there?

Everything seemed connected, yet . . . it wasn't. Or was it?

He watched the tides for a while, contemplating those questions. No answers came.

But he would find them.

CHAPTER
THIRTY-ONE

The Skull ran his fingers over the doctor's skin. Smooth and silky, just like a woman's should be.

Her hair was shorter than he liked. But her body reminded him of Janine's. Full and voluptuous. Big breasts. Nice hips. Curvy waist.

He trickled oil over her arms and smoothed it in with his hands, then dribbled some on her belly and down her legs. Inch by inch he rubbed the oil into her skin, appreciating her beauty.

She suddenly opened her eyes and yanked at the chains securing her wrists and ankles to the wall. The bed where he'd laid her was centered in the room so he could watch her from all angles. But he'd moved her to the tub for the cleansing.

Fear flashed in her eyes, and she screamed, frantically trying to free herself.

"Fight all you want," he said as he removed the gag. "No one will hear you." He gestured toward the skeletal heads hanging from the ceiling. "Except for them."

Her eyes followed to the dangling skulls, and then she began to plead and beg.

He simply smiled and let her get it out of her system. Soon she would be too tired to fight. She'd realize it was futile.

Then he could do whatever he wanted.

Just like he had with the others. Like he'd wanted to do with Janine. Except his father had stopped him.

His father had only teased him for wanting her. Then he'd cut him off. That had been cruel. Worse, then his father had dropped him off at that farm.

If you have dark needs, fuck one of the animals.

Bitterness welled inside him. He hadn't wanted to fuck a damn farm animal. He'd wanted *her*.

He'd been so enraged that first night he'd snatched one of the chickens from the pen and snapped its neck. The popping sound had given him such relief that he'd chosen another and killed it, too.

One, two, three . . . he snapped their necks, then slashed the heads off and stowed them on a shelf in his room.

The next day, he put the bodies in a box and sent them to his father and mother.

CHAPTER
THIRTY-TWO

A rumbling sound jerked Tinsley from sleep. She bolted upright, disoriented. She'd been dreaming she was back in that room with him.

Except this time Joyce was in a cage beside her. He forced her to watch as he dragged Joyce from the cage and raped her. Joyce's screams bounced off the cold walls and made her feel sick inside.

She twisted the sheets between her fingers, her breathing erratic. Slowly, reality returned. She wasn't in that room—she was at the cottage, her home for the last eleven months.

But Joyce was with him.

Fear and sorrow clawed at her, nearly immobilizing her.

The rumbling noise echoed again.

She slipped from bed, grabbed her robe, and pulled it on. Shivering, she slipped her feet into her bedroom shoes and padded into the living area.

No intruder. Just Wyatt stretched out on her sofa, deep in sleep.

She paused in the doorway, mesmerized by the sight of his big body. One muscular arm dangled from the side of the sofa while the other was thrown across his stomach, where he clutched a throw pillow. His legs were too long for the couch; one foot was braced on the floor, while the other was propped on the armrest.

He looked out of place against the cottagey blue and white, yet . . . somehow, he also looked at home. As if he belonged.

She hadn't shared her place with an overnight guest since she'd come home from the hospital. Carrie Ann had invited her to stay with her, but her sister was fragile herself. Tinsley's nightmares had been too much for Carrie Ann to handle.

She hadn't wanted to burden Carrie Ann.

Wyatt's wide mouth was open, his normally tense jaw slack, his eyelids fluttering as if he was dreaming.

She eased closer, her pulse racing as she moved to stand alongside him. For a long heartbeat, she studied his handsome face. Not perfect features. His nose had been broken at least once. His jaw was wide, with thick beard stubble. A cleft deepened his chin.

He was big and strong and . . . almost scary-looking in his masculinity.

She stepped toward him anyway. He was all those things, but he was also brave. Protective. Kind.

Her gut told her he was a man of his word.

Slowly, she reached one hand out and let it hover near his cheek. His breathing steadied, and he moaned softly, then licked his lips. That mouth was so sensuous.

She couldn't resist. She gently laid the palm of her hand against his cheek. His skin felt warm, rough with morning stubble. But a tenderness lay beneath that strong face.

Perspiration beaded on the back of her neck. Her body felt strange, hot and needy.

He opened his eyes and blinked, and then his gaze lifted to hers. His breathing rattled out as he watched her, but he didn't make a move to touch her.

Her heart stuttered at the intensity in those deep-brown eyes. Sensual eyes that made her want to kiss him.

♦ ♦ ♦

Wyatt forced himself to lie perfectly still. Any sudden movement would spook Tinsley.

His lungs strained for air, though.

He didn't know what had prompted Tinsley to touch him, but her sweet, tentative touch stirred emotions—and an arousal—he had no business feeling for her.

He needed to remain objective for both their sakes. She was scared and vulnerable. He could not take advantage of that.

Her chest rose and fell with her sharp intake of breath. Their gazes remained locked, a sea of emotion in her eyes. Her long blonde hair lay in a tangled mess over her shoulders. Her cheeks looked pink from sleep. Her rose-colored lips were parted slightly.

She was the most erotic woman he'd ever seen.

God . . . he hadn't been this attracted to anyone in ages. Maybe never.

But he'd felt a connection to her the moment they'd met. No, even before, when he'd studied her pictures.

Now he felt her need as if it were his own.

He couldn't help himself. He slowly lifted his hand to cover hers. She went still. Tense. Her eyes wide as if caught doing something naughty.

Then she jerked her hand away. "I . . . I'm sorry," she said brokenly.

She raked her fingers through her hair in an attempt to smooth the unruly strands. Her shy movement made her even sexier.

"You were snoring," she said softly.

Embarrassed, he pushed to a sitting position and rubbed his hand over his eyes. He probably looked like a big damn bear on her couch.

"I'm sorry," he said. "I didn't mean to disturb you. I know it took a long time for you to fall asleep." He stood, needing some cold water on his face. And to tamp down his burgeoning hard-on.

A blush stained her cheeks. "Nights are not always good for me."

He wanted to change that.

"I've had a few nightmares of my own." Ones of her and the night he'd found her. The night he'd almost lost his leg.

The night the Skull had escaped.

A loud knock at the door made him jerk his head to the side. Tinsley startled and hugged her arms around her waist.

"I'll see who it is." The intimate connection he'd felt with her a few moments earlier dissipated as fear haunted her eyes.

He strode to the door, then cursed.

"Who is it?" Tinsley asked.

He slanted her a worried look. "Marilyn Ellis."

Tinsley sighed wearily. "I should have known she'd come here."

She *was* a vulture. He looked at his rumpled shirt, then at her robe. "Put on some clothes. I'll get rid of her."

Tinsley's face heated as if she'd forgotten she wasn't wearing clothes. Then she fled into her bedroom and closed the door.

He eased the door open and stepped onto the porch. Last night's rain shimmered off the trees and sand, although more dark storm clouds were rolling in.

"Special Agent Camden?" Marilyn's tone reeked of surprise . . . and blatant suspicion. She stretched on her toes to see inside the house. "I came to talk to Ms. Jensen."

"She doesn't want to talk to you," he said bluntly.

She gave a pointed look to his rumpled shirt. "Then maybe you can. Has the man you call the Skull made contact with Ms. Jensen again? Is that the reason you're here? You believe that he kidnapped Joyce Ferris and that he's coming back for Ms. Jensen?"

He thought exactly that. But he motioned for the cameraman to turn the camera off. "I can't comment on an ongoing investigation. Besides, you already told the public that anyway."

She shrugged. "I wouldn't have to fill in the blanks if you'd give me the story."

He glared at her. "You want the truth?" His voice turned sharp. "Then tell the public that you're a person of interest. That you have connections to Cat Landon, and that you have a way of showing up at crime scenes as if you know the crime occurred before we announce it. That could mean that you're responsible."

She gaped at him angrily. "That's ridiculous."

"Do you have an alibi for the time Milt Milburn was murdered?"

Her breath heaved out. "I was with a source."

"Right. And you can't reveal that source because of your job." He huffed in disgust. He wasn't going to cross her off his suspect list, though. "Now leave Ms. Jensen alone, or I'll arrest you for harassment and obstruction of justice."

He stepped back inside, then slammed the door in the woman's face.

A quick shower woke Tinsley's sleep-ridden brain, although as she ran the loofa over her body, an awareness of the man in the next room surged to life. His handsome face. His strong muscles. His sensuous mouth.

Surprisingly, the fear that normally paralyzed her at the thought of a man's touch waned when Wyatt was near.

Don't be foolish. He's just working a case. How can you think of anything right now except what Joyce is going through?

Her friend's face jolted her back to reality. She hurriedly dressed in jeans and a pale-blue blouse, then dried her hair and braided it. She fastened her sea turtle necklace around her neck, a reminder of her sister. Of all she'd once had and lost.

Their mother had loved crafts and helped them make picture frames with shells they'd collected from the beach. She'd embroidered Christmas dresses for her and Carrie Ann, tied ribbons in their hair, and let her and Carrie Ann play dress-up in her costume jewelry.

Her father had built a playhouse outside for them. Had bought kites to fly on the beach. Had taught them both to swim.

They had been a happy family. Until her parents had died.

The next few months had been hell. Then one day Gram had bundled them up and carried them to the park, where the local PAWS group was hosting an adoption event.

The moment she and Carrie Ann had seen that golden retriever, they'd squealed and begged to have her. Gingersnap. She'd been sweet and playful and liked curling up in their bed at night.

The vet working the rescue event had been kind and encouraged them to bring Gingersnap to dog obedience class. They had, and Tinsley had fallen in love with all the animals at the clinic.

During summer break, she'd volunteered at the clinic. That summer, she decided she wanted to be a vet.

Although later on, money had been tight, and she'd given up that dream to help her sister. But still, she loved the work she did and wouldn't change it if she could.

God help her, she wanted to return to the life she loved.

Wyatt's footsteps echoed from the living room, and she went to face him.

"I don't know how that blasted woman gets her information, but she's at every crime scene. Somehow she knows that we're investigating the possibility that the Skull has been here."

Wyatt's cell phone buzzed, and he checked it, then returned a text.

"Is that about Joyce?" she said, hope stirring.

He shook his head. "Afraid not. Just a message about the boys fall ball team I coach."

Tinsley hesitated. Wyatt knew almost everything about her, but she knew nothing about him. Except that he'd nearly died saving her life.

"What team?"

A smile sparked in his eyes. "It's sponsored through the Boys' Club." He showed her a photograph of a group of boys in baseball uniforms, ages seven to nine, on his phone. Another man stood at one end, while Wyatt was at the other. He sported a big grin as he looked down at the kids.

"It's nice of you to help out," she said, her admiration for him mounting.

"The kids are great and need attention. It's a win-win for all of us."

Affection laced his tone as he pointed out the different boys' names and circumstances. Most were from troubled or single-parent homes and had no father figure.

The love in his eyes was powerful. "You want children yourself?" she asked.

"A whole team," he said with a chuckle.

Her insides quivered with longing. Once upon a time she'd dreamed about having a big family herself.

That dream had died when the Skull had brutalized her.

All the more reason she should stop fantasizing about getting closer to Wyatt. He was such a good man. He deserved to have that family.

A family she could never give him.

♦ ♦ ♦

Wyatt had no idea what just happened, but Tinsley seemed to shut down in front of his eyes.

Maybe she didn't like children.

Disappointment railed through him. Why, he didn't know. He'd pictured her as being a natural with kids.

Then again, he wasn't in the market for a family at the moment. His job was too damn dangerous.

Of all people, Tinsley needed to be with someone safe.

His phone buzzed with a text. Korine.

Would like to drop by to work on that profile with Tinsley.

Wyatt texted back, telling her to come on over.

Then he rushed to his SUV for the change of clothes he kept in a duffel bag.

"I'll make coffee and breakfast while you shower," Tinsley suggested.

The space suddenly felt small inside. The air was charged with tension.

"Is something wrong? I don't have to clean up here. I can go back to my place when Korine arrives."

She shook her head. "Don't be silly. I'm just worried about Joyce."

Of course she was. "Maybe the profile will help."

CHAPTER
THIRTY-THREE

Wyatt ran his portable electric razor over his face, then took a two-minute shower in Tinsley's bathroom and dressed in clean clothes.

The scent of coffee and cinnamon wafted toward him as he entered the den again.

Tinsley handed him a cup of coffee. "There're fresh cinnamon rolls if you'd like one."

His stomach growled. He couldn't remember when he'd last eaten. And those cinnamon rolls smelled heavenly. The doorbell rang, though, so he went to let Korine in.

Korine had met Tinsley during the investigation into the vigilante murders. "It's good to see you," Korine said, giving her a hug. "I'm sorry it's under these circumstances."

Tinsley smiled, although the smile looked forced. "You really are pregnant," she murmured.

Korine patted her big belly. "I certainly am and have the swollen ankles to prove it."

"Congratulations," Tinsley said. "I'm sure you and Hatcher are excited."

"We are." She squeezed Tinsley's hands. "How are you holding up?"

Tinsley lifted her chin. "I'm worried sick about my friend. I don't want to lose her to that monster."

Korine removed a small notepad from her purse and settled on the couch. Tinsley offered her coffee and a cinnamon roll, and Korine took the pastry but asked for water. "Then let's get started."

She waited until Tinsley joined her and settled into a chair. "I understand this is difficult," Korine said, "but I also know you want this man found."

"I do," Tinsley admitted.

"I've read the notes Wyatt took about your abduction, but I need you to tell me everything again. Maybe you'll recall something new this time."

Wyatt's phone buzzed. Hatcher. "I'll take this while you two talk."

He stepped outside. "Yeah?"

"I've been looking over the murder book on Felicia," Hatcher said. "The agent who took over her case failed to interview Norton's coworkers. Bernie sent info on one of them that we should question. She also dug up pictures from that orphanage."

"Anything happening with the Milburn case?"

"Korine's going to talk to Cat Landon this morning after she finishes with Tinsley. She thinks Cat may know if someone assumed her role as the Keeper."

Wyatt ended the call, then went to tell Tinsley and Korine.

When he entered the room, the silence was thick with tension. A candle flickered with soft pale light.

Tinsley opened her eyes and glanced over at him, but the glazed expression indicated she was still in the nightmare of her memory.

"You did good," Korine told her.

He arched a brow. "Are you ready to give the profile?" Wyatt asked.

Korine nodded. "We can always adjust later when new information comes to light, but with Dr. Ferris missing, we need to move quickly."

He agreed.

"This is what I have," she said in a matter-of-fact tone. "Judging from Tinsley's description, I'd say the Skull is a white male, probably late twenties to midthirties."

"Most serial killers start out around that age," Wyatt agreed.

Korine tapped her pen on the page. "The fact that he's waited so long between abductions and hasn't been caught indicates that he's patient, a planner, and organized. He has obsessive-compulsive tendencies exhibited in the fact that he shaves his body and his victims. Tinsley remembered the scent of strong soap, like in a doctor's office or hospital, so he may have a job in a medical or medically related field. There's also a component regarding animals that suggests that he works or has worked with animals, or that someone in his family did." She paused to take a breath.

"Norton worked with animal recovery," Wyatt said. "Hatcher and I are going to talk to one of his coworkers now."

She considered that. "The fact that he treated his victims like animals, caging them, indicates he not only wants control but also may have ambivalent feelings, or even resentment, toward animals. Most likely, he started by killing small animals when he was young. That whetted his appetite for the human kill."

Tinsley shivered. "Is that the reason he chose me? Because I rescue animals?"

"That's possible," Korine said. "Especially in light of the fact that he abducted Dr. Ferris." Korine crossed her legs. "There's something else to consider: his victimology. Serial killers often choose a certain type of victim—it could be related to race, ethnicity, age, hair color, or profession, such as a killer who targets prostitutes. It could be any of a number of characteristics. Identifying the profile of the victim may help us prevent another woman from becoming his next target."

"Dr. Ferris has blonde hair," Tinsley said. "It's darker than mine, but it is blonde."

Korine nodded. "Often the serial killer focuses on a certain type because the victims remind him of someone from his past who hurt him. It could be an abusive parent or an adult in his life—in this case, his mother or even a teacher or other relative."

"He cried afterward," Tinsley said. "And apologized to his mother."

"She was the source of his emotional upheaval, then," Korine said. "He's conflicted by her. He loved her, but he also has rage toward her."

"Why rape me if I remind him of her? Is he raping his mother?" Tinsley asked.

"Quite possibly. He may have had sexual fantasies about her and projects those fantasies onto his victims. Afterward, he cries and apologizes because deep down he knows it's wrong to lust for a parent."

Silence fell for a full minute, wrought with tension as they contemplated her statement.

Korine cleared her throat. "Remember, we're just creating theories here based on what we know so far. But this could help us find him, Tinsley."

She angled her head toward Wyatt. "Tinsley said there were skulls of three women in the room where she was held. Did you identify those victims?"

"The skulls were never recovered," Wyatt said. "With the number of missing persons cases and no other information to go on, we haven't narrowed down that list." He paused. "We're also still waiting on IDs of the skulls stolen from Seaside Cemetery."

"I'll get this profile out and share it with Bernie. Maybe someone on one of the lists you requested from the vet clinic or rescue center will fit."

He turned to Tinsley. "A uniformed officer is on his way to stand guard until I return. Hatcher has pictures of Norton when he was at the orphanage. He wants you to look at them and see if anything rings a bell."

"I told you I never saw his face," Tinsley said.

"Maybe not. But it's possible that you crossed paths with him at another time. Seeing these pictures might spark a memory."

She shrugged. "It's worth a shot."

"I'll stay here until the officer arrives," Korine said.

Adrenaline surged through Wyatt. *They might have a chance to catch this bastard.*

CHAPTER THIRTY-FOUR

Carrie Ann paced the motel room, coffee in hand as she flipped on the news.

She'd checked into the Beachside Inn on the island to be closer to Tinsley. Although Tinsley had no idea . . .

No one knew where she was. Or who she was. Not around here.

She liked it that way.

She'd hated the media attention after her sister had been kidnapped. Cameras in her face everywhere she went. Media parked on the lawn. Reporters nosing into her personal life and asking how she felt about her sister's abduction.

How the hell did they think she felt? Terrified at the thought of what might be happening to Tinsley, that's how. She'd been a nervous wreck. Hadn't slept for weeks. Had started pulling out her hair in a nervous tic. The doctors called it trichotillomania. It was an impulse-control disorder. One that fucking bitch reporter had described in her stupid story.

She'd wanted to kill the woman for it.

Then the story of Tinsley's months in captivity came out, and no one was interested in Carrie Ann's hair-pulling.

More press hounding her. Vultures demanding the gritty details.

That reporter was on the TV again. "This is Marilyn Ellis with updates on our previous story about the possible return of the serial predator the Skull. Police and FBI are investigating the possibility that he has kidnapped another victim.

"Dr. Joyce Ferris, the veterinarian who runs Best Friend's Animal Clinic in Savannah, has been reported missing. Sources have confirmed that a photograph of her was sent to Tinsley Jensen, the only known surviving victim of the Skull."

Carrie Ann froze as the picture appeared on screen.

"Dr. Ferris has received numerous awards for her humanitarian efforts with rescue animals and donates services both to PAT and PAWS," the reporter continued. "If you have any information regarding her disappearance or the man known as the Skull, please call your local police or the FBI."

"No, no, no!" Horror washed over Carrie Ann, and she paced the room again, yanking at her hair. It wasn't supposed to happen like this.

He wasn't supposed to take another woman!

She balled her hands into fists on her head, trying to stop herself from pulling out more strands of hair. *God* . . . He must have seen the story about the skulls on Tinsley's porch.

He'd realized an impostor had surfaced.

That had been the plan. The cat-and-mouse game. Play to his ego.

And it had worked.

Only . . . only he wasn't supposed to go after another innocent woman.

She thought he'd be so upset he'd make a mistake. Come after Tinsley while the police were guarding her.

Then they could catch him.

Guilt made her legs buckle, and she dropped to her knees, buried her head into the bed, and screamed into the pillow.

She had to do something. Fix this. Help save the woman.

But how could she do that without revealing everything she'd done?

Her plan had been a good one. It should have worked.

Heart pounding, she wiped at her tears. It still could work.

She just had to readjust.

She was not going to give up. If the vet died . . . God, she couldn't think about that. She had to find the Skull herself. Forget the police. They'd done nothing but screw up everything so far.

The Keepers wouldn't fuck it up, though. They knew how to get justice.

They wouldn't let him get away this time.

CHAPTER THIRTY-FIVE

Wyatt scrutinized Jim Oliver as the man shook a pack of Marlboros against his hand, pulled one out, and lit it up. According to the file Bernie sent, Oliver had no education beyond high school, no family. He'd worked with the local roadkill collection agency for ten years.

Hatcher introduced the two of them and asked the man how he'd gotten into the business.

Oliver shrugged, then jammed the cigarette pack back into the pocket of his dingy jacket. Stains, which looked like either blood or animal guts, darkened places on the coat, although the man didn't seem bothered by it. And he certainly didn't apologize.

"Hard to get a job when you've served time," Oliver said with a grin that revealed a missing front tooth.

"Now why're you here?" He flicked ashes onto the ground. "I been clean since I got out. Just ask my parole officer."

Hatcher spoke through gritted teeth. "Actually, we know that you worked with a man named Norton Smith."

Oliver's face paled to a milky white. "I didn't know what that crazy ass was up to."

Hatcher exhaled. "He didn't talk about his plans to kidnap a woman or his friendship with the man they call the Skull."

"Hell no." Oliver blew smoke into the air. "Listen, I had my problems. Got hooked on drugs and started dealing, but I cleaned up in prison." He patted the logo on his jacket. "This job ain't glamorous, but my old lady had a kid when I was in the pen, and I want to be around to see him grow up."

"So you're rehabilitated?" Wyatt asked.

Oliver's eyes narrowed to slits. "Yeah. Picking up dead animals ain't my idea of fun. But at least I make enough to pay the rent. And it's honest work."

"Did Norton ever talk about any of his friends? Maybe someone he was going to have a beer with or watch a ball game with?" Wyatt suggested.

Oliver shook his head. "Norton was an odd fuck. He enjoyed recovering the dead animals, maybe a little too much. Said he grew up dealing with animal crap so it didn't faze him."

Wyatt contemplated that comment.

"Did you ever go to his house or apartment?" Hatcher asked.

Oliver shook his head. "Like I said, he was a sick fuck and kept to himself. I got the impression he was into some weird shit."

"What do you mean—weird shit?" Wyatt asked.

Oliver cut his eyes between the two of them. Another man in overalls walked outside the animal-control center, gesturing toward a hand-held radio. "We got a call. Let's go."

Oliver started to walk away, but Wyatt grabbed his arm. "What kind of weird shit?"

Oliver shrugged. "Sometimes he'd sit and study the dead ones we picked up, even take pictures. Once I found him rocking a dead fox in his arms like a baby. Had blood all over him, but he didn't seem to care."

"What did he do with the pictures?"

"I didn't ask. But I saw him texting them to someone."

The hair on the back of Wyatt's neck prickled. What if he'd sent them to the Skull? Maybe the two of them had bonded over their sadistic urges.

◆ ◆ ◆

Tinsley felt helpless as Korine left. Dr. Ferris was out there, tied up, hurting, going through hell. And there wasn't a damn thing she could do about it.

Except try to remember more about the man who'd done the same thing to her.

She didn't know how Wyatt did his job. Moving from one ugly case to another. Putting one man behind bars, only to have to hunt down three others.

She skimmed her website and found more posts about the rapist. Then another that made a shiver run through her.

> Some of us stand tall through a storm. We may come out weathered and broken, but we survive.
>
> Others crumble like grains of sand blowing in the wind. Grains dragged out to sea to be swallowed in the ebb and flow of the tides. Like the lost souls in the marsh at Skull's Crossing, we hang in limbo.
>
> Not really alive. Not quite dead.
>
> The day my sister was rescued, hope lifted me from the darkness that had become my life during the long months she was missing. I thought we would hug and cry, but that we would mend.

But we are further away from each other now. We
both drifted into an endless sea of despair, drown-
ing in our own pain.

Finding the one who did this to her—to us—is what
I live for.

Destroying him is the only way to bring my sister
back.

Tinsley's heart pounded. That post . . . it sounded like something
her sister could have written. As if she could be talking about them . . .

Carrie Ann had tried to contact her lately. Had made efforts.

But Tinsley had pushed her away. Partly for her own safety. Partly
because she couldn't stand the pain and disappointment in her sister's
eyes.

She knew Carrie Ann wanted her to be happy again. To be . . .
normal. But she hadn't been able to give her that gift.

Could her sister be posting on her website as a way to reach out
to her?

She reached for her phone to call her, then halted and dropped it
on the table. Even if Carrie Ann wanted to reconcile, she was safer if
she was nowhere near Tinsley.

◆ ◆ ◆

Wyatt and Hatcher met at the field office to pick up the photos of the
orphanage and confer with their analyst about the profile.

Bernie ran her hands through her short, spiked black hair. "I've
been searching volunteers and workers who knew Tinsley at the rescue
center and comparing them to the group working on the upcoming
fund-raiser with Dr. Ferris."

Rita Herron

Wyatt crossed his arms. "And?"

"A couple of names popped up. The first, Seth Samson."

"He's Hispanic?"

"His grandmother was Hispanic." She pulled up the file on the computer, and he and Hatcher studied the man's profile. He was average height, short brown hair, a goatee.

"Tinsley said the Skull shaved himself all over. Even his head."

"He could be wearing a hairpiece and fake goatee."

True. "What else do you know about him?"

"He volunteered at the fund-raiser Tinsley organized and has been helping organize the upcoming one. He also works as a psychiatric nurse at the facility where Cat Landon is housed."

Wyatt's pulse clamored.

"Samson's grandmother raised him," Bernie continued. "She died a little over a year ago."

About the time the Skull abducted Tinsley. "Text me his address." Wyatt felt antsy to leave. This might be a real lead.

"The other name is Wade Hinke. He's a doc at a pain clinic. And he was denied adoption. Dr. Ferris made a note that something was off about him."

"He had access to meds," Wyatt said.

She nodded. "I just sent you the pain clinic's address."

"Thanks. See what else you can dig up on Norton Smith. Check rescue centers, vet clinics, pet stores, grooming businesses, any place that involves animal care. Find out if he knew Hinke or Samson."

Bernie wiggled her fingers and set them on the keyboard. "On it."

"Keep us posted." Wyatt took the envelope of photographs, and he and Hatcher headed to the door.

Outside, they picked up their pace to his SUV. Hatcher returned a call to Korine on the way.

When his partner hung up, a frown deepened the grooves around his eyes. "What's wrong?" Wyatt asked.

188

Hatcher rubbed a hand over his jaw. "Korine was at the doctor's office. Her blood pressure is too high, and she's showing signs of early preeclampsia. He advised bed rest until the baby is born."

Korine and this baby meant everything to him.

They had to be all right.

"Go home to her," Wyatt said. "I'll drop the pictures by Tinsley's."

Hatcher pulled a hand down his chin. "Thanks. I can't let Korine down."

Like he had his first wife. The words hung between them.

He thought Hatcher had let go of the guilt. But hell, that was easier said than done.

Where Tinsley was concerned, he had his own share.

Hatcher veered toward his own vehicle, and Wyatt climbed into his SUV. He'd drop the pictures at Tinsley's so she could look at them while he questioned Samson.

CHAPTER THIRTY-SIX

The Skull sipped his vodka tonic from a barstool at Nomad's, an eclectic restaurant near the place where he used to work. Some days he missed that job.

Although he'd found another place to work where no one asked too many questions. It wasn't in the best area of town, and they'd been robbed twice by druggies, but he was still helping people.

Someone at the bar asked the bartender to turn up the volume on the TV, and he cursed into his drink.

That damn bitch-assed reporter was on TV, yakking about the missing vet again. Bunch of bleeding hearts would be on the lookout for him now.

He pressed a hand to his face, making sure the facial hair was still in place. He had to be careful. Keep up the disguise.

The beast inside him was screaming again, though.

But not for the vet.

A sketch some idiot police artist had drawn flashed on the TV screen.

Thankfully it looked nothing like him. The eyes were too close together. The forehead too high.

How could Tinsley have described him anyway when she'd never seen his face? At least not that she remembered.

That had hurt. That she hadn't recognized him when he'd wanted her for years. When he'd compared every girl he'd met to her. She'd set the bar high, and no other female could measure up.

A short young woman in a low-cut top glanced from the TV to him, and he froze. Did she recognize him in that damned artist's drawing?

Then she offered him a smile, flirting like she had before. He didn't find her attractive, but he smiled at her anyway. Didn't want to attract suspicion.

But she wasn't his type. Hair too black. Makeup too thick. Skirt too short.

He'd heard her talking to her friend on the phone earlier. Naughty, filthy language. She was a cunt.

Not a good girl like Tinsley.

"Help us find this maniac and save Dr. Ferris," the reporter said. "She has won several awards for her efforts in rescuing animals injured and lost in Hurricane Irma . . ."

Her voice faded, the tribute to the doctor nauseating. He tossed cash on the bar to pay for his drink, then slipped out the back door.

Rage filled him as he drove back to the good vet. She wasn't what he wanted. She could never fill Tinsley's shoes.

That was the reason he hadn't taken anyone in months, not because he'd been arrested or was back on his meds or had moved to another city or state, as the FBI had suggested.

Taking Dr. Ferris had been impulsive, a reaction to the impostor who'd left those skulls on Tinsley's porch.

To the fucking cops who'd implied he was a coward.

His anger mounting, he swung his car into the drive and jumped out. His boots crunched gravel as he strode toward the door.

Five minutes later, stripped of his work clothes and the damn fake hair and in his skull mask, he entered the dark room where his captive awaited. She lay on the floor in the cage, limp, curled into a fetal position.

His heart pounded with dark desires.

Yet as he approached and she opened her eyes to look up at him, anger robbed him of feeling anything for her but disgust.

She was all wrong. She didn't stir his blood or his body. She wouldn't feed his hunger.

Because she wasn't Tinsley.

Memories of his father punishing him returned to haunt him. Suddenly he was thrust back to that chicken farm. His father thought working on the farm would teach him about life, about hard work, and would cure him of his sinful thoughts.

Instead, he'd gotten off on chasing the chickens and watching them run and squawk. He could still hear the bones cracking and the screech of the bird as he snapped its neck.

Smiling, adrenaline churning, he walked toward the cage. The doc's eyes widened in terror as he opened the door and stepped inside. She cowered, kicking and screaming, as he grabbed her by the throat.

CHAPTER
THIRTY-SEVEN

"Tinsley, it's Wyatt. Open up."

The sight of Wyatt's handsome face as she let him in was so comforting that she almost threw her arms around him. But she caught herself before she did.

Too much was riding on her helping Wyatt find Joyce Ferris for her to act foolish. He had been kind to her, but he was just doing his job.

Wyatt closed the door. "We interviewed one of Norton's coworkers. He claims he didn't know what Norton was up to or anything about the Skull. But we got the name of a psych nurse that I'm going to question when I leave here."

He laid an envelope on her desk. "Here are pictures our analyst pulled from the orphanage where Norton grew up. She also included some of his classmates and boys he worked alongside doing community service."

Nerves gathered in her stomach as she watched him remove the pictures. "Do you want coffee?"

"Actually, I can't stay. Hatcher had to check on Korine, so I'm on my own at the moment."

Rita Herron

Tinsley glanced at a picture of a group of boys. "Is everything okay with Korine and the baby?"

"Her doctor wants her on bed rest. Hatcher tried to play it cool, but I don't know what he'd do if he lost this baby or Korine."

She could understand that.

Every morning this summer, she'd watched families on the beach, and her heart had ached for one of her own.

Wyatt pointed to one of the kids. "This is Norton. Does he look familiar?"

Tinsley focused on the skinny preteen. He was tall and lanky with bony shoulders, a jagged scar on his left cheek and a burn scar on his arm. His eyes looked bleak, dead, as if he had nothing to live for. "I don't think so. I don't remember meeting any kids from an orphanage."

Wyatt removed a file from the envelope and gestured toward the contents. "Bernie also dug up copies of his school records, as well as the social worker's report on him. According to her, he was a loner. Didn't make friends. Kept to himself. He was abused by a foster father who claimed he tried to beat sense into the boy. The man insisted the beatings didn't even faze Norton. That he laughed when they were over. The mother was afraid of Norton, said something was off, so they turned him back over to the state. Same story about his behavior with two more families. He ended up in a group home until he aged out."

Sympathy for the child moved Tinsley, yet she couldn't feel sorry for the man who had killed Felicia.

"After vandalizing some property, the judge ordered Norton to do community service. He worked cleaning up the roads, then later cleaned cages at an animal rescue shelter."

Tinsley jerked her head toward Wyatt. "You think he and the Skull met at a rescue shelter?"

Wyatt shrugged. "It's possible."

"And that's how he met me," Tinsley said.

194

"Could be. Something about you drew him, and he became fixated on you." His dark eyes raked over her. "Our analyst pinpointed a possible suspect who fits the profile. A man who works at a pain clinic. He also applied to adopt a pet last year at your event, and he applied again this year. He was declined both times."

"Why?"

"Dr. Ferris made a note that something seemed off about him. He also refused a home visit, so he could be hiding something."

"You think he was angry because we denied his application?"

Wyatt shrugged. "Not sure that's enough of a motive. He could have bought a pet somewhere, gotten one online or at another rescue center."

"That's true."

"But I want to question him. Will you be all right looking at these while I'm gone?"

She lifted her chin and nodded. She'd do whatever it took to help find Joyce.

He reached out his hand, his fingers hovering just over her cheek. She ached to have him touch her again, something she thought she'd never want. But she craved his gentle fingers on her skin.

Their gazes locked for a moment. Heat and tension simmered between them.

But Joyce might be suffering this very moment, and it was her fault.

She took a step back. Dropped her gaze. Silently willed him to leave before she forgot what she needed to do.

Focus.

He told her he'd be back in a while, then left quietly. The sound of the door closing brought tears to her eyes. She wasn't whole, and she never would be.

And she couldn't pretend. Wyatt deserved better.

Pushing her feelings for Wyatt aside, she turned to the photos. Her finger shook as she arranged them on the table. Was the monster who ruined her life in one of these shots?

◆ ◆ ◆

Wyatt squashed the lingering need to stay with Tinsley as he parked at the pain clinic where Wade Hinke worked. On his application to adopt, he said he was a doctor at the clinic, but the name Hinke wasn't listed on the directory on the door of the building.

If he worked here, he had access to drugs that he could use to subdue victims.

That thought sent anger through him.

He was starting to care too much for Tinsley.

Hell, who was he kidding? He'd cared too much the moment he'd started hunting for her when she went missing a year ago. All those photos and stories about her made her too real. Too personal.

A few cars were scattered in the parking lot. A dark sedan pulled away. A gray-haired woman pushed an elderly man in a wheelchair toward a van.

Wyatt entered the building, went straight to the receptionist's desk, and identified himself. Her name was Penelope. "I'm looking for Wade Hinke."

The perky brunette tapped her finger on the appointment book. "Dr. Hinke?"

"Yes, I was told he worked here."

She raised a brow. "He used to, but he was let go."

"What happened?"

She leaned closer. "I'm really not supposed to talk about it."

Wyatt gave her a stern look. "I understand, but I'm investigating the possibility that he may be linked to a kidnapping. Anything you can tell me about the man might help."

Her eyes widened. She shifted her gaze to the side to make sure no one was watching or listening, then spoke in a hushed tone. "Well, some of the patients complained about him."

"What kind of complaints?"

"Penelope!" Footsteps sounded, then a man in a white lab coat appeared. "What are you doing?"

Panic streaked across the young woman's face. "Um, this is Agent Camden from the FBI. He wants to know about Dr. Hinke?"

The doctor narrowed his eyes. "We can't divulge information about patients or staff. That is, unless you have a subpoena."

Wyatt frowned. "Not yet, but I can get one."

The doctor glanced at Penelope. "Then we're finished until you do."

♦ ♦ ♦

One by one, Tinsley studied each photograph. Norton seemed familiar.

Then again, she'd seen his face on the news after Felicia's death.

Four other boys were lined up in the picture, a black-and-white shot that made the sad looks on the kids' faces even more depressing. The FBI analyst had included names and backgrounds on each of them.

To Norton's left stood a scrawny redhead named Curtis Dubinsky, and a chubby kid with braces named Pedro Ramirez. She checked the file for updated information and saw that he'd died of a drug overdose when he was seventeen. Curtis Dubinsky had moved to LA and owned a food truck that specialized in chili.

To Norton's right were two others—a grungy, angry-looking boy who stood a foot taller than Norton. Eke Torres. His eyes looked beady, and his face bore scars—she checked the file—from abuse. According to the file, Bernie hadn't been able to locate where he was now. It was as if he'd disappeared into thin air.

Could he be the Skull?

Nerves tightened her shoulder muscles as she studied the last kid. Ed Weakley. He was ten at the time. Choppy brown hair, a snarl on his face, a brace on one leg. The Skull hadn't worn a brace.

She glanced at Norton again, then at the date of the photograph. Norton was thirteen when the picture had been taken.

Her breath caught. She'd been twelve at the time.

Twelve—the worst time of her life, until she'd met the Skull.

Memories dragged her back to the night she'd lost her parents. It had been a warm spring evening. Flowers bloomed outside, birds sang, a happy time. Her parents had planned to take them on vacation to this very island the next day. Their bags had been packed. The bathing suits, beach towels, bicycles, and boogie boards all ready. She and Tinsley had been practicing their knot-tying for days in anticipation of a sailing trip.

Her grandmother was babysitting while her parents attended a fund-raiser for prostate cancer awareness that had been planned for months.

She and Carrie Ann had huddled in bed together. Too excited to sleep, they'd drawn sketches of sand art they planned to create—a whale, a sea turtle, maybe even a big castle with a moat around it. Their grandmother had kept popping her head in and reminding them that they needed to stop whispering, but the twinkle in her eye suggested that she understood. The love of the beach and ocean was in their blood.

Tinsley couldn't wait to hunt for the treasures that washed up on the beach with the tides. Carrie Ann had rattled on and on about which ice cream flavor she wanted to get at the Seahawk Island Sweet Shop. The homemade peach cobbler ice cream was Tinsley's favorite. In spite of the fact that sugar and chocolate made her sister hyper, Carrie Ann always wanted something with chocolate and sprinkles.

Finally, they'd exhausted themselves and drifted off to sleep. But a scream woke them sometime in the night. She and her sister bolted from bed and ran for their grandmother. She was leaning into a policeman at the door, sobbing.

Horror washed over Tinsley, and Carrie Ann started crying. Before Gram or the police could relay what happened, Tinsley had known their parents were dead.

Her world had shattered. So had Carrie Ann's.

They'd been so devastated that they'd retreated to their separate twin beds. No more laughter or giggles in the night. No more whispers about the future.

The silence had been ominous and filled with grief. Neither had wanted to go to school. She'd retreated into a shell, while Carrie Ann had started acting out. They'd both had nightmares and couldn't sleep.

Three months later, when Gram wanted to bake cookies with them and Carrie Ann threw the cookie cutters on the floor, Gram said she'd had enough. She was heartbroken, too, but they had to find a way to move on. Their mama and daddy would want it.

So she'd bundled them up and driven them to the park. Balloons had waved in the wind by tables decorated with treats for sale. The park had been filled with families and activities, a bouncy house for little kids, face painting, and a costumed pet parade. Another area had been roped off with animals offered for adoption.

The moment Tinsley had seen the beautiful golden retriever, her heart had melted. When the dog licked her sister's face, Carrie Ann had smiled for the first time in weeks. They'd begged Gram to take her home, and she'd easily agreed. On the way, they'd tossed out names but settled on Gingersnap because she was the color of the cookies their mother had always baked at Christmas. Gram stopped for a dog bed, dog food, chew toys, and bones.

Although Gingersnap never used that bed. She and Carrie Ann pushed their twin beds together—no more being separate. They made room for Gingersnap in between them. The big, lovable fur baby had warmed their beds and hearts with sloppy kisses, a tail that constantly wagged, and puppy-dog eyes that earned her whatever she wanted.

Gram said that they had saved the dog. But it was the other way around—Gingersnap had saved them.

But they'd eventually lost Gingersnap, too, just a year after they adopted her.

Another car accident. Gram rushed the dog to the vet, but Gingersnap didn't make it.

Tinsley steered her mind back to the task. The Skull had targeted her at the fund-raiser for the rescue center. And now he'd kidnapped Joyce, who was vital to this year's event.

She peered at the boys' faces again, then at Norton as an adult.

Another memory tickled her consciousness. A boy's face. Dark eyes. Watching her. A boy near the vet's booth. The vet had offered treatment, shots, spays, and neutering to any pet adopted that day.

Could that boy have been Norton? Or . . . if he and the Skull were friends, could they both have been at the park that day?

◆ ◆ ◆

Wyatt scanned the area around the dilapidated wooden house as he parked in the overgrown drive. Weeds and marsh grass choked the yard, and weather had damaged the wood. Rotting boards hung loose on the porch, the shutters had been ripped away in one of the storms, and a blue tarp covered the roof where it had obviously suffered damage.

The place was deserted. Wooden boards were nailed over the windows, and a condemned sign was tacked on the side of the house.

He texted Bernie to ask her to dig up anything she could find on Wade Hinke, especially another address where the man might live.

He opened the car door and stepped into the ankle-deep weeds, surveying the property for an outbuilding or someplace the man could hold Ferris hostage. The scent of damp earth and rotting vegetation drifted to him in the breeze that stirred the humid air.

He swatted at the gnats swarming around his face as he strode toward the house. Just because Hinke wasn't there at the moment didn't mean he hadn't left Joyce Ferris inside.

He worked his way to the front porch, stopped, and searched for a crawl space or basement but didn't see one. He cut to the left and scanned the exterior of the house and surrounding land for signs of the doctor or that someone had been there recently.

A few areas looked as if the marsh grass had been mashed down, but the recent rains had destroyed any footprints. A shadow fell across the house as clouds moved in, but a sliver of light shimmered off something red near the back door. He hurried toward it, heart hammering as he realized it was a woman's scarf.

With gloved hands, he examined it. It was dirty, wet, and dotted with blood.

He removed a baggie from his pocket and stored the scarf inside. The back windows and door were boarded up. But a closer look revealed loose nails on one corner of the door.

Someone had recently been inside.

Heart hammering, he yanked at the plywood until he uncovered the door. Senses alert, he jiggled the doorknob. The door squeaked open.

He inched inside. A rancid odor hit him, and he yanked a hand-kerchief over his mouth and nose.

Something—or somebody—had died inside.

CHAPTER THIRTY-EIGHT

Cat hated being confined. She missed her work at the bureau. She was too damn smart to stare at the walls and do nothing.

If someone wasn't crazy when they came into this place, they would be after twiddling their thumbs.

Nothing except think. And talk. And talk about what you were thinking about.

A bunch of lame-assed, mumbo-jumbo psychobabble.

She'd tried telling the psychologist, the psychiatrist, the counselors, and that medical doctor who wanted to pick apart her brain that she'd talked about her problems for years and it hadn't done a damn bit of good.

She had been molested as a child. There was no erasing that.

How the hell did they think a shrink could heal her when it was one of their own who'd stolen her innocence as a child? Korine Davenport's fucking father.

A child shrink who was supposed to help her get over the loss of her father. Or the fact that she'd never known him.

He hadn't loved her enough to stick around.

Liz Roberts said it wasn't her fault he'd abandoned her. That he was flawed, not her.

More bullshit.

She didn't trust anything the people in this nuthouse said. Or anyone else, for that matter.

Well, except for her new friends, the Keepers.

A soft knock sounded, and she shoved the unopened letters from her mother under the bed.

"Cat?" The door opened, and Marilyn Ellis poked her head into the room. "I need to talk to you."

Cat chewed her bottom lip. She'd been wary when the reporter had first approached her for her story. Her mother, Esme, had sworn Cat to silence over what had happened in her childhood. Esme had worried about what people would say, how they'd look at Cat. She'd been ashamed.

But hiding the truth was more shameful to Cat.

Marilyn had helped change that. She told the truth about what happened to Cat.

And she told the truth about the Keepers—if the cops did their jobs right, there would be no need for the Keepers.

Marilyn slipped inside. "It's about the Skull."

Cat waved Marilyn in and motioned for her to close the door so they could talk.

CHAPTER
THIRTY-NINE

Wyatt grabbed a flashlight, then jogged back to the house. Slowly, he inched his way inside, not surprised at the garbage and filth on the floor.

Judging from the bird droppings and animal feces in the corner, no one had lived in this house in quite some time.

Had Hinke used it as his home address at work to make it more difficult to find him?

It was off the grid, secluded, and could be accessed via a small boat by the creek out back, a creek that led to the Intracoastal Waterway.

The ancient refrigerator looked rusty, and an acrid odor hit him as he neared it. With one gloved hand he opened it and aimed the light into the interior. Some undistinguishable rotting meat was inside. Too large for birds. A deer maybe?

He closed the door, coughing at the stench, then scanned the living room. A threadbare sofa, stuffing from the cushions spilling out. A bird had made a nest of leaves, twigs, and the stuffing on the windowsill. Two dead pigeons lay in the corner.

He inched down a narrow hall. The first bedroom was empty except for a mattress on the floor, another roosting place for birds, or maybe a family of raccoons. The stench of death and blood hit him as he stepped to the last bedroom door.

A large dark stain discolored the scarred wood floor. Blood? He shined the light across the room, then noticed a closet on the far side. His heart beat a staccato rhythm as he crossed the room and gripped the doorknob.

If Hinke was their unsub and he'd brought the doctor here, she might be in that closet.

He held his breath as he opened the door. His gut clenched at the sight of three large dark garbage bags piled inside. Dead bugs littered the floor.

An image of the skulls Tinsley described flashed behind his eyes. Skulls that she said belonged to three women the Skull had killed.

They had no idea who those women were.

Their bodies had never been found.

He cursed, stepped back from the closet, then went outside for some air as he called the ERT.

Had he just found them?

♦ ♦ ♦

Tinsley's phone buzzed. She held her breath as she checked the number, hoping it was Wyatt saying he'd found Joyce alive.

Not Wyatt. Susan Lemming, one of the volunteers at the rescue shelter.

She answered on the second ring. "Susan?"

"Hey, Tinsley. Have you heard anything about Dr. Ferris? We're all worried over here at the shelter."

"I'm worried, too. Hopefully the FBI and police will find something soon." Although they'd been too late for Felicia. And months too late to save her from the agony of that man's brutality.

A slight hesitation. "Do you think we should cancel the upcoming adoption day?"

Maybe they should. Tinsley wanted to honor her friend.

But wouldn't continuing the event be the best way to do that?

"I think Dr. Ferris would want us to move forward with it. She was determined to find every lost animal a forever home."

Tinsley also wanted to prove to the Skull that he couldn't stop them from their work. That good people couldn't be destroyed by him.

Maybe the Skull would even show up. She made a mental note to ask Wyatt to post officers at the event.

"I agree, but it'll be difficult," Susan said. "Dr. Ferris always drew a crowd. She planned a demonstration on dog obedience tips before the pet parade."

The vet where she and Carrie Ann had taken Gingersnap had held dog obedience classes at her clinic years ago.

"I thought we might make missing person fliers to hand out with Dr. Ferris's picture on them," Susan said.

Outside, the sun was setting. The beachgoers had left for the day, yet Tinsley spotted a canoe in the distance, dipping with the waves.

"Tinsley?"

"That's a good idea." She desperately wanted to attend the event herself. If she was there, she could watch the crowd, look for someone suspicious.

For him.

She hadn't seen his face, but she thought she'd know him if he came near her. If she heard his voice . . .

She curled one hand into a fist, angry with herself for being such a coward.

Susan hung up, and Tinsley looked out the window. A jogger with a black lab ran down the beach and disappeared around the jetty. Seagulls swooped in search of food at the edge of the water. A helicopter from the coast guard station puttered above, then zoomed across the ocean toward Jekyll Island.

The canoe crept closer, bobbing and swaying with the waves. She peered through her binoculars for a clearer view. A lone figure was inside the canoe, rowing steadily, his face lost in the shadows as the sun dipped lower and streaked the sky with orange and pinks.

Nerves on edge, she stayed glued to the window until the colors began to fade and night set in.

The canoe drifted closer. The gray of evening swallowed the man in shadows so she couldn't distinguish his face. Suddenly the canoe made a slight turn and headed straight toward the beach directly in front of her cottage.

Just as he reached the shore, he looked up at her as if he could see her. There was something in the boat with him. A large, dark bag.

Fear pulsed through her as he shoved it over the edge of the canoe.

She gripped the binoculars, praying she was just being paranoid. But no . . . the man in the canoe was wearing a mask.

A skull mask.

It was him.

Dear God . . . Was Joyce's body in that bag?

She had to do something. Go out and stop him. Tell the officer. Call Wyatt . . .

But her legs buckled instead. She grabbed the window ledge to keep from sinking to the floor.

Outside, the bastard pressed his fingers to his mouth and blew her a kiss.

♦ ♦ ♦

Wyatt directed the ERT to search the property and the house. "There are three garbage bags in the closet in the second bedroom. I'm not sure if they're human or animal remains, but they've been there awhile."

Cummings frowned. "We'll get them to the lab."

Wyatt grimaced, glad he didn't have that job. "Process this scarf as well." He handed Cummings the bag. "There's blood on the floor inside and on this scarf. If we get DNA, maybe we'll be a step closer to catching this bastard."

That was assuming the Skull had been there. Or . . . Hinke. And that they were one and the same.

His phone buzzed. Bernie. "Yeah?"

"That house does not belong to Wade Hinke. He wasn't renting it either. Seems he got evicted from an apartment in Pooler nine months ago. No sign of where he's been living since."

"But he could have holed up here for a while."

"That's possible. The property belongs to a man named Fisher Eaton. Died thirteen months ago. His father was a lighthouse keeper on Seahawk Island."

"Any clue as to where Hinke might be?"

"Not yet. I'll keep looking. And I'll send his picture out to all law enforcement agencies."

"Good. Keep me posted." His phone was buzzing with an incoming call, so he thanked her and connected the call.

"Wyatt . . ."

He tensed, alert. "Tinsley? What's wrong?"

"H-he w-was here."

Shit. "Where? Is he still there?"

Her choppy breathing echoed over the line.

"Outside, the water," her voice broke. "A canoe . . . he dumped a big garbage bag on the beach. I . . . think it's a body."

Oh hell.

"I should have gone out after him—he's getting away!"

"Listen to me," he said firmly. "I'm going to hang up and call the officer on guard duty." From now on, they'd station a guard in a boat to watch the cove. "I want you to stay put, keep the door locked, and your phone with you. You understand?"

A low cry escaped her.

"Tinsley, do you understand? Do not open the door or go outside. I'll have the officer check the perimeter and the beach, and I'll be right there." He walked toward Cummings as he talked. "Did you hear me?"

"Y-yes . . . I'm sorry, Wyatt." Her voice cracked again. "I just froze . . . I panicked."

"It's not your job to go after him," Wyatt told her. "You did exactly what you should have. Now, I need to call the coast guard and see if they can fly over. Maybe they'll spot him."

She murmured okay, then hung up. He called the coast guard first, then the officer and explained the situation.

"Why didn't she come and get me?" the officer asked in a huff.

Wyatt gritted his teeth. "This man tormented her for months. She's traumatized and frightened, and she has a right to be." Besides, he didn't need to be coddling this damn officer. "Check around the cottage and get down to the beach. Tinsley thinks he may have dumped a body there."

Dread curled in his stomach as he raced to his vehicle. He had a bad feeling that Joyce Ferris was in that bag.

Leaving her body for Tinsley was just the kind of sick game the bastard liked to play.

◆ ◆ ◆

Tinsley thought her chest would explode with panic. She paced the room in front of the window, struggling for air as she silently prayed.

Dear God, please don't let that be Joyce's body on the shore.

The officer ran down the path to the beach. The canoe had rounded the jetty and disappeared from sight.

Emotions choked her. No . . . he couldn't get away. A rumbling sound startled her, and she looked up at the lights blinking in the dark sky.

The coast guard chopper.

A flashlight on the beach drew her eyes back to the officer. He'd reached the bag, was stooping over it, his flashlight bobbing up and down.

She clenched her hands together and prayed again, willing the bag to be empty or full of sand.

Not her friend.

Please not her friend.

Her phone buzzed, startling her, and she checked the number.

Her sister again.

Good grief, she didn't have time to deal with Carrie Ann right now. The Skull might be close by. He could have stowed the canoe around the jetty and snuck back on foot. He might be outside, hiding somewhere in the shadows of the trees or the neighboring houses, waiting on them to find what he'd left.

Maybe it was even a distraction to occupy the police so he could sneak up and attack her.

The windowpane rattled, startling her, and she jumped. She raced to the door to verify that it was locked, then hurried to her bedroom to check the lock on the window.

All secure, she released a pent-up breath and returned to the window. The chopper sailed above the ocean around the jetty, growing more distant. Maybe they'd spotted the canoe and were following him.

Hope surfaced, killed instantly when she looked down at the officer. He was shaking his head as he spoke on the phone. She aimed her binoculars on the bag but couldn't see what was inside.

Cold fear immobilized her, and she sank onto the window seat and stared helplessly into the night. Seconds ticked by. Then slow, painful minutes where she couldn't breathe.

Suddenly a soft knock sounded on the door. She swung her gaze toward it, then the beach. The officer still stood by the bag.

The knock again. "Tinsley, it's Wyatt."

Relief surged through her, and she raced to the door. Her hands were shaking as she fumbled with the locks. Finally, they gave way, and she jerked the door open.

Wyatt stood in the doorway, grim-faced, his stance rigid. A small shake of his head, and then he murmured, "I'm sorry."

Her world fell apart again.

How many more women had to die at the Skull's hands before they stopped him?

Rage shot through her, and she covered her face with her hands and silently screamed into them. She'd never been a violent person. She'd never thought she'd be capable of taking a life.

But if she had the chance, she'd kill the Skull and spit on his grave.

CHAPTER
FORTY

Wyatt didn't have to think about it—he pulled Tinsley up against him and stroked her back. A low cry escaped, one that sounded as if it had been wrenched from her gut.

He wanted to whisper promises and assure her things would be okay. But how the hell could he do that when clearly nothing was okay? He'd failed her when he hadn't found her before that monster tormented her. And a second time when Felicia had died. Now a third time.

"I'm so sorry," he murmured.

Sobs racked her body, and she clung to his chest. He held her tightly, letting her purge her emotions.

"You're sure it's her?" she asked brokenly.

He had spoken to the officer outside before he'd come to the door. The picture he'd texted Wyatt confirmed Tinsley's fears. "I'm afraid so," he said. "A team is on the way to take care of her body, and the coast guard is searching for that canoe."

She gulped back tears, her eyes filled with agony. "They're following him?"

"They lost him but are searching the area. He bailed on the canoe, left it afloat and disappeared. They're going to haul the canoe in for processing. Maybe he left a print or forensics inside it."

Tinsley wiped at the tears streaking her cheeks. "How could he get away so quickly?"

"He may have stashed another boat somewhere around the pier, or swam to shore and had a car waiting nearby."

Anger flashed across her face, mingling with pain. "I can't believe this," she cried. "He was so close." She pushed away and paced, her hands balled into fists. "It's my fault he escaped. I should have gone out there. If he'd seen me, he might have come for me."

Fear jolted Wyatt. He gripped Tinsley's arms and turned her to look at him. "The safest thing for you was to stay inside and call for help, just like you did."

"I was a coward," Tinsley said, a self-loathing note to her voice. "He took Joyce because of me."

"He took Joyce because he's a sick bastard," Wyatt said emphatically.

"But he wants *me*," Tinsley said. "He promised that I'd never leave him. Don't you see? He kidnapped her because guards are surrounding me." She pressed her hand over her heart. "That's why he brought her back here. To punish me for escaping him."

The odd gleam in her eyes raised the hair on the back of his neck. "That may be true," Wyatt said, "but he also took a risk by coming here. That means he's rattled and off his game." He rubbed her arms. "Did you get a look at him this time?"

"He was wearing that mask again and dark clothes. I couldn't see his face, but I swear he was smiling. He looked straight at me and blew me a kiss."

Creep. "He's growing bolder, either because he wants to get caught or he's out of control."

"Then let's play into that," Tinsley suggested. "Call off the guard. You can set a trap."

Wyatt's heart raced. He didn't like where her mind was going. They could try to set a trap for the Skull, but something could go terribly wrong.

He'd do anything to keep that maniac from getting his hands on Tinsley again.

Anything but use her as bait to catch him.

◆ ◆ ◆

A knock jarred Tinsley from her thoughts and sent Wyatt to the door.

He opened it, then turned to her. "This is the evidence response team. I'm going to talk to the officer on the beach and take a look at Dr. Ferris."

Tinsley winced but nodded that she understood. And she did. He had a job to do, and more than anything she wanted him to do it.

Concern darkened his gaze. "Will you be okay?"

"Of course." Chilled to the bone, she rubbed her hands up and down her arms, but nothing could erase the icy coldness that had invaded her when she'd seen that monster dump her friend's body on the beach.

Tension knotted her insides as she moved back to the window and watched Wyatt walk down to the beach. Mr. Jingles rattled his cage, perching on the edge, watching her as if he expected her to do something crazy any minute.

"You can leave the cage," she whispered. The parakeet simply stared at her as if saying she could leave, too.

A noise outside drew her back to the beach. A helicopter. The coast guard? Had they found him?

She watched Wyatt, saw him answer his phone. Then he shook his head at the officer.

Her hopes died. They hadn't found him. He'd escaped again.

Damn the Skull for ruining the peaceful sanctuary she'd created here.

Her phone rang, and she rushed to see who it was. Susan again? If so, she didn't think she could tell her about Joyce yet.

No. Her sister's name appeared on the caller ID screen. Why did Carrie Ann keep calling?

Irritation mingled with worry. But she didn't have time to deal with her sister's problems at the moment.

The phone rolled to voice mail, but a second later, it rang again. Carrie Ann.

Tinsley snatched the phone and connected the call. "I told you to leave me alone."

"We have to talk, sis. I'm coming over."

Tinsley's gaze remained glued to Wyatt as he stooped down and opened that bag.

Tears clogged her throat. Sweet Jesus, what had the Skull done to Joyce?

"I'll be there in ten minutes," Carrie Ann said.

God . . . Carrie Ann was near Seahawk Island? "No," Tinsley shouted. "Don't you understand? I don't want you here, Carrie Ann. For God's sake, the man who abducted me kidnapped my friend and killed her."

A tense second passed. "What?"

"You heard me," Tinsley cried. "He killed Dr. Ferris and left her body on the beach in front of my cottage. Now get out of town and leave me alone."

She ended the call, a sob escaping her. She hated to hurt her sister. But she didn't intend to lose Carrie Ann to that monster.

Wyatt cursed the Skull for what he'd done to Dr. Ferris. She hadn't deserved to die.

The fact that he'd been close to Tinsley was worse. In the city or near the restaurants in Savannah or the Village on Seahawk Island, security cameras might have captured images they could use to identify him.

Out here on the beach and in most of the older neighborhoods, security cameras were nonexistent. Of course the Skull knew that and used it to his advantage. He made a mental note to ask the owner about installing cameras on the cottage.

The ERT fanned out to search the beach, the access walkways from the street, and the public areas. He'd already phoned local authorities and asked them to search the park and the Village for anyone suspicious.

The medical examiner adjusted his glasses as he knelt by the body. "You're sure it's Dr. Ferris?"

Wyatt nodded. "Afraid so. We haven't pulled her from the bag yet, but it's her."

The ME rubbed his chin. "If you have your pictures, let's get her to the morgue, and I'll examine her there. No need in opening her up here."

True. The doctor deserved privacy and respect. On a public beach, a family or any number of people could come by. Besides, Tinsley was watching from her cottage. He didn't know the extent of the doctor's injuries, but he didn't want Tinsley to see her friend like this.

"Good call," Wyatt said. "I don't want the scene contaminated." Although this was definitely not the kill site. Finding that would be helpful.

He and the officer stood guard while the medical examiner directed a recovery team to the body. They loaded her on a stretcher and carried her up the beach and the walkway to the ME's vehicle.

His mind turned to the bags he'd found in that house on the marsh.

He needed to know what was inside them. If they were human, victims of the Skull, maybe he'd left some DNA and they could use it to nail him.

♦ ♦ ♦

Tinsley's heart squeezed as she watched the team carry Joyce's body up the beach. What had that monster done to her?

He'd held her for less than twenty-four hours. Why such a short time?

He'd kept Tinsley and the other three women longer. She'd seen and felt the carvings in the wall they'd made. Carvings marking the days they'd had to endure his filthy, vile presence.

Each day had meant a new brand of torture. Mental. Physical.

At least Joyce had been spared those excruciating days filled with pain and terror.

But why kill her instead of dragging out the agony as he'd done with her and the others?

Wyatt was following the medical examiner and the team with the body up the beach. Would he go with them to find out exactly what had happened to Joyce?

Her doorbell dinged. Thinking it had to be Wyatt, she raced to open it.

Marilyn Ellis stood on the other side, her cameraman behind her.

Tinsley started to slam the door in the woman's face, but the reporter caught the door with her foot. "You can't run forever, Tinsley. I know that your friend is in that bag going to the morgue. He killed her, didn't he?"

"How . . . did you find out that?" Tinsley whispered.

"I have my sources." An odd smile tinged her eyes. Sympathy? Victory? The thrill of the hunt for another gruesome story?

"Don't you think it's time you stood up to the man who assaulted you and killed your friends?"

Tinsley gasped in shock at the woman's blatant personal attack. "You don't know anything about me," Tinsley said. "Not what I've been through, and certainly not how I feel."

"I know you were traumatized and brutalized by a monster," Marilyn continued. "For that, I truly am sorry. No woman should have to endure that kind of suffering."

"No, they shouldn't," Tinsley agreed in a raw whisper.

"The police are doing what they can, but you must want to stop him before he hurts anyone else."

Tinsley wrung her hands together. More than anything she wanted to stop him.

"Talk to me." Marilyn made a motion, asking if she and her cameraman could come in. "Talk to *him*."

Hadn't she considered doing that? Setting a trap for him . . .

"You need to leave." Wyatt's loud voice boomed from behind the reporter. "If you don't, I'll haul you to the station myself."

Marilyn whirled on him, her TV smile in place. "You can't arrest me for talking to someone."

"I can arrest you for harassment and for interfering with an ongoing investigation."

"How am I interfering?" Marilyn asked sweetly. "I want the truth, just like you do, Agent Camden." She gestured toward Tinsley. "Just as Ms. Jensen does."

Wyatt shoved the camera down, ordered the cameraman off the porch, and stepped inside the doorway to make it clear to the reporter that she wasn't getting in, or getting to Tinsley.

"If you want me to go away, then tell the public exactly what's going on." She lifted her chin defiantly. "Explain how and why a notorious criminal like the Skull kidnapped and killed Dr. Joyce Ferris and evaded the police. How he later dropped off her body in front of Ms. Jensen's house, right under your noses."

Wyatt's nostrils flared with anger. Tinsley had never seen him so furious.

"As a matter of fact, I have been working several leads on the case," Wyatt said sharply. "Which brings me to the question of how you learned about the murder so quickly."

"You know I can't reveal my source," Marilyn said.

"You hide behind that bullshit," Wyatt said. "But your quick presence makes me wonder if you aren't more involved in these crimes than simply reporting them after the fact."

Marilyn's eyes narrowed to slits. "Just what are you implying, Agent Camden?"

Wyatt leaned closer with an intimidating stare.

"We always suspected that Cat Landon was working with someone else, that she wasn't the only one in this Keeper group who decided to take justice into her own hands."

Marilyn hissed between her teeth. "How dare you imply—"

"I'm not implying anything," Wyatt said sharply. "I'm asking you point-blank, Ms. Ellis. Have you assumed Ms. Landon's role as the Keeper?"

CHAPTER FORTY-ONE

Carrie Ann threw her phone onto the bed, panicked and terrified.

The doctor wasn't supposed to die! She was never supposed to have been taken.

She'd started the game of cat and mouse with the Skull to lure him out of hiding so the police could find him. So her sister would finally be free and join the real world again.

So they could walk up and down the beach and collect seashells like they'd done as children. So they could be best friends again.

She doubled over with pain as the loneliness washed over her. She needed Tinsley.

Why did Tinsley hate her so much?

They'd bickered as kids and then had made up and eaten ice cream and laughed about it. They'd pinkie-sworn that they'd always be best friends.

And when their parents died, they'd been each other's lifelines.

She rubbed her finger over her sea turtle necklace.

Then last year that crazy, awful man had stolen her sister from her, and she'd never come back.

She'd thought eventually Tinsley would come around, that she'd forgive her for not saying the right things at the hospital, for not being what Tinsley needed her to be.

But months had dragged by, and now almost a year. And Tinsley had just screamed at her to leave her alone.

Tears streamed down her cheeks, the helplessness overwhelming. She yanked at her hair, rocking herself back and forth. No . . . she wasn't going to give up.

She was going to make things right, even if it killed her.

The image of that vet's face haunted her. How could she make things right when a woman was dead because of what she'd done?

Lungs squeezing for air, she studied the picture of her and Gingersnap and Tinsley. They'd had so much fun together. The Three Musketeers, she'd dubbed them.

Tinsley had idolized the vet who'd given Gingersnap obedience lessons. She'd volunteered at the clinic. They both had. Being around the animals had been the bright spot in that first summer without their parents.

Yet a dark memory from the clinic intruded. The vet's son had been odd. She'd seen him snap at a terrier when his mother wasn't looking.

He'd also filled the dogs' food bowls with rocks. When he saw her watching, he'd said he was playing a prank on his mother, not to be a tattletale. She'd been scared of him.

She hadn't told the vet, but she'd told Tinsley. After that, they made it a point to show up at the end of the day to make sure the dogs had food.

Another time, she'd seen him hit a poodle. And he'd liked to pull the cats' legs and hear them squeal.

She'd been relieved when the doctor said he'd gone away.

She spun around and snagged her phone. She didn't have time to think about the past now. None of that mattered.

All that mattered was finding the Skull and . . . killing him.

She just hoped that Tinsley would never find out.

CHAPTER
FORTY-TWO

Wyatt studied Marilyn Ellis as he waited on a response. A myriad of emotions played across her face, making it hard to get a read.

"Are you and Cat working together to keep the Keepers active?"

"My conversations with Cat Landon are private," Marilyn said tightly.

"You mean the part of the conversations that you want to keep private," Wyatt said with a challenging glint in his eyes.

"If you think you can coerce me to give you dirt on Cat, you're wasting your time."

Wyatt crossed his arms. "So you killed Milt Milburn because you thought he deserved it."

Marilyn gave a wry laugh. "Nice try. But there's no way you can pin that crime on me."

"Because you're conspiring with someone else and covering for each other?"

Marilyn exhaled sharply. "You're fishing. Why don't you look for the real bad guy here? The man who dumped that poor woman's body on the beach a little while ago?"

He silently cursed. She was right. He was wasting time with her. Still, he couldn't resist one more question. "How many Keepers are there? One, two, a dozen?" Or was the group even more widespread than that? With the Internet, they could be building a damn empire on the dark web.

Marilyn simply smiled at him, a smile that was full of secrets and a sense of victory, as if she knew he had no concrete evidence against her. "Like I said, instead of giving me a hard time, why aren't you looking for the Skull?" She gestured toward Tinsley, who stood quietly behind him, looking shaken and distraught. "You don't care if the River Street Rapist is dead, do you, Ms. Jensen? All you want is for the Skull to be locked up—or dead—so the women of Savannah are safe."

Tinsley didn't respond. She walked back to the window and looked out into the night.

Wyatt knew the answer to Marilyn's question, and so did she.

His phone buzzed. "As a matter of fact, you're keeping me from doing just that."

She squared her shoulders defiantly. "No matter what you think of me, all I want is justice. The public deserves to know the truth."

His dark gaze met hers. "Just how far would you go to get it?"

Her wry smile returned. He didn't wait for a response. He gripped the door to shut it.

Marilyn stood on tiptoes to look past him at Tinsley. "Call me when you want to talk, Ms. Jensen."

Marilyn's shout echoed through the door as he slammed it in her face.

He cursed the woman for getting to him as he answered the call.

"It's Bernie. I've been digging into Samson."

"What did you find?"

"His grandmother, the one who raised him, died two years ago."

The timing fit when they believed the Skull had abducted his first victim.

Wyatt stiffened. "He also has access to drugs at the psych hospital where Cat is."

"Exactly. I checked, and he didn't show up for his shift tonight. He called in sick. I'm texting you his address."

He started to hang up, but Bernie stopped him. "There's something else. Forensics turned up a strand of hair at Tinsley's. Haven't had time to run the DNA, but it's female."

His heart stuttered. "It could belong to Tinsley."

"This one is shorter, a darker blonde." Liz Roberts had been at Tinsley's, but her hair was light blonde and waist length. "I can't see some woman helping the Skull."

"Could be some woman fell for him before she knew who he was. There have been cases where a submissive female helped her boyfriend or husband capture his prey."

True. Other times, the female was the dominant one, and the man was following her commands.

"There's another possibility," Bernie said. "The person who drugged Tinsley's tea and put those *papel picados* on her porch was not the Skull."

A copycat. He'd considered that in the beginning. Now they had information to support that theory.

So who was this impostor?

The conversation with Marilyn Ellis echoed in his head. She was ambitious, would do anything to get her story. Anything to get justice.

And she had blondish hair.

Surely she wasn't that devious. Was she?

◆ ◆ ◆

Tinsley listened quietly as Wyatt relayed the news the FBI analyst had given him.

"I don't understand," she said. "You believe someone is working with him now?"

"It's a theory—a copycat drugged your tea to make it appear as if the Skull was back in order to draw him out."

"But who would do such a thing?" Tinsley asked.

Wyatt hesitated to make accusations, but he couldn't shake the idea that the reporter was involved. Or hiding something. "The only person I can think of is Marilyn Ellis."

Tinsley gaped at him in shock. "I know she wants a story, but I can't believe she'd go that far."

"I can," Wyatt said. "She's made her name by exposing the underbelly and tackling controversial topics. She slanted the story about the Keepers to paint them as heroes. With the interest in the Keeper story being replaced by more urgent pieces, she needed a new story to get back into the spotlight."

Marilyn Ellis did like attention. That was obvious.

"If she stirred up the news that the Skull was back with an impostor," Wyatt continued, "she not only caught the public's eye but also caught the eye of the real Skull."

Horror engulfed Tinsley. "You mean she intentionally angered him so he'd come out of hiding?"

"Exactly."

"That's the reason he kidnapped Joyce."

Wyatt nodded. "The timing supports that theory. Now I just have to prove it."

Anger emboldened Tinsley. Her friend had died because Marilyn Ellis wanted to be the center of attention on the nightly news? "Do you think Marilyn has had contact with him?"

"I don't know, but I'm requesting warrants for her DNA and her home and office computer and phone."

Tinsley couldn't wrap her head around the idea that Marilyn—or any woman—would be so heartless as to intentionally draw the Skull back to her door. Marilyn had to have known how traumatic that was for her.

She obviously didn't care, though. Media attention meant more to her than Tinsley's sense of safety.

"If she drugged me, then she dug up those skulls and left them on the porch, too," Tinsley said.

"Seems probable. She wanted you drugged so you wouldn't recognize her if you saw her outside."

Anger railed inside Tinsley. "If she did this, I want her charged."

Wyatt agreed. "I still haven't talked to that psych nurse who works with Cat. He fits the profile." He gestured toward the door. "I'm leaving an officer to stand guard here while I go to his house."

Tinsley assured him she'd be fine, but she wasn't fine. Not only was her friend dead, but the reporter's selfish need for attention might have been what cost Joyce her life.

◆ ◆ ◆

Wyatt phoned Hatcher to fill him in as he drove toward Samson's.

"The contractions have stopped, but the doctor insists Korine stay on bed rest. I may have to tie her down to keep her at home, though."

Wyatt laughed. "Isn't that how you got into this situation, man?"

"Very funny," Hatcher said, although his partner didn't mind the ribbing.

"All joking aside," Wyatt said, "do whatever necessary to take care of them."

"Thanks, buddy. Now what's up with the case?"

Wyatt explained his findings at Hinke's. "The lab has those bags and are analyzing the contents. I also got word that Tinsley's tea was drugged and that the person who did it might be a woman. If Marilyn Ellis intentionally lured the Skull out of hiding, she hurt Tinsley and caused Dr. Ferris's death. We could charge her with involuntary manslaughter."

Hatcher made a low sound in his throat. "If she really wants justice as she claims, she'll turn herself in."

"Somehow I don't think she's that altruistic."

"I'll request warrants while you check out Samson," Hatcher offered. "Just be careful, man. If you need backup, call it in."

Wyatt agreed and hung up; mentally he reviewed what he knew about Samson as he approached the man's neighborhood.

The house was a small wooden cabin that looked rustic against the backdrop of the marsh. A little Baptist church sat on a hill to the right, the old-fashioned cemetery filled with stone markers and overrun with weeds.

Deserted and abandoned, this house or the church and graveyard would be a perfect place to hide or bury a body.

Except if Samson was the Skull, why not leave Joyce's body here instead of risking capture by dumping her in front of Tinsley's cottage?

It wasn't about the kill, he realized. It was about letting Tinsley and the police know that he was back, not the impostor. He was narcissistic and wanted credit for his activities.

Wyatt parked and walked up the dirt drive, senses alert in case Samson was watching. The house appeared dark, with only a dim light burning from one of the back rooms.

A beat-up black hearse sat near the house, parked at an odd angle.

Samson could have easily put Joyce's body in a garbage bag, loaded her in the hearse, and driven her to where he'd stashed a boat. Or hell, he could have stolen the canoe.

He aimed his mini flashlight across the exterior and then the interior of the car, searching for blood or anything suspicious. A stain on the passenger seat. Dark. Could be blood.

No one in the front.

With gloved hands, he opened the latch on the back, then the door.

He shined the light across the interior and found a stretcher. Stains darkened it, and a blanket lay piled on the floor, also stained with something that could be blood.

Enough to get him a warrant.

Now, for the house.

Hoping it was unlocked, he crept toward the front door. Mud from the last hurricane still caked the bottom of the steps and sides of the house. A dead tree lay on its side, branches and limbs that had been ripped from the trees a chaotic mess in the backyard.

One of the wooden steps was missing, so he climbed over it, swatting at mosquitos and gnats swarming near the screened door. The door was unlocked, so he gave a knock, then announced himself.

"Samson, FBI. I'm coming in!"

No response, so he pushed the door the rest of the way open, then paused to listen.

No voices. But a low wailing sound echoed from the back room. A crying sound like an injured animal—or person.

The moment he stepped inside the living room, he spotted it: an altar for the Day of the Dead ceremony. But he didn't have time to examine it now. The wailing sounded again, and he crept down the hall, his gun at the ready. The light came from a naked bulb shining in a bedroom to the left. No one inside.

The wailing came from the opposite room. A dark room that reeked of a foul odor.

He aimed the flashlight across the bedroom space, searching. Nothing. The wailing continued, driving him to the closet door.

He slowly pulled it open, his anger mounting at the sight of a metal cage jammed in the back, covered by old blankets.

It was too dark to see what was making the sound.

He yanked away the dirty blankets, dread coiling inside him.

CHAPTER
FORTY-THREE

Marilyn stormed into the newsroom and did her segment, furious with Camden.

He thought she wanted the story—Tinsley's; Korine's; Cat's; the Skull's—because she was a media piranha.

He had no idea. She wanted it because she connected with the victims.

But he would never know how deep her connection was. Exposing the truth would expose her own family secrets.

Secrets she wasn't ready to share.

But she had a plan.

Her coworkers doused her with compliments as she finished. A male anchor who'd expressed interest in her invited her to go for a drink, but she declined.

She had too much on her mind to sip martinis and make chitchat about his career goals. Typical male who only wanted to talk about himself and what she could do to help him.

Men with that kind of drive were admired, when an aggressive woman with ambition was deemed a bitch.

She'd heard the whispers behind her back.

Not that she cared.

She rushed outside and barreled toward the house in the boonies. No one knew about her visits here either.

No one ever would.

She parked at the house, then checked the Keeper page. Several people had commented on the River Street Rapist, then others on the disappearance of Dr. Joyce Ferris.

Please help us. The law does nothing. We want our children and daughters to be safe.

So did she.

Justice had to be served, no matter the cost.

Satisfied she was doing the right thing, she forced herself to go into the house. It was dark, musty, and smelled old. The windows rattled as the wind shook them, dust motes floating in the air.

A noise rumbled from the back room. The smell of sickness and evil wafted toward her in a mind-numbing wave of disgust and bitterness.

The pathetic lump of a man who lay in the bed wheezing for a breath turned his head slightly and looked over at her. Recognition and a sliver of hope lit his eyes.

Dumb fuck kept expecting her to grow a heart and leave him alone.

His eyes darted toward the prescription bottle on his nightstand. His frail hand trembled uncontrollably as he stretched it toward the pills.

She knew what he wanted. For her to ease his suffering.

Rage seethed inside her. She picked up the medication and claimed the chair by the bed.

His helpless moan punctuated the air.

No one knew the things she did about him.

Or his dirty little secrets.

But they would.

His pitiful wail came again. A pleading in his eyes that she'd never seen before.

Hate swelled within her. How dare he try to make her feel guilty, like she should take care of him.

She moved the pain pills on the table, just out of his reach.

A twisted look flashed in his eyes. If he had the strength, he'd jump out of that bed and strangle her.

But he didn't have the strength, and he knew it. He also knew he was at her mercy.

She removed the recorder from her purse and set it on the table by the pills. Anger radiated in his growl.

He earned a pain pill when he told his story. And it had to be the truth, not the lies or bullshit he'd told others.

CHAPTER FORTY-FOUR

Wyatt tossed one dingy blanket after another onto the floor. Four in all. Had Samson thought they would muffle the sound of someone crying inside that cage?

Furious, he threw the last one aside, then stooped and shined his light into the cage. Relief filled him when he realized it wasn't a woman.

But on the heels of relief, anger set in. A dog lay inside, his bones pushing at his sagging skin, a mangled chew toy on the cage floor.

"Hey, buddy," he murmured. "It's going to be all right."

Had Samson adopted this dog from the rescue center? If so, why treat him like this?

He slowly reached out his fingers and let the dog sniff them as he talked in a low, calming voice. "Are you ready to get out of this place?"

The dog tilted his head, his eyes sad.

"I know you got a raw deal here, but your life is about to change." He released the latch on the cage, then held out his hand again. "That's it, boy, I'm your friend." Slowly the dog nuzzled his hand, and Wyatt stroked his back.

It took several minutes to coax the poor guy from the closet, but finally they made it to the living room. That altar for the Day of the Dead ceremony reminded him why he was here.

He phoned for a team to search the house and the graveyard in case Samson had buried victims on that hill or in the marsh.

His phone buzzed as he hung up. Hatcher. He quickly filled him in.

"The judge gave us a warrant for Marilyn Ellis's DNA but denied ones for her phone and computer. If her DNA matches the DNA on the tea bottle, he'll reconsider."

Wyatt didn't like it, but it was a start.

"I talked to the ME and that forensic specialist," Hatcher said. "She said the skulls left on Tinsley's porch match the bones from that graveyard. She's trying to get an ID for us now."

Wyatt considered that information.

If Marilyn had dug up those bones, separated the heads from the skeletons, then left them on Tinsley's porch, she might be mentally disturbed herself.

"How about the bags of remains at Hinke's?"

"Dr. Patton is analyzing the contents. Severe decomp is complicating the analysis."

Those remains might be the break they needed. They could belong to the Skull's first three victims. "I'm going to request BOLOs for Samson and Hinke." He glanced at the dog, who was looking at him with pleading eyes.

Both men had questions to answer.

♦ ♦ ♦

Tinsley blinked again, and the face of the man on her porch slipped into focus. The officer. *Thank God.*

She was just being paranoid. The Skull wasn't there after all.

Although he had been. Right in front of her.

The information she remembered about her captivity had helped create a profile. If she remembered more details, it might help.

Body wound tight with tension, she returned to the pictures on the table and studied them again. Something was bothering her.

Something about Norton and his job.

But what was it, dammit?

The answer teetered on the edge of her consciousness but evaded her.

She rifled through the information the FBI analyst had collected on the four boys. None of them seemed familiar . . .

Or did they? Had she met Norton or one of the others when she was younger?

If so, where?

She'd never been to that orphanage. Maybe at an animal rescue event? But there were dozens and dozens of people who attended. How could she possibly remember them all?

Her phone dinged, and she checked it quickly. Maybe Wyatt had news.

Her sister's name appeared, then a series of texts.

I'm so sorry for everything, sis. I wish I'd been stronger when the police found you. You needed me to be there for you, and I failed you.

I don't blame you for hating me and not wanting me in your life.

You'll hate me even more when you find out the truth.

Even so, I'm going to try and fix this.

I still wear my sea turtle necklace and think about those lazy days when we combed the beaches with Dad and Mom.

I remember hugging Gingersnap between us and whispering secrets in the dark.

I have secrets now. Secrets that will hurt you, I'm afraid.

But everything I did, I did for you. I want you to be happy and free again.

Love always, Carrie Ann

Tinsley swallowed hard against the lump in her throat. Carrie Ann didn't understand at all. She didn't hate her. She wanted to protect her.

What secrets was her sister talking about?

Her heart ached. It had been so long since she'd seen Carrie Ann. Since those days when they'd been best friends. Thanksgiving and Christmas had passed last year with the two of them separated. The anniversary of their parents' death as well as Gram's had come and gone, two days they'd promised to always spend together.

Carrie Ann wanted to reconnect. So did she.

Her finger hovered over the reply box.

Worried Carrie Ann would do something erratic, she sent her a text.

I don't know what secrets you're talking about, but we'll talk. I can't now, though, am trying to help the police find the Skull. None of us are safe until he's caught.

Hopefully that would satisfy her sister for a while. Once this was over, she'd find out what was going on with Carrie Ann.

But now was the wrong time. Joyce had been killed because of her connection to Tinsley.

She wouldn't allow her sister to fall prey to that same monster.

A knock sounded at the door, and she hurried toward it.

"It's Wyatt," a gruff male voice called.

Relieved, she unlocked the door. Her breath caught at the sight of how handsome he looked. A dog stood beside him, so thin he was almost skeletal. His coat was a sandy brown, eyes big and soulful, his body trembling as if he was scared to death.

She heaved a breath. God, he reminded her so much of Gingersnap that she instantly dropped to her knees and held out her hand.

The dog inched toward her, a whimper coming from him that tore her heart in two.

♦ ♦ ♦

Wyatt's throat thickened as he watched Tinsley hug the dog to her. He'd taken the poor fella by the emergency vet clinic to be examined. Other than being half-starved, he was actually healthy.

He nuzzled up to Tinsley as if he'd known her all his life. Or maybe he just sensed a kindred soul who'd take far better care of him than the man who'd locked him in that cage.

Tinsley looked up at him with questioning eyes. "What's his story?"

Wyatt stepped inside and closed the door, then explained about finding him at Samson's. She rubbed the dog's back and coaxed him over to the sofa. Wyatt followed, and the dog crawled up on the couch, dropped his head in Tinsley's lap, and whined like a baby.

She whispered comforting words to the mutt, stroking his head until he settled down. "I don't know what happened to you, but you're safe now, buddy."

The tenderness in her voice made him warm inside. He'd never seen her smile before. She was beautiful.

"I can't believe this man volunteered at the rescue center and adopted a dog, then treated him like this." She laid her head against the animal's. "And he's a psychiatric nurse?"

"I know. Bizarre." Wyatt claimed a seat on the other side of the dog and laid his hand gently on the dog's back. "We issued a BOLO for Samson. We also obtained a warrant for Marilyn Ellis's DNA. I went by her loft to get it, but she wasn't home, so I left a message telling her to go to the police station tomorrow and leave a sample."

"Do you think she will?"

He grunted. "If she doesn't, I can haul her ass in. So yeah, I think she will. If she was the one who drugged your tea and left the skulls on the porch, she intentionally terrorized you and incited the Skull to abduct Dr. Ferris."

Tinsley lifted her head and looked at his hand on the dog's back. The fear in her eyes softened slightly. "That's a lot to do for a story."

"Sometimes ambition makes people do ruthless things. But she crossed the line. And if she killed Milburn or knows who did, she has to answer for it."

Tinsley nodded, although she didn't look convinced. Fatigue and grief for her friend had painted exhaustion lines around her eyes and mouth.

But when she looked down at the frail dog, a small smile curved her mouth. A sad smile, but a sliver of the darkness had vanished.

"Thank you for saving him," she said softly.

He shrugged. "He's yours if you want him."

For a moment, her eyes lit with joy. But a second later, the joy turned to sadness. She patted the dog's head, dropped a kiss on his face, then stood and walked to the window. The shutters were closed, but she stared at them as if they held answers.

Wyatt's heart pounded. "What did I say wrong?"

"Nothing," she said in a choked whisper. "It's me . . . I'd love to take him, but I can't."

"Why not?" Wyatt asked. "You'd be good for each other."

Emotions darkened her face. "He deserves better than me."

He opened his mouth to argue, but she fled into her bedroom and closed the door.

Wyatt was baffled. She obviously wanted the dog. And the dog had taken to her immediately. He needed love.

If Tinsley would admit it, so did she.

But he couldn't force anything on her after all she'd suffered. Tonight, she was grieving for her friend.

She needed space and time.

And answers. Most of all, he needed to find the bastard who'd forced her to lock herself in this house.

He stepped outside and told the officer to go home, that he'd stay the night. No way was he leaving Tinsley here alone. Tomorrow he'd carry the dog to his mother's. She'd keep him in a heartbeat.

He returned to the photographs, then called Bernie and asked her if she'd matched them with Hinke or Samson. But she had nothing new.

Exhaustion weighed on him, and he laid his gun on the end table and stretched out on the couch. The dog curled up next to him and started snoring.

Wyatt flipped off the lights and closed his eyes. He doubted he'd sleep, but he was flat worn out, and his head ached from mentally struggling to piece together the truth about the case.

A few minutes later, a scream jarred him, and he bolted upright.

Tinsley?

He grabbed his gun and ran for the bedroom.

CHAPTER
FORTY-FIVE

Wyatt stormed into Tinsley's room, scanning left and right for an intruder. The shutters were closed, the room dark except for a night-light in the bathroom.

Tinsley was thrashing at the covers in the midst of a nightmare.

He slowly approached the bed, then lowered himself onto the edge of the mattress and gently stroked her arm. "Tinsley, wake up, sweetie, you're having a nightmare."

She whimpered and clawed at the covers, drawing his attention to the scars on her hands. Rage at those scars and how she'd gotten them shot through him. But he reminded himself to be gentle as he raked her hair from her face. "Tinsley, it's Wyatt. Wake up now. You're safe."

Her eyes jerked open, but she was obviously still lost in the nightmare—or memory.

"You're safe," he murmured again.

Tears filled her eyes. "But Joyce is dead, and he's still out there."

"We're getting closer to finding him," he said gruffly.

For a long, tension-filled heartbeat, she simply stared at him. Nothing he could say could change what had happened to her.

It was the most helpless feeling he'd ever had, because he wanted to erase the pain from her past and promise her a future full of nothing but happy memories.

But he couldn't do that. "Go back to sleep."

He stood, closed her door, then walked back to the living room. The dog lay snoring on the floor by the couch. He stretched out again, but there was no way he could sleep.

Not when his heart was in that room with Tinsley.

The door to Tinsley's bedroom creaked open. Footsteps padded. He lay perfectly still, wondering what she was doing.

Maybe this was her nightly ritual. She'd wake and prowl the house. God knows he'd had a lot of nights like that himself.

Instead of going to the kitchen or back to the bedroom, she paused by the sofa where he lay.

He didn't move. Didn't want to frighten her away. Her shallow breathing echoed between them. He felt her watching him.

A second later, she stooped and stroked the dog. He gave a contented whimper, and Wyatt bit back a smile. She wanted the dog.

So what was holding her back?

He released a breath that he didn't realize he'd been holding. She'd go back to bed in a minute. He just had to lie still a bit longer.

But she didn't return to the bedroom. Instead, she shocked him by lying down beside him. His breath caught, but he didn't move.

Then she snuggled up next to him.

Her hand curled on his chest, sending a surge of desire through him. It took all his strength and self-control not to kiss her.

She made a soft sound and snuggled deeper against him. Tenderness for her kept him from acting on his growing hunger.

But he couldn't resist sliding one arm down around her and pulling her closer to him. She breathed deeply, and he feared he'd made a mistake.

But she burrowed her head against him and let him hold her. Seconds later, she drifted to sleep.

He closed his eyes and savored the moment. Earning Tinsley's trust meant more to him than jumping her bones.

Although he wanted that.

But Tinsley's feelings were more important. She needed to feel safe.

His job dictated that he deal with the worst of the worst on a daily basis.

There was no future between them.

He could never live confined to a small space as she did. And she could never live in the ugly world of evil that was part of his job.

Still, he'd give his life to save her.

♦ ♦ ♦

Tinsley stirred from sleep, warm and cozy. A rumbling sound echoed around her, and she realized she was lying next to Wyatt, curled in his arms.

But he wasn't the one snoring.

She glanced at the floor and noticed the dog sleeping by her side, his eyelids fluttering. A smile curved her mouth. She missed having a fur baby of her own.

But reality returned as she looked up at Wyatt and his dark eyes met hers. A dog needed long walks and to run on the beach and in the park. She couldn't offer him that.

Wyatt shifted, and she realized she was warm because his big body was next to her, giving her comfort.

"I'm sorry," she said, suddenly embarrassed that she'd crawled next to him without an invitation.

"Don't be," he said in a husky tone.

An awkwardness thrummed between them, the kind that made her want to touch his cheek. Made her want to kiss him.

Shaken by the thought, she swung her legs over the side of the couch.

"No, I shouldn't have . . . have—"

"What?" He gently rubbed her shoulder. "Shouldn't have come in here?"

She pressed her lips together, her cheeks heating. "You know what I mean."

He chuckled. "There's nothing wrong with two people giving each other comfort. It's natural, Tinsley."

It wasn't natural for her.

She headed to the coffeepot. She needed caffeine, but more than that, she needed to occupy her hands before she touched him the way she wanted.

Don't be a fool. He's just protecting you.

How could he be attracted to her when she was such a wreck? When she was scarred inside and out?

"Tinsley?"

"I don't want to talk about it."

He petted the dog for a minute, then stood and walked toward her. "It was nice," he said. "Didn't you think so?"

She dropped the coffee filter, then closed her eyes to regain her composure. She heard his clothes rustling as he stepped up behind her, and then he laid a hand on her back and rubbed her shoulders.

The tension knotting her muscles dissipated slightly, although another kind of tension coiled inside her.

She was just about to turn and do what she'd wanted to do earlier. Feel his cheek. Maybe stroke his lips with her finger.

But his phone trilled from the end table.

He gave her an apologetic look; then he stepped outside to take the call.

What in the world was wrong with her? She shouldn't enter-
tain thoughts about touching Wyatt when her friend had just been
murdered.

She opened the shutters to let in the morning light. The jogger was
there, the man with his dog that she watched every morning. The sight
had become her routine, the regulars on the beach her family.

But they were strangers. They didn't really know her or care
about her.

Damn the Skull for terrorizing her. Damn *her* for letting him.

She started the coffee, then rushed to her bedroom to shower. The
cold water would hopefully jolt some sense back into her. Just as she was
stripping her pajamas, her phone buzzed from the dresser. Liz Roberts.
She needed to talk to the counselor about these feelings she was having
for Wyatt.

She connected as she started the shower water. "Liz?"

"We have to talk. I'll be right over."

Tinsley didn't have time to respond. The phone clicked into silence.

◆　◆　◆

"An officer from the island police station is outside to stand guard,"
Wyatt said as he returned. "I'm going to drop the dog at my mother's,
then meet with the ME and forensic specialist. Will you be all right
here?"

"Sure. Liz Roberts is coming by. She said she wanted to see me."

Wyatt arched a brow. "What about?"

Tinsley shrugged and sipped her coffee. "I don't know. She probably heard about Joyce and thought I needed to talk to someone."

She offered him coffee, and he took a to-go cup and a piece of
toast, then headed out the door. She stooped to hug the dog goodbye,
and his heart went to his throat. He wished she'd keep the guy. Maybe
when this was over . . .

He loaded the boy in his SUV, then drove him to his mother's. She welcomed him with open arms, but he made a mental note to ask Tinsley again about keeping him once the Skull was caught.

Ten minutes later, he stood in the ME's office with Dr. Patton and Dr. Lofton.

"You have news?"

Dr. Patton nodded. "First, I'll let Dr. Lofton speak on those skeletal remains recovered from Seaside Cemetery."

"Two of the sets of remains belong to sisters."

She'd mentioned that before. "How long have they been there?"

"I still don't have the exact timing, but I would estimate a decade, possibly two."

Wyatt chewed the inside of his cheek. "Too long to be victims of the Skull?"

She nodded.

"The fact that they were in unmarked graves suggests murder," Wyatt said. "I'll get the Glynn County Sheriff's Office and Detective Brockett from the Savannah PD to start digging into it."

The Skull was his priority.

He scrubbed his hand over his face, wishing for a shower and more coffee. "What about the three bags of remains I found at Hinke's?"

"Human. Females," Dr. Patton said. "The heads were missing."

Jesus. "Tinsley saw three skulls that the unsub kept where he held her."

"It's possible they belong to these remains. My guess is that one of them was there just over a year. The other two go back months before that. Maybe two years."

"You can't identify the victims?" Wyatt asked.

"I'm working on it, but without teeth to compare dental records to, it's difficult. Your analyst is supposed to be researching missing persons reports. Maybe we'll get lucky."

Wyatt sighed. "It always bothered me that we knew there were other victims but had no families looking for them. We theorized that the girls might have been estranged from their families, or that they didn't have families."

"That could explain it," Dr. Lofton murmured.

Adrenaline spiked through Wyatt. They actually might have an ID on the Skull. "The ERT is searching that graveyard by Samson's, but if Hinke left those bodies in that closet, he's our man."

Still, he had to cover all the bases. "What about Joyce Ferris? Cause of death?"

"Asphyxiation. Dr. Ferris was strangled."

"Was she sexually assaulted?"

Dr. Patton nodded. "I'm afraid so."

Wyatt rubbed his chin as he considered some of Tinsley's injuries. "Burn marks. Torture?"

"She had defense wounds where she tried to fight him. Her nails were cut, skin bleached."

"To destroy DNA where she scratched him."

"Looks that way," Dr. Patton said.

"This guy knows what he's doing," Wyatt said. "Hinke had medical training."

And he could have stolen medication from the pain clinic where he'd worked. But he had raped and tormented Tinsley and held her hostage for months.

Why had he killed the veterinarian so soon after kidnapping her? Why not keep her and torment her?

His phone buzzed, and he stepped aside to answer it.

"It's Bernie. I compared Marilyn Ellis's DNA to the hair we found. They're not a match."

"What?"

"Sorry. I ran the test a couple of times, but they're not even close."

Damn. He'd been so sure she'd drugged Tinsley and planted those skulls on her porch.

If she hadn't, then who the hell had?

Tinsley took one look at Liz Roberts's face and her stomach churned. "What's wrong?"

Liz paced to the couch, then sank onto it. "I . . . probably shouldn't be here. I . . . can't really talk."

"What?" Tinsley poured the counselor a cup of coffee and carried it to her. Liz cradled it between her hands as if she needed to warm herself.

"Tell me what's going on," Tinsley said.

"It's about the copycat, the one who drugged your tea and left that *papel picado* and the skulls on your doorstep."

"What?" Tinsley rubbed her forehead. "You know who did it? Was it Marilyn Ellis?"

Liz shook her head, then leaned her face into her hands. She looked miserable.

"Turn on the TV," she whispered. "Marilyn is about to do a special live interview."

Confusion mingled with fear. Why didn't Liz just tell her who this copycat was?

Her phone buzzed with a text. She stood, flipped on the TV, and grabbed her phone.

Wyatt. Hair DNA not a match for Marilyn. Another woman.

Fear shot through Tinsley, and she glanced at Liz. Liz had been at her house for tea and could have drugged her. And she'd just mentioned the skulls . . .

No . . . surely Liz wasn't responsible. Not the woman she'd begun to think of as her friend . . .

CHAPTER
FORTY-SIX

Wyatt texted Bernie to deepen the search on Hinke. He wanted to know everything about the man, including any houses or properties he or his family might have owned.

She informed him that Samson had shown up for work at the psych hospital, so he drove there and went straight to the director of the hospital. So far, he had no evidence that Samson had killed anyone or that he was the Skull, but he didn't like the way he'd found that dog. Cruelty to animals was often a precursor to violence against a human.

Samson worked with Cat, which meant he could have knowledge of the latest Keeper, the one who'd killed Milburn. He could have even committed the crime for her.

"Seth Samson is a good employee," Heard said. "He keeps to himself, treats the patients with kindness and respect."

That didn't fit with the image of the man Wyatt had created in his head—an image painted by the starving dog locked in that cage in the closet.

"He works on the floor where Cat Landon is, doesn't he?"

Heard shifted. "He does. I warned him and all the employees to be cautious around her. She can be very charming."

So could sociopaths.

Wyatt raised a brow. "You think they have a sexual relationship?"

Heard looked surprised at his bluntness, but Wyatt didn't have time to beat around the bush.

"Ms. Landon doesn't like men, at least not in that way," Heard said.

"I'd like to talk to Samson," Wyatt said.

Heard pressed an intercom button and paged Samson. Several minutes later, when the man hadn't shown up, Heard motioned for Wyatt to follow him.

Just as they exited the elevator, Wyatt spotted Samson ducking into the stairwell at the end of the hall. Heard called his name, but Samson broke into a run.

Wyatt jogged after him. He passed a nurse with a medical cart and ran around it, then ducked into the stairwell where Samson had disappeared. Footsteps pounded the cement steps. He followed.

One flight, then a second, then a door screeched open. The exit. He dashed down the last few steps and raced through the door. Samson was sprinting across the grass toward the parking lot.

Wyatt's leg throbbed, but he ignored the pain and sped up. "Stop, Samson, I'm FBI."

But the man didn't even slow down.

Wyatt yelled his name again, then dove at him and knocked him to the ground. Samson heaved for a breath, finally going still when Wyatt dug his knee into the man's back to make him stop fighting.

"I didn't do anything!" Samson shouted.

Wyatt snapped cuffs around the man's wrists, securing his hands behind him, then rolled him over.

"Then why the hell did you run?"

Samson's eyes darted sideways, a guilty reaction that made Wyatt even angrier.

"What didn't you do?" he said between gritted teeth.

"I don't know, whatever it is you think I did."

"I'm not here to play games, Samson," Wyatt said. "Did you kidnap Joyce Ferris and kill her?"

"What?" Samson's eyes widened in shock. "No, God no. I would never hurt anyone."

Wyatt narrowed his eyes. "You locked your dog in a cage and starved him."

Samson's erratic breathing punctuated the air. "I wasn't starving that animal. I was training him."

"That is no way to train an animal. It's called abuse." Wyatt yanked him to a standing position. "And I intend to charge you with animal cruelty."

"You're arresting me for not feeding my dog enough?" Samson bellowed. "Don't you have more important things to do?"

"Abusing animals is a precursor for abusing others. Even murder."

"I didn't murder anyone," Samson said. "I'm a nurse. I help people."

Heard ran up, his breathing labored.

"Then I'll ask you one more time," Wyatt said as Heard stopped beside them. "Why did you run?"

Samson glanced at his boss, then down at his feet. "I didn't want to get fired."

"Why do you think you're going to get fired?" Heard asked curtly.

Samson shifted, his expression strained. "For helping Ms. Landon."

The image of Milburn's body flashed in Wyatt's mind. "How did you help her?"

"I gave her a phone," Samson said. "She wanted to communicate with her mother. I didn't think it would harm anything."

Heard folded his arms. "You know our policy, Samson. Giving a patient a phone or a tablet is considered contraband."

"Cat wanted to call her mother?" Wyatt asked pointedly. "But she hates her."

Samson gave him a wide-eyed look. "That's what she told me. She was crying the other day and said she wanted to make amends with her."

And he'd fallen for her act. "I doubt she was talking with her mother," Wyatt said icily. "She was most likely communicating with the Keepers."

Shock streaked Samson's face again.

"If she orchestrated the murder of Milt Milburn, then you helped her do it."

"I had nothing to do with that. I swear I didn't."

Wyatt grunted. "You provided her with the means to put a murder plan in motion. That can be considered conspiracy."

The implication that he could be charged as an accomplice sank in, and Samson moaned a protest.

Wyatt jerked him to his feet and shoved him toward the hospital. He'd haul him into the field office later.

But first he wanted to see that phone. If Cat was running the Keepers from inside the hospital, they might be able to trace it to Milburn's killer.

CHAPTER
FORTY-SEVEN

Nerves clawed at Tinsley as she read Wyatt's text message. Liz was wringing her hands together, her expression tormented. Mr. Jingles sat perched on the bar by the door to his cage, his eyes darting back and forth as if he knew something was wrong.

"Who was that?" Liz asked, her voice tight.

If Liz had drugged her, she wanted an explanation. Liz was supposed to be helping her overcome her trauma. "Wyatt. He got test results back on the tea bottles. I was definitely drugged."

Liz's eyes widened. "Who drugged you?"

"It wasn't the Skull," Tinsley said. "A woman's hair was found outside with those skulls. At first we thought it was Marilyn Ellis's, that she made me think the Skull was back just to get a story."

Liz sighed. "But it wasn't."

Not a question but a statement.

"How did you know that?" Tinsley asked. "Do *you* know who drugged my tea?"

Liz averted her gaze. "I can't say. I wish I could, but I can't."

"It *was* you, wasn't it?" Tinsley said, unwilling to let it go. "I poured my heart out to you and trusted you, and you sabotaged me. Why?"

"No." Horror tinged Liz's voice. "I swear, Tinsley. I would never do anything to hurt you, much less terrorize you. I'm your friend."

"Then why are you acting so strange?" Tinsley cried.

Emotions clouded Liz's face as she grabbed the remote and turned up the volume. "Just watch this special newscast, and you'll understand."

Tinsley wanted to scream, but Liz turned up the volume as the camera zoomed in on Marilyn Ellis.

Tinsley gaped in shock.

Her sister was sitting beside the news anchor. What in the world was going on?

"This is Marilyn Ellis with this breaking story—an exclusive interview with Carrie Ann Jensen. Ms. Jensen is the sister of Tinsley Jensen, the only known surviving victim of the man the police call the Skull." She angled the microphone toward Carrie Ann.

"Oftentimes people don't realize the far-reaching effects a victim's trauma has on his or her loved ones. The devastation is like a poison that spreads to anyone associated with the victim, whether family, friend, neighbor, or coworker." Ellis paused, her voice softening. "Today we're going to hear firsthand just how deeply impacted Tinsley Jensen's family was."

Tinsley twisted her hands together. "How dare that reporter do this segment without my permission. And why would Carrie Ann agree?"

Liz took her hand in hers and squeezed it. "I'm sorry, I know your life was ripped apart. Unfortunately, so was your sister's. She wanted to do this."

"You know Carrie Ann?"

Liz nodded. "I met her in a group counseling session. She's had a difficult time this past year."

Oh God. Tinsley had been selfish and had thought only about herself. She'd believed she was doing the right thing by pushing her sister away; instead, she'd hurt her.

Carrie Ann straightened her shoulders. "I'm not telling my story to earn sympathy. In fact, I didn't handle things well after Tinsley was rescued. I was selfish and childish and wanted *her* to assure *me* that everything was all right."

But she hadn't done that, Tinsley thought. She'd been too lost herself.

Carrie Ann continued, "My sister was abducted almost twelve months ago. With that gruesome anniversary approaching, and with my sister still locked away in fear, I was desperate to do something. To find the man who tore apart our lives."

Tinsley's heart pounded.

"So I concocted a plan to draw him out. The Skull had gone radio-silent, but I knew he'd come back for her one day. The wait was destroying both of us. So I figured if he thought someone was copying his crimes, he'd take notice. Maybe get mad. Come out of hiding."

"What did you do?" Tinsley whispered.

"So I dug up some skeletons and put the skulls on my sister's porch to get his attention. This bastard is narcissistic. His ego drives him. He wants people to know who he is. I knew he'd hate it if someone else took credit for being him."

She wiped at a tear and faced the camera as if she was directing her words to Tinsley. "I'm so sorry, sis," Carrie Ann said. "I knew it would scare you to think he was back, but I thought it might push you to leave the house. To move in with me so you wouldn't be alone anymore."

Tears filled Tinsley's eyes.

"I had no idea my actions would endanger anyone else. No idea this maniac would kidnap Dr. Joyce Ferris and hurt her, much less kill her. I'll . . . never forgive myself for that." Carrie Ann inhaled sharply, defiance in her expression. "So whoever you are, hiding behind that Skull mask, if you want to retaliate against anyone for posing as you, then here I am. My sister had nothing to do with it. It was all me."

Horror ripped through Tinsley. Her sister had drugged her tea and left the skulls on her doorstep.

And now she'd challenged that monster to come after her.

This was Tinsley's worst nightmare.

"I thought I was protecting her by pushing her away," Tinsley said in a hoarse whisper.

Instead, she'd pushed Carrie Ann right into the hands of a madman.

◆ ◆ ◆

"I don't know what you're talking about," Cat said. "What phone?"

"Give it up, Cat," Wyatt said. "You and I both know that I won't buy your act."

"Ms. Landon, unless you want to spend some time alone, and I do mean alone with no privileges," Heard said, "then hand it over."

Cat fumed but stormed over to the corner in her room, unscrewed the vent, and removed the phone. She seared Wyatt with a furious look when she slapped it into his hand.

"You won't find anything in there," Cat said.

Cat was a tech expert, a genius in the field. She'd probably already erased anything incriminating.

"Your replacement at our field office is smart and honest," he said, hoping to put Cat in her place.

She simply glared at him, then tapped her foot. "Maybe so. But instead of hounding me about Milburn's killer, why aren't you tracking down the real monsters out there?"

"We are doing that," Wyatt said. "So if you have any idea who the new Keeper is, tell us."

Cat's devious look chilled him. "How could I know? I've been locked in this hellhole for months."

"Maybe you orchestrated Milburn's death with that phone Samson gave you."

"That's a stretch."

"Are you talking with the new Keeper? Or is there a group of you out there?"

"I told you before that I acted alone."

"I don't believe you. I think you and the Keepers are hunting the Skull so you can put him to death before we can make an arrest."

Her smile lifted. "He deserves to die."

He couldn't argue with that. "Don't stonewall us, Cat. If you know who the Skull is or where he is, tell me so I can stop him before he hurts anyone else."

"I wish I could help you, but I can't."

"Can't or won't?"

She folded her arms again and turned her back on him. Samson stood at the door, looking shaken, like he would run again if he had the chance. A night in jail would do him good.

Wyatt tucked the phone in his pocket, shoved Samson into the hall, and followed Heard out of the building to his SUV. He secured Samson in the back seat and drove straight to the field office, then threw the man into a holding cell.

He handed the phone over to Bernie, and she immediately went to work on it.

"You think Cat knows the Skull's identity?" she asked.

He shrugged. "I think she's working with the Keepers again. Word was before that they have a list of targets. The River Street Rapist was on that list. My guess is that the Skull is, too."

"So how would they find him if we can't?"

"Good question. She and Marilyn Ellis seem to know a lot of things before we release information."

Bernie was busy tapping keys and running a search.

"Damn, you're right. She tried to delete her posts to the Keepers. But I found one connection."

"To whom?"

Bernie drummed her fingers on the desk. "To a woman named Carrie Ann."

Wyatt went still. "Carrie Ann Jensen?"

"No last name listed, but . . ." She tapped a few more keys. "Yes, Jensen." She swung her chair toward Wyatt. "That's Tinsley's sister, right?"

He nodded. "What exactly did you find?"

"Looks like she joined the Keepers."

Wyatt's phone buzzed. A text from Hatcher.

Turn on the news. Tinsley's sister is on with Marilyn Ellis.

"Find the news," Wyatt told Bernie.

Bernie leaned in, studying the information spilling onto her screen, then clicked a few keys on the computer monitor.

He sat dumbfounded as Tinsley's sister addressed the reporter and admitted that she was the impostor who'd terrified Tinsley, that she'd done so to smoke out the Skull.

Fuck. Carrie Ann's ploy had pissed off the Skull and driven him to kidnap Dr. Ferris.

Earlier he'd wondered why the bastard had killed her instead of holding her hostage and torturing her.

The truth hit him like a knife in the gut.

He'd killed Joyce Ferris because she wasn't Tinsley.

Which meant he was coming for Tinsley.

He snatched his phone and punched Marilyn Ellis's number. He needed her to make sure she kept Carrie Ann at the station.

Then he'd call the officer guarding Tinsley and put him on alert.

CHAPTER
FORTY-EIGHT

Cat paced her room, furious with Camden. He was too damn by-the-book. She would have thought that he and Hatcher would understand the reason she'd resorted to taking justice into her own hands.

They saw firsthand the devastating effects when they failed to get justice for a victim.

Just look at Tinsley Jensen and the River Street Rapist's victims.

But Camden had confiscated her phone. She'd covered the bases and deleted anything that might lead back to the Keepers, but if that new analyst was as good as Camden said, as good as *her*, then she'd eventually find a link.

She might be locked up, but she'd protect the others at all costs.

Antsy, she dug out the letters her mother had written.

Her hand trembled as childhood memories of Esme baking Christmas cookies with her taunted her. For a few short years, she'd had a happy childhood. Even without a daddy, Esme had loved her enough to make up for it.

Until the shrink who was supposed to help her had taken advantage of her.

Sure, Esme had apologized, but . . . it didn't change things.

Tears blurred her eyes as she turned one of the envelopes over in her hand. She studied the handwriting. Knew what Esme would say inside.

Esme wasn't a bad woman. She'd done her best. One day she'd tell her that.

Cat pressed her hands against her eyes to stem the stupid tears.

She couldn't afford to be weak.

Couldn't start letting emotions interfere with the cause.

The Keepers were doing the right thing. Making up with her mother would only compromise their plans.

Weak people didn't achieve anything.

The Keepers were more important than anything personal Cat wanted for herself.

CHAPTER FORTY-NINE

Carrie Ann waited to the side as Marilyn Ellis finished her segment. Some folks didn't like Marilyn. She hadn't either at first, not when she'd bugged Tinsley.

But she admired her guts and tenacity.

She wanted to be strong like Marilyn. And she wanted to comfort Tinsley instead of relying on her sister to take care of her.

Once she'd started reading *Heart & Soul*, she couldn't stop herself from reading every single post. The tormented cries from the women who'd posted had hit home.

And her sister . . . her soulful cries from her self-imposed prison had made Carrie Ann ache inside. She'd known she had to do something to end the hold that maniac had on her.

So she'd devised a plan. Had befriended the Keepers. And Marilyn.

But things had gone wrong. And Tinsley was going to hate her now.

God help her, she hadn't meant for anyone else to get hurt.

Hopefully today's plan would work. She just hoped she didn't get herself killed in the process.

But if she did, at least Tinsley would finally be free.

Marilyn finished and strode toward her, an odd look in her eyes. "You did good today, Carrie Ann. But putting yourself out there is dangerous."

Carrie Ann bit her bottom lip. "It's time someone stopped him."

"I agree." Marilyn squeezed her arm. "Talk to Agent Camden and have him assign you a protective detail. If the Skull comes after you, the FBI might catch him and end this."

She nodded. She'd consider it.

Although prison would be too good for him. He deserved to die.

She thanked Marilyn for the segment, then rushed toward the door. Her phone was buzzing as she exited the building. Tinsley.

Damn. She'd probably seen the show. She'd wanted to talk to her so badly these last months. But now it was too late for talking.

Besides, her sister would try to persuade her to go into hiding until the Skull was apprehended.

Her skin crawled. She'd rather die than be locked up like Tinsley.

She let the call roll to voice mail, then hurried toward her car. A fall breeze kicked up, stirring the tree branches. A blanket of orange, red, and yellow leaves covered the sidewalk, crunching beneath her feet.

Another sound made her jerk her head around. Two women pushing strollers toward the park. Other people rushed to work or to shops and restaurants. The coffee shop on the corner had a line, the sign for pumpkin lattes prominent. A group of teens stood smoking by a streetlamp in front of a souvenir shop that specialized in pirate memorabilia. She'd been in that store before.

Tomorrow would mark the one-year anniversary of her sister's abduction.

Nerves gathered in her stomach, and she crossed the street, then made her way down by the riverfront. Her car was where she'd left it in a lot behind a tattoo shop. No one lurking around.

The hair on the back of her neck prickled as she reached for her car door to open it. Suddenly she felt someone behind her. One hand went to her pocket where she'd stored the gun she'd stolen from Tinsley's. She had a knife in her boot.

But she had no time to retrieve it. Strong hands grabbed her, then she felt the sharp jab of a needle, and the world spun into darkness.

CHAPTER
FIFTY

Wyatt cursed. Carrie Ann Jensen had just done a reckless thing with her TV appearance. If the Skull was watching, he'd probably go after her.

He'd killed Joyce Ferris because she wasn't Tinsley. And he might think that Carrie Ann's appearance was a trap.

So he might try to take Tinsley.

Thankfully, an officer was watching her.

"Check that BOLO on Hinke, and let's find Carrie Ann Jensen," Wyatt told Bernie. "Get me a phone number, address, anything you can find on her. I'll call the TV station and see if I can catch her before she leaves."

Bernie went to work, and he phoned the station and identified himself. "I just saw Carrie Ann Jensen's interview. Is she still there?"

"She just left."

"Then let me speak to Marilyn Ellis."

"Hold on, please."

He gripped the phone with sweaty hands as he waited. Bernie scribbled a number onto a sticky note and pushed it in front of him. Carrie Ann's phone. He gestured for her to call it.

"This is Marilyn Ellis."

"You should have told me you were going to put Tinsley's sister on air."

Her sigh punctuated the silence. "I didn't ask her; she came to me."

"Do you know where she was going when she left?"

"No. She mentioned that she's staying in an inn on the island. She didn't say which one."

There were only two. He'd check both.

Dammit. "You know you may have just pushed her into the hands of the Skull."

A heartbeat passed. "Then you'd better find him fast."

"You may not like me, Marilyn, but if you hear anything, you have to call me. Lives are at stake."

He hung up without waiting for a reply. Bernie was shaking her head. "No answer on Carrie Ann's phone. I left a message for her to call you."

"Thanks. Marilyn Ellis said Carrie Ann left. She's staying in an inn on the island. Find out which one and see if she's there. Also find out what kind of car she's driving and get an APB out on it."

He punched Tinsley's number, but it rang and rang, and she didn't answer.

His gut churned. "I'm going to Tinsley's."

He jogged to his car, then called the officer standing guard as he started the engine. No answer there either.

What the hell? Where was he?

Panic shot through him, and he clenched the steering wheel in a white-knuckled grip and sped onto the highway.

♦ ♦ ♦

Tinsley tried her sister's phone again. No answer. Wyatt had called as Liz was leaving, but just as she saw his number, a text came through.

She stared at the photograph in the text in horror.

Her sister. A gag in her mouth. Hands bound. She lay on the floor of a cage unconscious.

The cage where the Skull had held her.

Another photograph appeared. This one of the three skulls dangling from the ceiling in clear sight of her sister. Except this time Carrie Ann's sea turtle necklace was hanging from one of the skulls where the neck should have been.

Cold terror washed over Tinsley as memories assailed her. His breath on her skin. His hands touching her. His throaty grunt as he shoved himself inside her.

His childlike chanting about the dead, then his sobbing when he finished with her.

Nausea flooded Tinsley, and she ran to the bathroom, dropped to her knees, and threw up. Trembling, she stood, used mouthwash, then splashed cold water on her face.

She was pale from lack of sun. Dark circles beneath her eyes. A shell of a woman.

Because she'd been too cowardly to face him, her sister might die.

She couldn't let that happen.

Stumbling on shaky legs, she hurried back to her phone. Another text from *him*.

It's you I need, Tinsley. It has always been you.

If you want to save your sister, come to me.

No cops or she's dead.

Heart hammering, she quickly sent a response.

Tell me where and I'll be there.

Precious, painful seconds ticked by. She tapped her fingers on the phone, anxious. "Tell me, dammit!"

Finally, a response.

Where we first met.

A picture of a dog followed. No . . . not any dog.

Gingersnap.

Her chest ached with the effort to breathe. What did he mean? Where they met?

How did he have a picture of the first dog she'd rescued?

She studied the picture again. The red collar around Gingersnap's neck. The cage where her sister was being held. Where he'd held her.

The stainless-steel bowls he'd used to give her bits of food.

She pounded her head with her fist. She had to think, but she was so terrified her thoughts were jumbled.

He'd told her he could give pain and take it away. That it was wrong that some people loved their animals more than their children.

Korine said that he might be infatuated with his mother. That he saw his victims as a reminder of her . . .

She glanced back at the picture—the red collar. Gingersnap.

The photographs of the kids at the orphanage flashed in her head again. Something had been familiar.

Where they'd met . . .

When she'd gotten Gingersnap, the vet . . . she and Carrie Ann had taken dog obedience lessons from her. Two boys had helped at the clinic, cleaning cages, walking the animals . . .

A year later when Gingersnap had been hit by a car, they'd taken her to that clinic. At first the vet had said Gingersnap would make it.

But she'd died that night.

She examined the picture of the orphanage boys one more time. The familiar face . . . Norton had been one of those boys. And the other, no, not at the orphanage. The photo of the boys doing community service . . . the vet's son.

Carrie Ann had mentioned that she'd seen the boy putting rocks in the dogs' bowls. Said he'd even hit one of the animals.

At some point, a cat had died suspiciously. She'd heard the vet talking to her son. He'd been in charge of the cat. The boy claimed the animal was suffering, that it was dying. He'd cried and said he hadn't wanted to see it suffer.

The next summer when she returned to the clinic, the boys hadn't been there. According to the receptionist, the vet had sent her son away, saying that he was dangerous. She'd suspected he'd killed more than one animal.

Tinsley pressed her hand to her mouth and forced a deep breath. That boy . . . oh God, he might have killed Gingersnap. He was the Skull.

She'd met him when they were barely teenagers. She'd admired his mother and followed in her footsteps. Except for becoming a vet. She'd wanted that, but she'd given up the dream to help Carrie Ann go to college.

Instead she'd focused on the rescue side of animal care.

That's how she reminded him of his mother. And Joyce . . . she was another vet . . .

The profile's words echoed in her head—the Skull had a twisted fantasy of his mother. He'd wanted her sexually but had known it was wrong.

He'd used her as a substitute for his mother and acted out that fantasy. Then he'd cried afterward because he knew he shouldn't lust after his mother.

She reread his text. If she wanted to save her sister, she had to go to him. If she brought the cops, he'd kill Carrie Ann.

Tears blurred her vision. How could she do that when she couldn't bear to go outside the cottage?

You have to go to save Carrie Ann.

Heart racing, she dug her car keys from the basket in her room. Her phone was ringing again. She checked the number.

Wyatt.

She started to answer. Tell him and let him go.

But doing that might get her sister killed.

Her mind raced. She had to get rid of the officer outside.

She sent him a text and told him she saw someone on the beach, someone who might be the Skull.

Please check it out.

He responded that he would, for her to keep the door locked.

She clenched her keys, then stopped to grab a kitchen knife. She jammed it in the pocket of her jacket, then rushed to the door.

She closed her fingers around the doorknob, but the room swayed, spun. She couldn't breathe.

Her legs gave way, and she slid to the floor, sweating and trembling.

Why wasn't Tinsley answering the damn phone?

He tried the officer on duty again and finally got him.

"Tinsley saw someone on the beach. I'm checking it out."

"Is she okay?"

"Locked up tight. I'll check back with her when I see who this guy on the beach is."

"If it's him, call for backup."

A call from Bernie beeped in, so he hung up.

"I found some interesting information on Hinke. Actually, Hinke is his mother's maiden name, not his father's name. She was a veterinarian."

That fit with the profile. "Does she still practice?"

"No, she passed away two years ago tomorrow."

Adrenaline spiked his blood. About the time they suspected the first victim had gone missing. Then Tinsley last year. It all fit.

"The mother's house was handed down to him," she said. "I'm sending you the address now."

"Good, now get me some warrants."

He pressed the accelerator and sped away from the field office, racing toward the address. He veered around traffic, speeding through intersections, his focus on one thing—finding this bastard before he hurt Tinsley or her sister.

His phone buzzed just as he swung onto the street leading to the man's house. Bernie. "Yeah?"

"I checked surveillance cameras around the TV station." Bernie's voice cracked. "Carrie Ann Jensen's car is still there."

His lungs tightened. "Maybe she took a cab?"

"I'm afraid not, Wyatt. We have him on camera. You can't see his face, but he has her."

He slammed his fist against the steering wheel with a growl. "Did you see what kind of vehicle he was driving?"

"No. He dragged her into an alley, and then we lost him."

"Look at traffic cams in the surrounding area. Let's find this bastard."

CHAPTER
FIFTY-ONE

Wyatt eased down the deserted street to Hinke's house, scanning the road and property. A dark sedan was parked beneath a carport, but he saw no signs of life outside. The curtains inside the house were drawn, the yard slightly overgrown, an ancient swing set to the side.

It looked abandoned. Set off the beaten path, it would be a good place to hide his victims. An outbuilding made Wyatt even more suspicious.

He parked, drew his weapon, his senses alert as he approached the house. The wooden steps creaked as he climbed them. He leaned against the door and listened, straining for sounds of a voice or a woman's cry.

Silence.

Body coiled with tension, he turned the doorknob. The door swung open.

He inched through the house, noting well-worn furniture. A faded spread hung on a spindle bed that looked as if it hadn't been slept in for a while.

A wall of photographs in the first bedroom held pictures of a menagerie of animals, most likely rescues the mother had brought home.

Where were the pictures of the son?

Curious, he examined the collection on the dresser, but a lone picture of a small boy was all he found.

Next, he stepped into a room that he assumed was Hinke's. A navy-and-brown-plaid spread covered a twin oak bed. The bedding was mussed, the pillow worn.

Instead of the desk in the corner holding sports paraphernalia or other childhood mementos, the corkboard was covered in photos of a young girl and a ginger-colored dog. He peered closer and realized that the girl in the picture was Tinsley. He'd seen a photo of her and her sister at her house.

Good God. Hinke *had* known Tinsley as a child. And he'd begun an obsession with her then.

He opened the desk drawers and discovered an album of pictures, very disturbing photographs of dead animals. A dog. A chicken. Two kittens.

Animals Hinke had killed?

He moved to the closet and opened the door. *Dammit.* The man had tacked pictures of Tinsley all over the inside of the door. Candid shots of Tinsley at the rescue events, at a vet clinic, at a park playing with a dog, on the beach with a lab.

Tinsley's cottage, a shot of her looking through the window. It had to have been taken from the beach. That bastard had known where she was all along. And he'd been watching.

Rage slammed into him when he glanced at the opposite door. More pictures of Tinsley, these from her captivity. Photographs of Tinsley tied in a cage, close ups of her face and body as she lay unconscious from his torture.

His first instinct was to rip them from the door and get rid of them. He didn't want to look at them, and he sure as hell didn't want Tinsley or anyone else to see them.

But they were evidence.

He couldn't do anything to jeopardize this case.

Stomach churning, he snapped pictures of the room and everything he'd found, then went outside to search that storage building.

The door was boarded over, but a noise echoed through the rotting boards. He hurried to his SUV, grabbed a tool from the trunk, then rushed back and pried open the boards.

The scratching sound came from the back.

He hoped Carrie Ann wasn't tied up in that dark corner.

♦ ♦ ♦

Perspiration beaded Tinsley's neck as she struggled to regain control. She closed her eyes, forcing deep breaths to stem the panic.

An image of the Skull taunted her. Then an image of her little sister tied up in that cage.

Fury replaced her panic.

She'd taken care of Carrie Ann when she was little, had kept the mean girls from teasing her when she wore braces. Had kept bullies from bothering her because she'd been tiny for her age.

She was not going to let the Skull torment Carrie Ann the way he'd done her.

She massaged her temples, her breathing steadying slightly as other memories bombarded her. She and her sister and father collecting sea-shells out there on the beach. Her mother helping them glue the shells to frames to put their pictures inside. The four of them crabbing in the marsh. Riding bicycles to the Village and watching fireworks at the park on the Fourth of July.

At night, she'd consoled her sister when she'd cried herself to sleep. Carrie Ann had tried to do that for her when she'd first been rescued, but she'd pushed her away.

"I'm coming for you, sis," she whispered on a ragged breath.

The wind howled outside, the sun slipping away. She knew what it was like to live in that darkness. To lose track of time and the days. To wait for him to come . . .

She gathered her courage and snatched her keys and purse where they'd landed on the floor when she'd fallen. Gripping them in one hand, she clawed at the door. Sweat trickled down the back of her neck as she turned the doorknob.

Cool air assaulted her as she pushed the door open. It had been so long since she'd been outside that she'd forgotten how refreshing the ocean breeze felt on her face.

She savored the moment, breathing in and out, then tried to stand. But her legs were wobbling, and the world tilted.

Baby steps. You can do this. You have to.

Instead of standing, she dragged herself onto the porch. Her vision blurred as she glanced down the steps toward the beach. The officer was too far away to hear her, but it wouldn't take him long to get back.

No cops or she's dead.

She had to hurry.

Dogged determination filled her, and she forced herself to her hands and knees and slowly made her way to the bannister. She gritted her teeth, gripped the railing, and pulled herself up to stand.

Her car was parked in the detached garage.

You can do this. Just think of Carrie Ann.

Those words became her mantra as she stumbled down the steps. Her legs felt weak, and she was sweating all over, but she managed to put one foot in front of the other and finally made it to the garage. She pressed the garage door opener and glanced back at the beach as the door slid up.

Summoning her courage again, she clung to the wall until she made it to her car. She threw the door open, praying the SUV would start. Her hand was shaking so hard that she dropped the keys and had to dig around on the floor to retrieve them.

Finally, she snagged them, then jammed the keys in the ignition. The engine chugged and sputtered, then died.

Tears of frustration filled her. She slammed the steering wheel with her fist. "Dammit, come on. I have to save Carrie Ann."

She twisted the key again, holding her breath as the engine struggled to come to life. She had to try three more times, but finally it started.

The message from Wyatt taunted her. She didn't have time to call but forwarded him the texts from the Skull. Maybe he could trace them, and he'd find the bastard. Or Carrie Ann.

She hadn't driven in months and had to remind herself what to do next. She wiped perspiration from her forehead and checked the rearview mirror, then eased the SUV into reverse and backed from the garage.

Her heart pounded as she swung the SUV around and onto the street. She checked for traffic, the last slivers of sunlight dipping below the horizon.

For a second, the world blurred again, and sweat drenched her neck. Carrie Ann's face materialized again. Then the sound of her crying when she was a little girl.

She saw the two of them petting Gingersnap, chasing her in the yard, tying a red, white, and blue bandana around her neck for the Fourth of July. Dressing her in a police dog costume at Halloween. Then a Santa hat at Christmas.

She wanted a dog again. Wanted her life back. But most of all she wanted her sister safe and back home. She couldn't let her die.

The vet clinic . . . she remembered exactly where it was. She'd volunteered there as a teenager. Had dreamed about becoming a vet and joining the doctor in her practice.

She blinked to focus, pressed the accelerator, and eased down the street.

She had seen a notice about Dr. Hinke's death two years ago. The clinic had closed.

Two years . . . Had his mother's death triggered Hinke to kidnap his first victim?

◆ ◆ ◆

A rat skittered across the floor of the outbuilding, and Wyatt jumped back. Another one squeaked from the corner, and two more raced along the edge of the wall, scurrying into a hole that led outside.

They were the source of the noise.

He shined his flashlight along the wall. An old refrigerator sat on the far side.

A padlock held the door closed, so he searched the storage closet and found bolt cutters. He pulled on gloves, cut the lock, opened the door, and shined his flashlight inside.

The sight of the decaying body sent nausea to his throat. He coughed and stepped back for a second, then forced himself to take a closer look.

The cooler temperature inside the refrigerator would have slowed down decomp, but the body had still decayed considerably.

Who was it?

He didn't know enough about forensics to be able to tell much, but a gold wedding band lay on the floor of the refrigerator. A man's ring.

He snapped pictures of the interior, then closed the door and stepped outside to call the ERT and medical examiner. Before he hung up with them, his phone was beeping with another call.

Bernie.

He quickly connected and relayed what he'd found. "If it's a male, it could be his father," Bernie said. "He disappeared about a month before the wife died. Apparently the wife reported him missing. When the police questioned her, she mentioned that they'd turned their son over to the state because he displayed signs of aggression and psychosis. Police questioned Hinke about his father's disappearance but didn't find anything to charge him with or hold him on. When no body surfaced, the case went cold."

So Hinke killed the father, and then the mother's death was his trigger. He kidnapped his first victim to replace her. When she didn't measure up, he killed her and took another.

A text made him hesitate.

Fuck. The Skull had texted Tinsley . . .

"Hatcher is going to the TV station to look at surveillance cameras," Bernie said.

That might give them a break. "Pull any recent pictures you can find of Hinke and the kind of car he drives and get them to every law enforcement agency in the state. We need everyone looking for him." He took a breath, fighting pure panic. "I'm forwarding you texts Tinsley just sent. Apparently the Skull contacted her. Get on these right away."

"Copy that."

His phone rang as soon as he hung up. The officer at Tinsley's.

"Agent Camden?"

Fear seized him at the sound of the man's choppy breathing. "What's wrong?"

"It's Ms. Jensen. She's gone."

Wyatt went still. "What do you mean *gone?*"

"I mean she left. She sent me to the beach, but the guy down there was just a local walking his dog."

"You mean he took her?"

A tense second passed. "I don't think so. Odd thing is that I heard an engine start and ran to see who it was. She was behind the steering wheel."

Shock immobilized Wyatt. "She was driving? How can that be? She's terrified to leave the house."

"That's what I thought."

Wyatt tried to process what the officer had said. Tinsley had been terrified to leave the cottage. She hadn't left it in months.

She wasn't faking the agoraphobia. He'd seen her terror when she'd tried to leave it the night she'd been drugged.

She might not leave the house for herself, but it was possible she had to save Carrie Ann.

"Let me get a BOLO on her car and a trace on her phone. The Skull has her sister."

CHAPTER FIFTY-TWO

Tinsley gripped her phone, terrified and desperate as she parked at the clinic. How could she face the Skull alone?

What if he'd already hurt—or worse, *killed*—her sister? Would she be able to fight him?

Gravel crunched outside the car. A noise . . . someone was out there.

She felt for the knife inside her pocket and closed her fingers around the handle.

Suddenly the door jerked open. She clutched the knife and swung around, determined to fight him and win.

She made it halfway to his chest with the knife before he slammed his hand down and knocked her wrist. Pain ricocheted through her arm, and she lost her grip on the knife. It fell to the floorboard.

She clawed for her keys to jab his eyes. But he was fast and wrenched her hand backward. Then he snatched the keys and threw them to the ground.

She pummeled her fists into him. "Let my sister go, and I'll stay with you, you bastard!"

A dark chuckle rumbled from him, and he jabbed a needle in her neck. She swayed. His body blurred into a fog, and her legs gave way.

A voice inside her head screamed for her to fight, but her limbs were so heavy she couldn't move.

She hung like a rag doll as he carried her inside the clinic.

◆ ◆ ◆

"So far, nothing on Tinsley's car," Bernie told Wyatt. "I'm working on tracing her phone."

Wyatt paced back and forth outside his vehicle, terrified that the Skull had Tinsley.

He blotted out the images of those pictures the bastard had kept of his sick, depraved acts.

"Tell me everything you found on him."

"He was a single child born to Janine Hinke and Clyde Dorchester. I dug all the way back to his childhood and managed to talk to a lady who worked with his mother at her vet clinic. She said the kid was withdrawn, quiet, and in her words—peculiar. Apparently he had a mean streak. The mother thought helping at the clinic with the animals would be good for him."

"Pet therapy," Wyatt mumbled.

"Something like that. Only it backfired. He was jealous of the time his mother spent with the animals. There were at least two instances where she suspected that he'd killed animals at the clinic. The parents put him in private therapy then. By middle school, he'd escalated. He set fire to part of the clinic. More animals were found dead, this time sadistically tortured. Something happened at home, too, although the parents wouldn't talk about it. But they sent him to an inpatient treatment facility."

"That's where he met Norton?" Wyatt asked.

"No. They met at the clinic. Norton's therapist arranged for him to work cleaning cages."

"And the boys' friendship was born." Wyatt scrubbed his hand over his face.

Bernie heaved a sigh. "Wait. I have a trace on Tinsley's phone."

"Where is it coming from?"

"The mother's vet clinic."

Dammit. He should have guessed that.

"I'm sending you the address."

"I'm on my way."

♦ ♦ ♦

The pungent aroma of flowers and scented candles swirled around Tinsley as she stirred from unconsciousness. She blinked, but everything was a blur.

"Tinsley . . ."

A whispered voice. Carrie Ann.

Reality returned in a terrifying rush.

She blinked again, struggling to sit up. A hand brushed her cheek. Not Wyatt's. Not Carrie Ann's.

It was the rough hand of the Skull through the bars of the cage.

Panic stole her breath and she cringed, shrinking away from him.

"We're finally together again." The sound of the Skull's voice made nausea rise to her throat.

She looked across the room. Three skulls dangled from the ceiling just like before. The flowers, the candles . . . he was preparing for the Day of the Dead celebration.

Now she understood what it was about.

His mother.

"I'm here," Carrie Ann said in a muffled whisper.

Tinsley turned her head toward the sound. Through a hazy fog, she saw her younger sister crawling toward her. They were locked together in one of his damn cages.

Carrie Ann's hands were tied, but she lifted them and raked Tinsley's hair from her face. "I'm sorry," she whispered. "I thought I could kill him and you'd be free."

The man's deep chant echoed through the room as he began the rituals again. He was lost in his own demented world.

Tears blurred Tinsley's vision as her sister stroked her cheek. She sucked in a breath to clear her throat. "Did he hurt you?"

Carrie Ann shook her head, but her face looked puffy from crying, and dark circles rimmed her eyes. "I'm okay."

"You shouldn't have gone on camera," Tinsley said, her voice breaking.

"I had to do something to save you," Carrie Ann said. "We both knew he was coming back for you. I wanted him to come after me instead so I could get rid of him."

"You're my baby sister," Tinsley said. "I'm supposed to protect you. That's why I pushed you away."

Confusion streaked Carrie's Ann's face, then understanding. "Oh God, Tins, I thought you hated me. You gave up so much for me and—"

"I loved you," Tinsley said. "I still do, more than anything in the world."

Carrie Ann leaned her head against Tinsley's, and for a moment they were lost in their tears and pain. They'd bonded as children. When their parents had died, they'd become even closer. They would get through this together.

Determination reared its way through the fear gnawing at Tinsley. "We're going to get out of here," Tinsley whispered.

"How?" Carrie Ann gulped. "He took my knife and the gun. Your gun."

"It's okay; we'll find a way." Tinsley curled her little finger and gestured for her sister to do the same. "Pinkie-swear. We're going to beat this son of a bitch."

Carrie Ann hesitated slightly, then hooked her finger with Tinsley's.

The Skull's chanting grew louder as he lit candles and lined sugar skulls around the altar. "Help me sit up," Tinsley whispered.

Carrie Ann used her hands to pull Tinsley to a sitting position. Tinsley motioned for her sister to turn around. Carrie Ann did, and Tinsley began to work at the ropes.

The knots were tight, but she and her sister had practiced knot-tying so much as kids that she could almost do it in her sleep. It took some time, but she wiggled and pulled the strands until she managed to unravel the rope and free her sister. Then Carrie Ann returned the favor.

They kept their heads bowed together to hide what they were doing. Candlelight flickered from the corner, illuminating the altar and flickering off the Skull's face. He looked like some kind of demon circling the fires of hell as he chanted and sang to the sugar skulls.

Tinsley inched to the cage door and tried the latch, but the padlock needed a key. She visually searched the room. The key hung on a chain around his neck.

Frustration made her want to scream, but she had to think, not panic.

She'd get Carrie Ann out or die trying.

Footsteps brought her gaze to the Skull. Carrie Ann gripped her arm.

"Nice to see you awake now, Tinsley."

She swallowed revulsion, forcing her mind not to relive the past. This time, things were going to be different. They had to be.

"I know who you are, Wade," she said. "So why don't you stop hiding behind that mask and show your face?"

"I'm not hiding. I wear it in honor of the celebration."

"You wear it because you're a coward," Tinsley said, baiting him. "You're nothing but a big bully. You were as a kid. And now you have to intimidate women to get what you want from them because no woman would want you for who you are."

Anger radiated from him as he glared at her. "You don't know what you're talking about. I help people. I take away their pain."

"You're delusional," Tinsley said.

He jammed the key in the lock and turned it. Tinsley braced herself for his attack. Carrie Ann's nails dug into her arm as they waited.

The door jerked open, and he yanked her arm. With her hand free, she punched him in the face with her fist. He bellowed and dragged her from the cage, but Carrie Ann dove out and hit him in the knees.

He sank to the floor with a shocked yelp.

Tinsley took advantage and ran for the knife he'd taken from her.

But he snatched her leg before she could reach it and dragged her toward him. "You're mine, Tinsley. If you fight me, I'll make it even more painful for your little sister."

Tinsley kicked back, slamming her foot into his face. Blood spurted from his nose through the holes in the mask, and he bellowed in rage but didn't release her.

Carrie ran toward the altar. He was pulling Tinsley beneath him, straddling her, his hands groping her. She kicked and bucked to shove him off her. He punched her in the face, sending pain through her jaw.

Stars swam in front of her eyes, but she refused to give up. She grabbed his balls and twisted them. He shouted an obscenity, then bent her wrist until she released him.

Carrie Ann dove onto his back and slipped a knife to his throat. "Let her go or you're dead."

He froze, still straddling Tinsley. She shoved off his mask. Without that cover, he didn't look as terrifying. In fact, he looked weak and pathetic. "You bastard. You're going to pay for what you've done."

He roared, then swung back and knocked Carrie Ann off him. The two of them wrestled for the knife, and it skittered across the floor. Carrie Ann tried to reach it, but he stomped on her arm, and she screamed in pain. Then he slammed his fist against the side of her head, and she passed out.

Tinsley wanted to get the knife, but the candles were closer, so she stood up, grabbed a burning candle, and threw it on him.

The flame caught his flannel shirt, and he yelled and beat at it, then growled and lurched toward her.

She lifted her leg to kick him, but he knocked her back into the table. The table collapsed. Candles slid off, quickly catching the rotting wood floor ablaze. He rolled them away from the flames and tried to drag her to the corner, but she fought and kicked with every ounce of strength she possessed.

He was stronger, though, and punched her in the jaw, then covered her body with his again. His weight on her triggered the memory of his brutal attacks the year before, and she pummeled him with her fists.

"Run!" Tinsley screamed. "Run!"

But Carrie Ann didn't listen. Instead, she snagged the knife and jumped Hinke from behind. This time she didn't threaten him.

Carrie Ann stabbed the knife into his back with all her force. Blood spurted as he grunted in shock and collapsed.

Tinsley tried to push him off her, but he grabbed her and rolled her to the side. Before she could escape, he snatched a burning candle from the floor and held it in front of her. Evil flared in his eyes.

Then hot wax dripped onto her skin as he waved the flame across her cheek.

CHAPTER
FIFTY-THREE

Wyatt threw his SUV into park, shoved his car door open, and jumped out, gun at the ready. Tinsley's vehicle was parked in the drive, the door ajar.

Her phone was on the ground.

Smoke curled around the edge of the clinic doorway.

He ran for the building and checked the front door. Locked.

Knowing the Skull might be waiting to ambush him, he carefully scanned the property and periphery of the building as he circled around to the back entrance. Dog runs and an outdoor play yard for pets occupied the far-left corner. All empty.

He eased up to the back door, then paused to listen.

A scream sounded inside. Then a man's shout.

He kicked open the door and raced inside. Cages lined the back room. He made his way through the hall. Exam rooms along the right. Then a surgical room and lab.

Smoke was coming from another room.

He eased toward it, then peeked through the edge of the cracked doorway. Flames licked the floor and wall. Noises came from the midst of the smoke.

He ducked inside, searching for Tinsley and her sister. A cry from the corner made him jerk his head toward the sound. Tinsley. Carrie Ann.

A man hovered over Tinsley, a burning candle in his hand. Hinke.

"Stop!" Wyatt aimed his weapon at the bastard.

Tinsley knocked the candle from Hinke's hand; then Hinke reached for her throat.

Wyatt didn't hesitate. He pulled the trigger. The bullet hit home, piercing the man's temple. The impact knocked Hinke backward, and he collapsed beside Tinsley, blood spurting from Hinke's wound.

"Tinsley? Carrie Ann?"

Carrie Ann lay on the floor, half-conscious, blood on her hands. Tinsley was dragging herself toward her sister. She looked shell-shocked and terrified, but she was alive.

He stooped to make sure Hinke was dead. Wood popped and cracked, the fire spreading. He rushed to Tinsley and helped her lift Carrie Ann to stand. Carrie Ann draped her arms around his shoulder on one side and Tinsley's on the other, and they ran outside.

He coaxed them far away from the building, and they sank down beneath a giant oak tree. Carrie Ann roused, and Tinsley wrapped her arms around her. The two of them hugged and rocked each other as he ran back inside to retrieve the Skull's body.

He beat at flames as he entered, covering his mouth to stifle the smoke. He could let the man's body burn.

He wanted to see him in the ground instead.

◆ ◆ ◆

Tinsley dabbed blood from Carrie Ann's forehead with Wyatt's handkerchief.

Wyatt looked down at them, his expression dark. "Police and ambulance are on their way. Are you hurt, Tinsley?"

She shook her head. "Just banged up. Carrie Ann needs stitches."

He nodded, then stepped away to answer his phone.

"I'm so proud of you for coming out of the house," Carrie Ann said as she looked into Tinsley's eyes. "That took courage, Tins."

Tinsley shook her head. "No, it took rage."

Carrie Ann squeezed Tinsley's hand. "He's dead. That's all that matters."

"What matters is that you and I are alive," Tinsley said. "And we won't have to worry about him anymore."

They hugged again, but when they broke apart, tears filled Carrie Ann's eyes. "Don't cry," Tinsley whispered. "We're free. We can get a place together now and make up for these last few months. If you want to stay at the cottage, we'll take long walks on the beach and sip wine at sunset and dream about the future like we did when we were kids."

Carrie Ann gave her a sad smile. "I want that more than anything, but I have to take responsibility for what I've done. If I don't, I can't start with a clean slate."

Tinsley cradled her sister's hands in hers. "What are you talking about? There's nothing to—"

"I was so upset these last few months that I became obsessed with your case and all the injustices in the world. I joined that group, the Keepers."

"No . . ." Tinsley shook her head in denial.

Carrie Ann lifted her chin. "I met Milburn in the bar that night and let him buy me a drink. When he came onto me outside, I was prepared."

Wyatt had walked over and was listening. Panic seared Tinsley. He was an FBI agent, sworn to uphold the law.

"Please, Wyatt—"

"I'm sorry, Tinsley," Carrie Ann said. "I have to stand up for all the women who've been victimized by men, both in bars and on the job or in schools."

Tinsley's heart ached. She couldn't get her sister back only to lose her to prison.

◆ ◆ ◆

Wyatt didn't like the latest turn of events. Carrie Ann could go to jail. He might have to arrest her. She could do hard time.

That would be another blow to Tinsley.

But if he didn't do his job, he'd be no better than the vigilantes.

He waited for the fire department and paramedics to arrive, along with the ERT and medical examiner, then followed the ambulance to the hospital.

He wanted Tinsley examined, too. She might have internal injuries, and those bruises needed tending to.

His heart was still racing from the terror that had driven him to this place. If Tinsley had been dead, he . . . didn't know what he'd do.

He was in love with her. He didn't know when it had happened. Maybe the first time he'd met her.

But he could no more deny his feelings than he could have denied the call to law enforcement. That was in his blood.

And now Tinsley was in his heart.

What the hell was he going to do about it?

He parked in the emergency room parking lot and hurried inside. At Tinsley's insistence, she was wheeled to the same exam room as her sister.

He paced the waiting room while they were examined, then phoned Kendall James. She was the attorney who'd represented Cat and had helped Korine when Mrs. Davenport confessed that she'd shot Korine's father.

Ms. James agreed to represent Carrie Ann, and he breathed a sigh of relief. Carrie Ann still might not get off. Milburn's asshole father was determined to make his son's killer pay.

And Carrie Ann had killed him. But self-defense and a history of PTSD would work in her defense. James would also use that as a defense in relation to Dr. Ferris's death.

A nurse led him back to Tinsley. "They want to keep Carrie Ann for observation tonight," Tinsley said. "She has seven stitches and a concussion."

"All right. I'll drive you back to the cottage." He raised a brow. "That is, unless you don't want to go back there." Too many bad memories of being locked inside.

"You're right," she said with a sad smile. "I don't want to go there tonight."

"Then a hotel?" He hesitated. "Or I could take you to my place. You'll be safe there."

She slid her hand into his. "Your place would be nice."

◆ ◆ ◆

Before Tinsley left with Wyatt, she assured Carrie Ann that she wouldn't go to prison. Marilyn Ellis wanted the story, and she and her sister would give her one. Ellis had made Cat look sympathetic. Hopefully, she'd do the same for Carrie Ann.

In fact, Carrie Ann had wanted to talk to the reporter. Tinsley wondered about those skulls from Seaside Cemetery. She'd told the police that she'd heard some old-timers in a bar talking about that graveyard and one of them had said graves had been uprooted. Still, something about her sister's story bothered her.

But the Skull was gone and Carrie Ann was safe, so she hadn't pushed for more information.

Maybe she didn't want to know . . .

She'd wanted to stay with Carrie Ann, but her sister insisted she go home and get some rest. The silence between them was over. They would see each other the next day when Tinsley came to pick up Carrie Ann.

The beach was calling both their names. But this time she'd be outside, strolling with her sister, collecting seashells, and looking for sea glass. They were going to attend the fund-raiser for the rescue center together as well.

She owed it to Dr. Ferris.

Still, as much as she wanted to believe that everything was going to be normal, she still had scars, and so did her sister. It would take time to recover from all that had happened. The guilt over Dr. Ferris's death was eating at both of them.

But this time they would work through their pain together.

"Do you want to stop by your cottage and pick up some things?" Wyatt asked as they left the hospital.

"Not tonight." She'd finally broken free and was terrified that if she returned, she'd never leave again.

She was not going to lock herself away anymore.

They rode in silence, the tension thick with uncertainty. When they arrived at his cabin, she admired the rustic atmosphere of the exterior. "This place looks like you."

He chuckled, a deep, hearty sound that warmed her insides. "It's a fixer-upper, but I haven't gotten to the fixing yet."

She smiled, grateful for his attempt at a joke. He parked and came around to help her out, but she managed on her own. A low quarter moon hung in the distance, the sunset long gone. The wind whispered with the scent of the marsh and promises of a life that she'd forgotten to live.

No more.

Wyatt took her arm, and they walked inside. The dark-brown tones of the leather furniture, the thick wood farm table, and the stone fireplace looked masculine. But it was cozy and inviting, a home.

The pictures on the mantel drew her eye. Wyatt smiling with a Little League team. Then another of him and a man in uniform. "Your father?"

Wyatt nodded, a bittersweet look in his eyes. "He was on the police force."

Then another of him and a woman and two men who resembled him. "Your family looks close."

"We are. Mom demands we all come for dinner every week." He shrugged. "But the truth is, we don't mind."

Her heart squeezed, her thoughts turning to her sister. "I'm worried about Carrie Ann. I . . . can't lose her, Wyatt."

He turned her to face him. "I promise I'll do everything I can to help her."

After her ordeal with the Skull, she thought she'd never trust another man. But she trusted Wyatt with her life. And her sister.

And her heart.

She wanted to be with him tonight. But the scent and feel of Hinke lingered on her skin. "Do you mind if I shower?"

"Of course not. I can probably dig up a T-shirt for you to sleep in." His smile returned. "It'll swallow you whole, but it should be comfortable."

"Sounds perfect."

He showed her to the bathroom and linen closet, then hurried to find her a shirt. She smiled at the sight of the big Georgia bulldog emblazoned on the front.

One of the bars on the island catered to the Georgia fans. She imagined Wyatt there, having a beer with friends as they watched the game.

It had been so long since she'd been out in public or to a restaurant that it seemed foreign, but she ached to do it.

One step at a time. She'd left the cottage today. That was a start.

Staying with Wyatt tonight would be another.

♦ ♦ ♦

Wyatt heard the water running and imagined Tinsley naked inside his shower. His body hardened, his hunger for her returning full force.

He could not act on that need, though. Tinsley had been through hell tonight, and she'd taken a big step in leaving that cottage. Pushing her would be selfish.

Besides, she hadn't come home with him because she'd wanted to sleep with him. She'd come because she'd been beaten and mauled by that sadistic son of a bitch, Hinke.

He found a bottle of wine he'd bought some time ago and opened it, then poured two glasses. Tinsley might want something to help her relax.

Hell, he could use a drink himself.

He walked to the back deck and looked out at the marsh. There were still details to tie up. The three skulls hanging in that clinic needed to be identified and their families notified. But they had the rest of the remains, so at least the women could be buried intact.

Dr. Patton had sent word that the remains he'd found in the refrigerator definitely belonged to Hinke's father.

The door creaked open, and he sensed Tinsley behind him. Desire shot through him as he saw her standing barefoot in his big T-shirt.

With her hair hanging damp over her shoulders and her face scrubbed clean, she was the most beautiful woman he'd ever seen.

"My turn." He had to get a cold shower to tamp down his libido. "There's wine on the counter if you'd like a glass."

She nodded, her blue eyes huge. He rushed into his room, stripped, quickly showered, then dressed in a pair of sweats and a T-shirt.

When he was finished, he found her standing on the back deck with a glass of wine, her look pensive as she stared across the marsh.

"I've missed so much."

"You're free now," he said gruffly.

She turned toward him, her eyes flickering with emotions, then something akin to desire. "I want to live again. To really live."

"You're strong and brave. You have time."

She stepped toward him, tilted her head, her gaze locking with his. "Maybe. But one thing I've learned is that all you can really count on is today."

He swallowed hard at her husky tone. "That's true." He'd almost lost her today. He wanted to savor every minute in her presence now.

She took his hand, lifted it, and kissed his palm. He licked his lips, aching for a taste of her. But she had to make the first move.

Then she did. She stood on tiptoe and pressed her hand to his cheek. His body went still, heart pounding, blood racing.

CHAPTER
FIFTY-FOUR

Wyatt closed his mouth over Tinsley's, the sweetness of her touch more arousing than anything he'd ever felt before.

She trailed her hands into his hair, and his heart hammered as he drew her closer. Her breath caught, and then she looked up into his eyes. Hers were dark with hunger.

He knew damn good and well that she hadn't been with anyone since that monster had violated her. That humbled him more than anything.

He kissed her again, tenderly this time, his hands gently stroking her back. He wanted her naked in his arms, her body writhing beneath him as he pleasured her.

But if a kiss was all she wanted, he'd take it.

She gingerly traced her tongue over his lips until he opened for her. Pleasure rocked through him when she clasped his face in her hands and coaxed him into a mating dance with their tongues.

He lowered his hands to her hips, his cock hardening when she rubbed her body against him. He held her tight, kissing her with all the pent-up emotions he'd held at bay, and was rewarded when she emitted a soft moan.

That simple sound of pleasure was almost more than he could bear.

He had to slow things down. Wrangle in his libido, which was quickly spiraling out of control.

Slowly, he ended the kiss, then leaned his head against hers. Their erratic breathing filled the silence, the tension palpable.

"You should go to bed," he said gruffly.

"You're right." She took a step back but shocked him by taking his hand in hers. "But I don't want to go alone, Wyatt."

He squeezed her hand. "I'll be right out here."

A wariness flashed in her eyes. "You don't want to be with me? I know I have scars—"

He shushed her by kissing her again, deeply, tenderly. When he pulled away, her cheeks were flushed, her breathing shaky.

"Don't misunderstand," he said. "I want you with every fiber of my being. I don't care about your scars. When I look at you, I see a beautiful, desirable, strong woman." He cupped her face between his hands. "But I don't want to hurt you," he said in a low voice.

"You could never hurt me," she said softly. This time she kissed him.

When she pulled away, she took his hand again, and he followed her to the bedroom.

♦ ♦ ♦

Nerves knotted Tinsley's stomach as she pulled Wyatt to the bed. For a moment, she feared he wouldn't find her attractive.

Although his sultry looks, and the way his body hardened when they were close, had given her hope. And courage.

She trusted Wyatt. He wouldn't hurt her. But he might break her heart.

Because they had no future together. He wanted a family, and . . . she couldn't give him that.

They had tonight, though. And she was going to make every minute count.

She'd closed herself off from the world, from people, from feeling for so long that one touch of his fingers stirred her passion.

She turned in his arms and saw him watching her. He was worried.

His concern made her want him even more.

She pulled his face to her for another kiss.

He wrapped his arms around her and kissed her again, this time more urgently. She raked her hands over his back, need building. His hard muscles bunched beneath her touch, and his heated breath bathed her neck as he trailed kisses along her throat. She threw her head back in abandon, offering him free rein.

His lips and tongue teased her; he kissed her again, a kiss filled with passion. She moaned and reached for his shirt. He helped her remove it, then tossed it to the side.

He was beautiful. A soft dusting of dark hair covered his broad chest. He was muscular and strong, but he used that strength to protect others, not to exert his power or hurt anyone.

His patience and tenderness and protectiveness had ignited a flame inside her. She was in love with him. She'd fallen hard.

She pressed her lips to his chest and leaned her head against him, savoring the warmth of his skin and the sound of his heart beating. He rubbed her arms, then kissed her forehead and threaded his fingers in her hair.

"We can stop anytime," he murmured.

She nodded. "I know." She looked up at him with her heart in her eyes. "I don't want to stop. I want you."

He made a low sound in his throat, part pleasure, part pain, then kissed her again. By the time he broke the kiss, her legs felt weak.

"Remember what I said," he whispered as he gently eased her onto the bed.

She raked her hands down his chest and pulled him on top of her. His weight should have felt suffocating.

Instead it felt comforting. And sensual.

She wrapped her legs around his, and they twined their bodies together, kissing and stroking each other until he reached for the bottom of her shirt. She held her breath, hating that she bore scars.

"I wish I was perfect for you," she said in a raw whisper.

"You are." He tilted her face so she had to look into his eyes. "You are beautiful."

She licked her dry lips, aching for more of him. "You make me feel that way."

A sexy smile curved his mouth. "And you make me humble." He kissed her throat, then inched the T-shirt over her head, exposing her breasts and belly and a pair of black bikini underwear that nearly made him lose control.

"God, you're sexy."

She closed her eyes and let him pleasure her. His tongue and hands roamed over her body, bringing her back to life with titillating erotic pleasure. He tugged one nipple into his mouth and gently suckled her, and she wrapped her legs around him, lifted her hips, and felt his thick erection bulging against her heat.

He teased one breast, then the other, then trailed kisses down her stomach to her inner thighs. He tugged at her panties with his teeth, then dragged them off her and threw them to the floor.

She felt naked and vulnerable and exhilarated as he pressed his lips to her center and tasted her. He didn't stop with one taste either.

He played with her clit with his tongue, driving her mad with erotic sensations. She couldn't hold back.

She cried out his name as her orgasm rocked through her. A million wonderful sensations splintered through her, triggering a burst of emotions that brought tears to her eyes.

He rose above her, passion glazing his eyes. But when he saw her tears, his face went ashen and he started to move off her.

"You should have stopped me," he said in a tortured voice.

"I wanted you," she said as she pulled him back to her. "I still do."

His gaze met hers, emotions and sexual tension simmering between them.

"I want you, too, Tinsley."

At his husky words, she untied the drawstring on his sweatpants and stroked his flat belly. He sucked in a breath, then helped her push them down his hips. For a moment, her breath caught at the sight of the long, jagged scar on his thigh.

He'd gotten it rescuing her a few months ago. He'd had surgery and physical therapy, and he had suffered terribly. All because of her.

Yet he'd come back and protected her without question.

"I told you I had scars, too," he said gruffly.

She traced a finger over the puckered skin. "They make you even more handsome," she said softly.

"You think I'm handsome?" he said with a teasing smile.

She laughed and pulled him to her. "Yes, and sexy, and I want you inside me."

She'd never thought she'd feel such abandon, but Wyatt had unleashed the passion she thought had died.

He held up a finger, then grabbed a condom from the nightstand. She considered telling him it wasn't necessary, but she bit back the words.

She didn't want to talk now. She wanted to make love to him.

◆ ◆ ◆

The moment Tinsley parted her thighs and took him inside her, Wyatt felt as if he'd come home.

Emotions nearly overcame him, but she clutched his hips with her hands and urged him deeper, and he forgot to think. He thrust inside her, first gently, but she urged him closer and deeper, and within seconds, they built a sensual rhythm that drove him mad with desire.

He wanted to prolong the pleasure, but she teased his nipple with her tongue, sending him over the edge. He called her name in a husky whisper as his release splintered through him.

She moaned, and he felt her riding the waves again, this time with him.

He wrapped his arms around her, holding her close and kissing her as the erotic sensations peaked.

She clung to his back, the sound of her soft moans of satisfaction twisting his heart. He held her for a long time, the two of them wrapped in each other's arms. When she grew sleepy, he slipped from bed, cleaned up, then returned to cradle her in his arms. She nestled against him, and her breathing grew steady. Then she purred his name, and he kissed her forehead and hugged her tighter.

He wanted her tonight.

He wanted her tomorrow and the day after . . .

CHAPTER
FIFTY-FIVE

The sound of a phone ringing jarred Tinsley from sleep. She blinked, disoriented. She was warm and cozy and had slept better than she had in ages.

Because she was in Wyatt's arms.

Her body tingled from their lovemaking. She wanted to make love with him again. And again. And again.

The ringing broke into the warm haze around her, and Wyatt rolled over and groaned as he reached for his phone on the nightstand.

"Hello." A tense pause. Wyatt rubbed his eyes and sat up, swinging his legs to the side. "What? She had the baby last night? Everything okay?" Another pause. "Good. We'll drop by, and I'll fill you in on the case."

He hung the phone up, then rolled back to her, leaned on his elbow, and took a strand of her hair between his fingers. She smiled as he played with it.

"Korine had the baby. A boy."

"Everybody all right?"

He nodded. "He's small, five pounds, but everything seems good. Hatcher sounded nervous and excited. I told him we'd stop by to visit."

Tinsley clamped her teeth over her lower lip. He'd said *we* as if they were a couple. She wanted that more than anything.

But he wanted a family. His own baseball team.

She couldn't give him that. Not ever.

Besides, he hadn't said he loved her. Only that he wanted her.

She tugged the sheet over her and pushed her hair from her face. "I need to see Carrie Ann."

"I'll drive you to the hospital."

She nodded, then reached for his shirt. "I'm going to take a quick shower first."

"I could join you," he said with a teasing glint to his eyes.

She wanted that. But every minute she was with him made it harder to walk away. And she had to do that for his sake.

She hurried to the bathroom. "I won't be long."

She closed it behind her, tears trickling down her cheeks as she stepped into the shower alone.

◆ ◆ ◆

Wyatt didn't know exactly what had happened, but as they drove to the hospital, he sensed something had changed with Tinsley.

Last night they'd made love, sweet and tender, erotic and passionate. He thought they'd bonded.

But this morning she seemed distant, as if she'd closed down again.

Dammit. He couldn't push her. He had to be patient. She'd taken a huge step by leaving that cottage and then by allowing him to make love to her.

They parked and walked up the steps to the hospital in silence. "Do you want to see the baby?" he asked as they entered the hospital.

A sad look flickered in her eyes. "This is a time for family and special friends." She shrugged. "My place is with Carrie Ann."

"I'm sorry, Tinsley, but she'll have to go to the police station and turn herself in. I'll call Kendall James and ask her to meet you there."

"I know. Thanks." She stood on tiptoe and kissed his cheek. "I appreciate everything you've done for me. For us."

The elevator dinged open, and she slipped inside. Maternity was on the fourth floor, but her sister was on the second. When the doors opened, she gave him another sad smile, stepped outside, lifted her hand up in a small wave, then turned and walked down the hall.

His stomach knotted. Why did he feel like she was saying goodbye?

♦ ♦ ♦

The next two weeks dragged by. Tinsley thought she'd been lonely when she was locked in the cottage, but she missed Wyatt like crazy.

He'd called dozens of times. Asked to come over. To see her. Invited her to his mother's house for dinner.

She'd refused them all, using her sister as an excuse. But his persistence made it difficult to say no.

Sometimes she dreamed that having children didn't matter to him, but in the light of day reality intruded.

She could never be what he needed. And she refused to put them both through the agony of trying to make a relationship work when in the end he'd probably resent her.

At least the case against her sister was settled. Wyatt had investigated Milt Milburn's father and discovered he also had sexual misconduct allegations against him. In addition to the incriminating videos they'd found at Milt's house, a warrant for Milt's father's house revealed a video of Milt bragging about the rapes along with other incriminating photos. Several women had agreed to come forward and testify against father and son.

The DA had struck a deal with Carrie Ann for no prison time, but she had to undergo extensive counseling.

Tinsley hoped it helped her sister. She'd needed it for a long time.

CHAPTER FIFTY-SIX

Wyatt stewed over what he'd done wrong with Tinsley as he nuked a frozen pizza that night. Dammit, Hatcher and Korine were bringing home their new son.

He wanted to be with Tinsley, for them to build a future and life together, too.

Why didn't she want him?

His mother had asked about her several times, and he'd admitted he'd fallen in love with her. She'd encouraged him to go after her, but he'd explained that Tinsley needed a safe haven, one he couldn't offer.

She assured him that even though she'd worried about his father every day on the job, the time they'd shared together had been worth it.

A knock sounded on the door, and he left the pizza on the counter, hope surfacing. Maybe Tinsley had changed her mind and come to see him.

He ran his fingers through his hair as he padded to the door. He couldn't appear too anxious or be pushy.

He inhaled as he opened the door, but his heart sank when he saw Carrie Ann standing in the doorway. She looked jittery and wary.

Panic followed. "Is something wrong with Tinsley?"

A tentative smile fought through the wariness. "Yes. She's lonely. She misses you."

"Right." Sarcasm laced his voice. "She won't even return my calls."

She shifted and tugged at her hat. Tinsley had told him about her sister's nervous condition, but hopefully now the Skull had been caught and she and Tinsley had reconciled, she could get it under control. Although she still refused to tell them why she'd chosen those graves to take the skulls, or to name any of the other Keepers. He sensed there was a group now working in secret.

"Can I come inside?"

He gestured for her to enter. Something was definitely up. Maybe she was ready to talk. "Would you like a drink or something?"

She fidgeted. "No drink. I have something to tell you."

He forced a calm voice. "Then spit it out."

"Are you in love with my sister?" she asked bluntly.

He gaped at her, tempted to lie and save his pride. But he couldn't lie about Tinsley. She meant too much to him. "It's that obvious."

She released a sigh as if she'd been holding her breath. "That's what I thought."

"It doesn't matter, though," he said. "She doesn't want me."

Carrie Ann rolled her eyes. "Men are so damn dense. She does too want you. She's in love with you. And trust me, Tinsley has never been in love."

"She was engaged," he reminded her.

"That was a mistake. Tinsley never lit up around him the way she does around you."

He swallowed hard. "Then why won't she talk to me?"

Carrie Ann paced across the room swinging her hands. "You have to understand Tinsley. When she was locked in that cottage, she pushed me away. I called and called, and she told me to leave her alone, that she didn't want me around. She did that to protect me."

He tried to follow her logic. "She doesn't need to protect me."

Carrie Ann paused in her pacing and folded her arms. "She is protecting you, or she thinks she is. She loves you and she knows you want children and she wants you to be happy, so she's pushing you away now."

He took a deep breath. "So what if I want kids? I want them with her."

"That's the problem, Wyatt." Sadness tinged her eyes. "Tinsley can't have children. Not since the attack." Her voice cracked. "You didn't know, did you?"

Emotions bombarded him. Disappointment. Anger. "She didn't tell me."

"It's been painful for her," Carrie Ann said. "She loves children, and she would be an amazing mother. I hate him most for taking that from her."

So did he. But what could he do about it?

◆ ◆ ◆

Tinsley left the fund-raiser with a lift to her spirit. In light of Dr. Ferris's death and her funeral, they had postponed the event. But it had been a great success today, and they'd held a special ceremony to honor the veterinarian.

Working with the people and animals had filled Tinsley's heart with warmth and love. She'd wanted to adopt all the dogs available, but she'd given her heart to that mutt Wyatt had brought over, and she'd asked him whether she could have him.

He'd dropped off the dog, whom he'd named Tanner, the night before and lingered as if he'd wanted to say something, but he hadn't.

Mr. Jingles had finally left his cage. He'd flown around the room, then landed on Wyatt's shoulder as if he approved.

Heaven help her, she'd wanted both Wyatt and the dog. But Tanner would have to do.

"We have one more place to stop," Carrie Ann said.

"Where to?" Tinsley asked.

"A surprise. You and Tanner will like it, I promise."

She rubbed Tanner's head while her sister drove across the park to the baseball fields.

Her nerves prickled. Little League baseball fields.

"What are we doing here?"

"Come on, there's something you have to see." Her sister's enthusiasm was hard to fight, so she and Tanner followed her to a set of bleachers where parents and fans sat, yelling for their favored teams.

The game ended, cheers erupted, and then the players met in the middle to shake hands.

Her gaze scanned the field. Wyatt. Big and handsome and sexier than ever. He looked so happy and relaxed with those kids.

The boys climbed and jumped all over him, and he threw them up in the air and swung them around as they grabbed snacks and dispersed.

Her heart melted. He was so wonderful with those kids.

Emotions clogged her throat. "Why did you bring me here?"

"Wyatt asked me to," Carrie Ann said.

"It was a mistake." She headed away from the bleachers, determined not to cry until she reached the car. But Tanner balked and dug in his paws.

She expected her sister to follow, but a male voice stopped her. "Why are you running from me?"

She exhaled, blinking back tears, and turned to face him. "I'm not. I . . ."

He paused to pet Tanner, who jumped all over him with excited licks. *Traitor.*

Wyatt patted the dog's head, then ordered him to stay. His dark eyes raked over her as he crossed to her. Damn if he didn't have the sexiest swagger she'd ever seen.

She struggled to compose herself. "You look like you're having fun. The boys obviously adore you."

"It's mutual," he said gruffly. "That's the reason I wanted you to see us here."

Pain wrenched her heart. "You deserve to be happy, Wyatt. You're a good man."

A muscle ticked in his jaw. "I'm also a man in love."

God, how she wanted to hear those words. But she shook her head in denial. "It would never work between us."

He pulled her toward him. "Why not? I love you. You love me?"

"That's not the point."

"Of course it is," he said in a deep voice. "Love is what makes families."

Her chest ached with the effort to breathe. She just had to spit it out, and then he'd leave. And she could start getting over him.

"And you should have that, a family, but I can't give it to you." She tried to pull away. She needed to run before she broke down.

He yanked her back to him. "You're missing the point. But first answer me, do you love me?"

She couldn't lie to him, not after all he'd done for her. Even if it would be the right thing to do.

"It's a yes-or-no question, Tinsley. Do you love me?"

"Yes."

A smile curved his mouth. "Then there is no problem."

"You didn't hear me. I said I can't give you a family, and I won't let you sacrifice having your own team for me."

"I have my team here," he said. "Those kids love me, and I love them."

"I know, but you deserve to have children of your own."

He wrapped his arms around her waist and dragged her to him. "You rescue animals, Tinsley. There are a lot of children out there who need rescuing, who need loving homes, too."

She searched his face. She'd thought he would want his own children—his birth children.

"You mean adoption?"

He nodded. "Of course. We could give a home to children who really need us. So no more being unselfish and making decisions for me because you think it's the best thing for me." He pressed his fist over his chest. "I know what's best for me."

A smile tugged at her mouth. He sounded so gruff, so determined, so fierce and loving. So Wyatt.

She raised a brow. "You do? And what is that?"

"You." He lowered his mouth and kissed her, and she looped her arms around his neck and kissed him back.

When they finally broke for air, he smiled against her. "Marry me, Tinsley."

She nodded. "Only if you promise to make love to me every night."

A chuckle rumbled from deep in his belly. "That's a promise."

EPILOGUE

Marilyn kissed Ryker and rolled over, still breathing hard from their lovemaking.

She and the detective made a good team. Especially in bed.

But he also understood her like no man ever had.

He slapped her on the rear, flipped her over, and drove his cock inside her again. She lost her breath as he thrust deeper and deeper. She clutched his tight ass and gave in to the passion, riding the waves with him until they spiraled into blissful oblivion.

He came inside her with a grunt, and she flipped him over and rode him until they were both spent.

Finally sated, she crawled off him and headed to the bathroom.

But he was insatiable and joined her in the shower.

She soaped his chest and wrapped her legs around him one more time. She could never get tired of fucking Ryker.

But he had work to do. And she had one more visit to make. Tonight, she would get the rest of the story.

Then she'd know the truth about the little darlings. That's what the old man called them.

The "Dead Little Darlings." They deserved justice.

Thanks to Carrie Ann for digging up those bones, she could do it without exposing herself.

Then the Keepers could continue.

ABOUT THE AUTHOR

USA Today bestselling author Rita Herron fell in love with books at the ripe old age of eight, when she read her first Trixie Belden mystery. Twenty years ago, she traded her job as a kindergarten teacher for one as a writer, and she now has more than ninety romance novels to her credit. She loves penning dark romantic suspense tales, especially those set in small Southern towns. Her awards include a Career Achievement Award from *RT Book Reviews* for her work in series romantic suspense, the National Readers' Choice Award, and a RITA nomination. She has received rave reviews for the Slaughter Creek novels (*Dying to Tell, Her Dying Breath, Worth Dying For,* and *Dying for Love*), her Graveyard Falls novels (*All the Beautiful Brides, All the Pretty Faces,* and *All the Dead Girls*), and for *Pretty Little Killers,* the first book in The Keepers series. Rita is a native of Atlanta, Georgia, and a proud mother and grandmother.